*A Novel*

# JULIA SPIRO

LAKE UNION
PUBLISHING

Published by Lake Union Publishing, Seattle

www.apub.com

Amazon, the Amazon logo, and Lake Union Publishing are trademarks of Amazon.com, Inc., or its affiliates.

ISBN-13: 9781542033572 (hardcover)
ISBN-10: 1542033578 (hardcover)

ISBN-13: 9781542033558 (paperback)
ISBN-10: 1542033551 (paperback)

Cover design by Kathleen Lynch/Black Kat Design

Printed in the United States of America

First edition

*In memory of Bailey.*

# Chapter 1

It's still dark out when we pile into the van. The leather seats are cold against the backs of my thighs. I shiver, regretting my decision to wear shorts. My stomach growls. Sarah slides the door shut once we're all in and hops into the driver's seat.

"It's just ten minutes away," she assures us.

We pull out of the manicured driveway of Island Wellness and turn right, up North Road. Though the sun has yet to rise, several cars pass us on the drive, their headlights a reminder of the people who make Martha's Vineyard run, the ones who are up before dawn to work the land, the animals, the construction sites.

My shoulders rub against Stephanie's, who is wedged between me and Rhoda. The two women look over at me when I release a heavy exhale.

"You okay?" Rhoda asks.

I nod. I don't have the energy to open my mouth and tell them the truth: that I'm not okay, that my entire life has imploded within twenty-four hours, and that I'm on the verge of a total and complete meltdown. I don't need to tell them, anyway. They know.

One of the leggings—a spandex-clad trio from the suburbs—leans forward from the back row, her face almost touching my cheek. I can smell her dry shampoo, a powerful scent of artificial pink grapefruit that makes my head hurt.

"This sunrise meditation better be worth it," she says to no one in particular. "I'm freaking *tired*." I look straight ahead, unresponsive.

"Uh-huh," Stephanie says. Of course, I'm tired, too. I don't want to go to this. I wanted to stay in bed and hide. But Stephanie and Rhoda dragged me. *This might be good for you*, they had said. *Take a break from all this . . . drama.* I even left my phone back in the cabin, and now, without it, I feel disoriented, my hands fumbling blindly for something that's not there. I imagine the messages coming in, the angry emails, the concerned calls, the press inquiries. I can see the headlines now: Ava Maloney, famous wellness influencer, exposed! I wonder briefly whether I could just change my name, move to Europe, disappear.

"Here we are," Sarah says as she comes to a stop at the end of a winding road. "Squibnocket." We step outside and huddle around one another, waiting for direction. The sun is still tucked away beneath the horizon, but it has cast a gentle glow in the air, allowing us to see the sprawling beach before us: a white shoreline of smooth beach stones met by low waves rolling toward it in slow, methodical movements.

Sarah and two other staff members lead us to a spot on the beach where several blankets are spread out on the sand. A woman in a linen jumpsuit waits for us there, and I recognize her as the same woman who led the sound bath for us a few weeks ago. I roll my eyes, certain this is a waste of time.

"Nice to see you all again," she says. "I'm Ophelia, for those of you I haven't met yet." She instructs us to get comfortable, sitting or lying down, and close our eyes. One of the leggings raises her hand to ask if there's coffee; the answer is no.

I sit cross-legged and pretend to close my eyes, but I keep them open just enough to look around me. Stephanie curls into the fetal position; Rhoda lies flat on her back. The middle-aged man in khaki shorts sits with his legs pulled into his chest; the young, stylish couple both lie on their backs with their hands neatly folded on their bellies; the twins are pressed flat against the ground like starfish, their faces turned sideways; the leggings all sit cross-legged as well, their expressions identical and frozen. Six weeks ago, these other guests were inconsequential to me. Now, they're all suspects.

I wonder what motive any of them could have had to come after me. Maybe one of the guests has a secret obsession with me that I don't know about; I've dealt with dozens of internet trolls already. It comes with the territory of being an influencer. And yet I just don't think any of the guests would do it. They're all too self-absorbed. After all, everyone at Island Wellness is there for a reason—to fix something, to heal something. Everyone is focused on themselves.

I think about the other people I've met here during the last six weeks: Carter, Sarah, Wanda, Naomi, Lucy and her team. How could I have been so blind to the possibility that one of them could have been plotting against me? What have I even been *doing*?

I glance over at the Island Wellness staff. They're watching us—always watching us. Between some of my missteps over the last few weeks and my initial application, they certainly have enough dirt on me to fill a lengthy exposé. But why me? Island Wellness has had plenty of celebrity guests far more well known and powerful than I am.

I consider my brother, my friend Becky, Ben, all the people I left behind in LA. What if the person who did this has been right under my nose even before this summer—for *years*? Maybe what's happened to me is far bigger than the last few weeks at Island Wellness. Maybe someone out there really, truly *hates* me.

But I suppose it doesn't matter who did it, in a way. The truth is out now, regardless of who put it there. The ugly, shameful truth that I've been fighting for so long is now right there for everyone to see and dissect. And there's nothing I can do about it.

What matters now is what comes next. What matters now is how I'm going to deal with it.

The sun starts to ascend, and I finally shut my eyes. The last thing I'm capable of doing right now is *meditating*, but I'm stuck here, so I might as well go along with it. Ophelia instructs us to breathe deeply, to fill up our lungs and hold the air in our bellies for a second longer than we want to, then to release it slowly and purposefully. She asks us to notice how the salt air smells as it enters our noses, how the breeze feels against our skin, what we see behind the blackness of our eyelids. She asks us to set an intention for our day. "What do you want from today? How do you want to feel?" she asks us. "What do you *need*?"

The answers for me are clear. I want to erase the damage that's been done over the last twenty-four hours. I want my business and my image back. I want to explain myself to the world on my own terms, in my own time. I want whoever did this to me to apologize and pay for it. I want to regain control of my body, my mind, my life. I want to get better.

But what I want more than any of that—in fact, the only thing I really want, the only thing that would make it all okay—is the one thing I can never have.

I want my mom.

# Chapter 2

*Six weeks earlier*

Before Ben even pours the wine, I think I'm going to puke. We've been dating for a few months now, and while we're nowhere near the *I love you* stage, I think we might get there eventually. We established exclusivity a few weeks ago, and it just feels *real*. I haven't been able to say that about anyone I've dated—ever.

Tonight, I'm going over to his place for dinner. We see each other at least a few times a week. It's not always a sleepover, but it usually is, often enough that I have a toothbrush and a few other essentials at his place, and he's got some at mine. Though his place is where we more often end up—he's undeniably got the better house. I still live in the same West Hollywood one-bedroom apartment that I've rented for six years, since I moved out west after graduating from Northwestern, while Ben lives in a Spanish-style house up in the hills, complete with a hot tub and a lush backyard surrounded by ivy-covered walls.

It's not that I think I'm going to puke because I feel ill. It's that I've planned it out that way. I've had to factor in the reality that, if I want to sleep over and have a good night with the guy I really, really like, I need to have an empty belly. *After* eating dinner.

Ben's a foodie, like me, which is something I love about him, but it's something that's also posed a few hurdles in our relationship. Tonight is a perfect example of his love of food. He said he was ordering pizza for dinner, but his version of that is a full spread from Mozza: piping-hot arancini, fresh burrata and crusty bread, a chopped salad sprinkled with salami and provolone, a glistening mushroom-and-fontina pizza, a spicy fennel sausage pizza, and two pots of luscious butterscotch budino for dessert. What's even more annoying, though I reap the benefits of it, is that he's not overweight at all. He belongs to Equinox and works out there a few days a week, though not obsessively. He's just naturally lean.

I don't have a key to the house yet, but Ben leaves the door unlocked when I'm coming over. When I enter the house, the aroma of the food hits me immediately. I ate a snack beforehand—a banana—so that I wouldn't feel the need to binge at dinner and then have to purge. But after I drop my things in the foyer and walk into the kitchen, I see the containers from Mozza and know that I'm screwed.

"Hi," he says as he pours me a glass of Sancerre, which he knows is my favorite. "You look great."

"Oh, thanks," I say, trying to come across as casual. The truth is, there is nothing casual about my appearance. I have worked for it and *spent* on it. After combing through my closet that afternoon and deciding that I had nothing to wear, I rushed to a store on Melrose designed for thin girls with fat wallets, and splurged on a dress that I couldn't really afford but felt I needed. I bolted to a salon after and begged them to squeeze me in for a quick blowout even though I didn't have an appointment. This date could dictate my *future*, I told myself, so indulging in an expensive mini-makeover was a small price to pay in the grand scheme of my life.

"You do, too," I tell him.

And with his freshly shaved face, close-cropped hair, rich-brown eyes, and perfectly fitted linen shirt, he does. But he always does. Ben is an architect. He appreciates detail and style like I do—maybe even more than I do. His house, which he bought just before we started dating, reflects this. It's filled with tasteful and unique furniture and art. Even the hand soap in the bathrooms is the expensive kind that smells like fresh herbs. The kitchen is my favorite part of the house. It's got hand-painted tiles in blues, yellows, and oranges that brighten up the black appliances and butcher-block countertop. The first time I came over, he made me an old-fashioned with a perfectly curled orange peel in a crystal tumbler, and we drank together in the kitchen. I had to force myself to stop imagining waking up together on Sundays and cooking eggs and bacon in his kitchen, both of us wearing his undershirts and boxers. Since then, I've tried hard to maintain a certain effortless appearance that fits into his seemingly perfect world. As long as I am buffed, waxed, polished, blow-dried, stylized, and depuffed, I think that I can fit in just fine here.

And I need to fit in because Ben is different. In Los Angeles, especially, Ben is like a *unicorn*: successful (but doesn't work in entertainment), smart, well educated, handsome but not *too* handsome, doesn't want to date a model, can cook but can also change a flat tire. Even the way we met—in line at Alfred—feels almost too good to be true, a real-life meet-cute in a world of digital introductions. But perhaps what I like best about him is that he doesn't judge me for what I do.

I really wish there were another name for it—something that sounds more serious, more professional—but it is what it is. I'm an influencer. Specifically, I'm a food-and-wellness influencer. And I'm a good one. As Ava Maloney, otherwise known as TheGratefulAvocado, I've got just over a million followers on Instagram, no easy feat in my hypersaturated field. But most people, and a lot of the guys I've dated in LA, don't understand that it's a *real* job, with real stakes. They treat it like it's a silly hobby. Ben, however, never has. He's inquisitive about it, always asking me questions about how the business works. He's supportive and encouraging.

On our first date, he nearly spat out his wine when I told him how many followers I had.

"A *million people?*" he said with wide eyes. "Wow. How did you get so many followers? I mean, how long did that take? I don't even have Instagram, so I don't know how this stuff works."

I gave him the spiel I'd given many times before: "I think it's my dedication to it that's really been the key to my success. My transparency, too. My followers know that I'm going to post pretty much everything I eat throughout the day, all my workouts, what I buy at the grocery store, what I order at restaurants. All of it." I paused then. In the past, this was where I'd lost most people in conversation, where their expressions ever so subtly indicated that they thought I was one of *those* women—dumb, vapid, and obsessed with social media—who perpetuates dangerous body-image disorders and obsessions with unrealistic beauty standards. The ones who pretend to be inclusive and supportive of body equality but are actually fatphobic, their seemingly benign posts about core strength and vegan smoothies somehow just making other women ultimately feel like shit. Obviously, not me. But Ben's expression conveyed only interest, so I kept going. "I used to have an eating disorder, you know. I was pretty severely bulimic, and my followers know that, so I think it's important to be a figure for people to look up to, especially other young women who are struggling."

Ben didn't say anything at first, only nodded. And I caught a flash of sympathy on his face. "I'm so sorry to hear that," he said. "But you're better now?"

"Yes," I assured him. "I'm better now. I mean, I'm not perfect. It's always going to be a struggle. But I've gone through therapy and come out the other side. Now, it's about balance. And it's about being real with my followers."

"Well, it's pretty amazing that you get to help people with their own issues, you know, having gone through it yourself," he said.

"That's the best part," I told him. "Knowing that I can help other young women get healthy. There's so much toxic diet culture out there that young women get exposed to. So many ridiculous ideas of body perfection. I think it's really important for me to show that there's no such thing as being perfect. That it's about finding your own healthy lifestyle."

After that, we never spoke of my eating disorder again. As far as Ben knows, it was something in my past, something that I heroically overcame, and something that I could now help others defeat, too. The lie that I told Ben—that I was *cured*—was the exact thing that made him most attracted to me, I think. And that was where it all went wrong. Because while everything that followed wasn't necessarily a lie, it was all veiled in the fundamental untruth that I established with him on that first date. Now, he thinks that I'm somebody I'm not, and I have only myself to blame for that.

"Wow," I say, eyeing the takeout on the kitchen counter. "Yum." I take out my phone and open Instagram, then pan the camera across the spread. "Thursday night Mozza," I sing into the camera. Then I flip the lens back on me and cheers my wineglass. I check the video twice before posting it. Ben doesn't say anything while I do this. He's used to it now. Other guys I've gone out with have been annoyed or embarrassed when I film or photograph food. They curve their heads away from me at the table, trying to hide in plain sight, ashamed to be out with another social media wannabe. Ben's openness is a relief, and it helps that he doesn't have Instagram himself. Sometimes I think that if he did—if he saw what I was posting each day—he might be turned off from me somehow. Or he might suspect that it's not the real me.

I had genuinely hoped to avoid throwing up tonight. It wasn't always the plan. I thought that if I ate just one piece of pizza, and maybe pretended to pick at a second one, I could be okay letting it digest. I don't *always* have to throw up. That's not how it works for me, anyway. But with the food Ben's ordered tonight, I don't see a way out. Even if I just had a few little bites of each dish, I'd be too full. I have no choice. Which means that I need to prepare and plot my steps.

We bring the food outside to the patio, where Ben has a table and chairs set up, complete with hurricane candles and potted succulents. It's a warm night in June, and the usual gray mist of the month has given way to a clear sky and a radiant sunset that we can see glimmers of through the treetops. I pour us both glasses of water, an essential part of what will come next.

"So, when does the article come out?" Ben asks as he passes me the plate of arancini. A few weeks ago, *Los Angeles* Magazine reached out to include me in a feature on the city's leaders in the wellness space. It was a short profile piece, less than five hundred words, with a focus on my realistic approach to healthy eating and exercise, and the positive impact I've had on my followers.

"I think the magazine comes out next week, actually."

"That's so great," Ben says. "It's a big deal."

"Thanks." It *is* a big deal, he's right, and I'm proud of myself. But it's one of the first times that my platform has been so publicly and formally acknowledged, and ever since the interview, I've had pangs of fear and guilt that override my excitement. Because I know, and only I know, that just as I lied to Ben on that first date, I lied to the reporter, too. I'm lying to everyone.

I continue eating dinner, sampling all of it, dragging my pizza crust in the salad dressing left on my plate, licking my fork clean of every bite. I refill my water glass and make sure to drink the entire thing. And when I feel my stomach inflate that extra little bit with hydration, I know it's time.

"Want to digest a bit before dessert?" I suggest.

"Definitely," he says. We rise and start clearing the dishes together, bringing them into the kitchen. I toss the empty cartons in the trash while Ben begins loading the dishwasher. This is my moment.

"How about some music?" I ask. Music—noise, in general—is always a good buffer.

"Sure," he says. "You pick." He points to his phone, and I unlock it by holding it in front of his face, giving him a quick peck on the lips after. If I had more time, I'd glance through his texts and photos while pretending to search for music. But I hastily select Mumford & Sons radio on his Sonos and turn up the volume.

"I'll be right back," I tell him. "Just running to the bathroom." Ben nods and continues cleaning up.

With the music on and Ben distracted in the kitchen, I now have the perfect five-minute window to do what I need to do. I've timed it out before, many times, and it can be done faster, but it just depends on how my body feels, how much water I've had to drink, how much time I need to wait after the fact for the flush of my face to subside. It's almost like a science.

The bathroom is toward the front door, and I practically run there, my phone in hand. I grab my clutch, which I'd left on the table across the hall, purposely, and duck inside. I'm immediately comforted by the confines of the bathroom: my place of peace. The first time I was over, I was grateful to discover that the bathroom has a lock. And even better, it has a fan vent. The toilet is somewhat old-fashioned, with a smaller, rounded rim and an antique-looking handle, which would generally frighten me a little (old plumbing can be treacherous), but I also know that I can do this anywhere, under any circumstance.

I loosely tie my long blonde hair back with the elastic around my wrist—which is always there, at all times, for this exact purpose. I grab a handful of toilet paper for immediate cleanup. I tug my dress down in the front to avoid any potential splashes. I position myself on my knees in front of the toilet.

I take a few breaths and relax my jaw. No matter how many times I do this, there's always a second where I'm so excited for what's about to come that I have to calm myself down, and relax my body, so that my throat will open up. But the anticipation is overwhelming; I'm on the cusp of immediate gratification, instant relief. I breathe deeply, and once I feel that the vibration of my body has settled, I stick my index finger into my mouth and all the way to the back, letting muscle memory take over.

It's always the first round that's the hardest. It sets the tone for the rest of the purge. Luckily, this one is fast, and my body doesn't fight me on it, in part because of all the water I drank. And it's a rush, as it always is—an overwhelming rush. That's the thing that most people don't understand about this disease, at least my version of it. It's not so much food that I'm addicted to. Sure, I abuse food, but food itself isn't really my drug. The purge is my drug. The purge is what gives me that unparalleled high, that liberating wave of freedom, that immediate and consuming euphoria. For me, it's like a magic trick. People say you can't turn back time, that you can't erase mistakes from your past. But that's exactly what I do when I purge: almost instantly, I'm able to transform myself, lighten myself, *free* myself from the damage I have previously done. As far as I'm concerned, the toilet is a time machine, and there, on my knees, I'm the genius who's figured out how to use it. Every time I stick my finger down my throat, I'm jettisoned back in time, past tonight's dinner, past that morning, all the way back to that last Christmas Eve with Mom.

When I'm done, I rise, feeling relief and comfort. I'm back to being my *best self*. Now I'm ready to reengage with Ben, ready for whatever comes next. I've managed to be the girl who can eat three slices of pizza and still have a flat stomach when she undresses half an hour later. Now, *I'm* the unicorn.

I wipe my mouth and finger with some toilet paper and then flush. I turn on the sink, lather up my hands, and start to wash out my mouth. I open my purse and take out my mini toothbrush and toothpaste, which I always have on hand. I check the time: four minutes. Not bad. But just as I'm about to start brushing my teeth, I glance down at the toilet, and everything goes wildly, madly wrong in a matter of seconds.

*"Fuck."*

The water and everything I dumped into it is rising, like an angry swarm of bees. "Fuck, fuck, fuck," I say again, my face starting to heat up. I can feel sweat immediately begin to spring from my pores. I lunge down toward the back of the toilet and frantically twist the water knob. It's old and somewhat rusty, and my knuckles whiten as I twist. I hear the water pressure dissipate, and just for a moment, I think I might have stopped it. There's a plunger in the corner behind the toilet, so I can fix this, I know I can. But it's too late. The water and my vomit begin to spill out over the toilet and onto the floor, rising up and cascading like lava down a mountainside. I grab at the washcloth hanging by the sink and start to wipe it up, but there's too much, and it's too fast. And now it's on my dress, my sandals, my hands, even the tip of my ponytail. The water finally shuts off, but the damage is done. I look under the sink for cleaning supplies: nothing. It wouldn't matter, anyway; I am beyond salvation.

Tears start to well up in my eyes. I'm trapped in a tiny bathroom, covered in vomit, while Ben waits in the kitchen, probably with a fresh glass of wine for me. I consider my options, quickly devising a story in my mind about sudden food poisoning, or a fake allergy to pine nuts, or maybe even something about bad period cramps causing severe nausea. Even *that* would be better than the truth.

But I know I can't bring myself to say any of these things. I can't bring myself to face Ben. He's too smart, too perceptive; he would know that I was lying. And, anyway, I'm too ashamed. I'm literally covered in my own waste; I couldn't be less attractive or feel like more of a phony. There's only one thing I can do now: leave.

I turn the lock on the bathroom door slowly and open it as quietly as I can. I listen, and hear Ben humming along to the music in the kitchen, the fridge door opening and closing. For a few seconds, there's a sense of normalcy. He doesn't yet know what's happened. He hasn't seen the disgusting mess that I've made—the disgusting mess that I am. I hold on to that moment for just a second longer. I want to call out to him and tell him the truth: that I'm sick, that I'm a liar, that I need help, that I have a problem, that dinner was wonderful and lovely but that he doesn't understand the feeling of needing to get something out of your stomach so badly that you think you might die. Maybe he would understand. Maybe he'd even be attracted to the notion of needing to help me. I consider it, but then I look back in the mirror behind me. My face is red, my dress is stained, my eyes are watery, and there's a line of sweat around my hairline. He'd never understand. He'd never want this version of me. The real me.

So I run toward the entryway table, frantically grabbing my sweater, and I bolt toward the front door, swinging it open.

"Ava? Where are you going?" I hear Ben's voice echo out as I slam the door behind me and run to my car. My hands shake as I start the ignition and hit the gas, nearly crashing into his neighbor's trash bins. As I careen down the winding roads of the hills toward the flats of West Hollywood, I begin to sob. My phone rings—it's Ben. I ignore it. There's nothing to say. I picture Ben now, standing in the doorway of the bathroom, the stench of my mess filling the air. My phone rings again, and again, and again. But I don't answer. I can't. And then the ringing stops.

Fifteen minutes later, I'm alone in my apartment. I shut the curtains. I strip my clothes off and dump them in the wash. I don't even notice that I'm crying until I realize that my face is dripping with salty tears, so big they're almost viscous. I wipe them away and open a bottle of red wine. Between gulping down the wine and choking back my own sobs, I start to assemble a grilled cheese sandwich and open a bag of Doritos. I only know how to comfort myself in this way: by eating and drinking and puking and then doing it again. So that's what I do. I binge and I purge, three times, until I finally pass out sometime around four in the morning, with the glow of my laptop on my salt-crusted face.

# Chapter 3

I dream about Christmas Eve that night. The last one with Mom, the night when everything changed.

I see her at the bottom of the stairs in our house in Cherry Hill. She's wearing the red satin blazer she wore every Christmas Eve, and I think she's the most beautiful woman in the world.

"You look gorgeous, Ava," she tells me. It's 2009 and I'm fifteen, dressed in a black crushed-velvet dress that she bought me on our last shopping trip.

My dad drives us to the steak house, the same one we go to every year, the kind with a buffet of prime rib, mashed potatoes, and freshly baked rolls, and an ice-cream sundae bar for the kids. My brother, Mike, and I sit in the back seat. Outside, snow falls. We pass by a shopping mall illuminated with hundreds of twinkle lights, and through a rotary with a giant fir tree in the middle, a gold star lit up on top. Maybe it's the Christmas decorations, but I feel a distinct sense of hope as we drive. The hope that things might be okay.

When we arrive, the manager greets us and takes our coats, though when he asks us all how we are, it's clear that he already knows the answer. Mom isn't doing well. And yet she's made every effort to disguise that fact. I know that she's spent hours looking in the bathroom mirror, perfecting her makeup. To me, she looks healthy—glowing, even. And the red blazer and black cigarette pants make her look powerful and strong, stylish and sexy. *Dress how you want to feel*, she always told me. I never saw her leave the house in anything but a meticulously polished outfit, even if she was just going to the supermarket.

I feel happiness as we get our food from the buffet and enjoy dinner together. I slather butter on a roll, douse my prime rib in gravy, dunk every bite in rich mashed potatoes. My father and brother rise from the table to get seconds. I begin to do the same, but my mother reaches her hand out and places it on mine, a silent instruction to stay put. *You don't need that.*

She's not wrong. I'm not hungry anymore. And in the previous months, my late-blooming prepubescent body had transformed from what a male classmate had described as "cardboard"—*flat from every angle*—to having boobs, a butt, hips, and a belly. The changes made me feel like a visitor in my own skin. My bones and flesh felt unfamiliar to me, at a time when I was already feeling rudderless and disoriented.

My mom's hand, cold and papery, still rests on mine when I look up at her. I suddenly realize that the red blazer is now far too big for her. It swallows her tiny body, and she looks like a child playing dress-up in an adult's clothing. The skin on her face sags on her cheekbones, tired and dry. Her complexion is washed out, and though she's tried to disguise it with blush, her face still conveys a white ghostliness. The scarf wrapped around her bald head suddenly looks less glamorous than it had to me just moments before; now, it's a reminder of the very thing she'd been trying so hard for us to ignore: that she's leaving us. It's not that I don't think she's beautiful; it's that I now see her mortality.

And so, I don't go to the buffet for seconds. Instead, I go to the bathroom, where, for the first of what would become thousands of times, I stick my finger down my throat and throw up. When I return to the table, something in the atmosphere has shifted. My mother looks healthy again. She fills out her red blazer, her skin is plump and soft, she's laughing with wet, joyful eyes. She looks over at me and smiles.

Somehow, my trip to the bathroom has restored my world to its normal state. Somehow, it has made everything better. Just like magic.

# Chapter 4

I wake up with a pounding headache, naked, and sweating. My skin feels cracked, and my eyes hurt; my mouth is dry and tastes like vinegar. I miraculously made it from the couch to my bed, though my laptop sits next to me, open and dead. I pick up my phone from the bedside table. I have two missed calls and a text from Ben:

Ava, please call me back.

I stare at the message. Even though I'm the one who ran out on him with no explanation and left his bathroom looking like a war zone, even though I'm the one who ghosted him, I get the distinct feeling that he's criticizing me, scolding me, rejecting me. I rub my eyes, burning with shame and embarrassment. I take a few deep breaths and decide to respond with a text. At this point, things with Ben can't get worse. So I might as well put my cards on the table and be honest.

I'm sorry. I have a problem. I'm still bulimic. Last night I panicked.

I'm so embarrassed I don't know what to say.

I hit "Send" and then force myself up and out of bed. I move the laundry along and wash my sheets. I need some food, but my fridge is empty, and I can't bring myself to venture outside and face the beautiful California sunshine, so I order two bagels for delivery: cinnamon raisin, toasted with extra butter, and an everything bagel with cream cheese and lox.

As I wait for Ben's response, a numbness settles over me. I feel so empty in every way—empty of tears, food, emotion—that there's nothing left to do but carry on. I need to make an endorsement post and a few stories, at least, so that I can project the illusion of normalcy.

I open up my album of stock photos—the ones I take in advance and keep on hand to post at the right times, or when I know I won't have time to take photos. It's one of the tricks I use, along with keeping my nails the same color and style for three manicures in a row, so that crafty little Instagram trolls can't catch me with different-colored nails on the same day and accuse me of posting something fake. I find a video I took a few days ago when I had good lighting, had just gotten my lashes redone, and actually went to the effort of making a latte.

"Good morning, *friends*!" I always refer to my followers as *friends*. "I wanted to tell you about a product that I've been using lately and *loving*. So, you know I have a supersensitive tummy and started limiting my dairy intake about a month ago . . . except for the occasional pizza. You guys know I can't live without my pizza." This is a lie—I only have a sensitive stomach when I treat it like a reusable barf bag. Otherwise, I have no allergies whatsoever, and I totally still eat dairy. All the time. But the timing of using this as a post couldn't be better since I documented last night's Mozza. "And ever since, my tummy has been feeling so much better. All that icky bloat I felt before is gone. But I really missed my morning lattes, and all the creamers I tried just weren't doing it for me. A lot of nut creamers have this weird chalky taste, you know?" At this point, I reverse the camera angle away from me and toward my kitchen counter, where I have a carton of oat milk and oat creamer from a new sponsor. "Until I found *this stuff*. You guys, this oat milk is so good. It's seriously delicious, and it has that same rich, creamy texture you get with real milk and cream, minus the indigestion. So, as you can see here," I say, moving the camera over to a latte I made, "I just whipped up my morning latte with their milk." I bring the camera back up to my face, now holding the latte and taking a sip. It took me a while to master that technique—being able to film and hold something at the same time, but now I've got it down pat. "And this has truly become my morning routine. So, you can swipe up to order it and use my code, Ava20, to get twenty percent off. Have a great morning, friends!" I watch the video a few times and decide it's good. I post it to my stories and a few minutes later post it to my feed as well, choosing a still shot of myself holding the latte, my skin looking fresh and glowing, thanks to my ring light. That's part of the endorsement deal. It's got to be on my actual feed, not just my stories. I add a caption that I already wrote last week and saved, basically a rehashing of everything I said in the video, but with all the necessary tags and hashtags at the end.

Within seconds, I have dozens of likes and thousands of views of my story. *Good,* I think. *I might have ruined my personal life last night, but not my professional one.* The oat-milk deal is a new partnership I just landed. They've agreed to pay me $1,000 for every post, one a month for six months. After that, if my posts do well, they might pay me more. I've got a handful of deals like this—some for a lot more money, some for less, at various levels of commitment. It all adds up, but it can all disappear quickly if I don't stay on top of it. Right now, I'm able to maintain a steady cash flow while not inundating my content with sponsored posts. I hate when influencers get so consumed with their sponsorships that all their posts are paid and nothing is real. Maintaining my authenticity is part of my brand. The key is finding a way to manufacture the "authentic" posts so that they feel completely real, even if they're just as premeditated and edited as a sponsored post.

My bagels arrive, and I hastily grab them from the deliveryman, glad that I can leave a tip on the app instead of in person. I do a quick story, twirling the lox bagel in my hand (which still has the same manicure as in the oat-milk post). Dairy-free cream cheese for the win! I type over the story. I make a mental note to document something "healthy" later, like a salad or a green juice, whether or not I'm actually going to consume it. I need to post something nutritious to offset the bagel and the pizza of last night. After all, if I only showed unhealthy food, my entire platform of balance would be gone. That said, I'm always careful to never deem foods "good" or "bad" to my followers, and I've gone on my account to address that vocally, head-on, during Q&As with my viewers or the occasional "get to know me" posts I do. "No food is 'bad,'" I tell them. "And I really think it's messed up that society has made us believe that. Girl, if you want the donuts, have the donuts and then move on!" My hypocrisy is not lost on me, though it usually goes undetected among my followers. Sometimes, though, a keen-eyed, often embittered troll will call me out on this. Someone once DM'd me in response to a pasta post: "If no food is 'bad,' as you say, then why do you always feel the need to remind us that it's okay to eat things like pasta? Isn't the subliminal message here that you actually think pasta IS bad and you're kind of like, making an excuse?"

I had decided to address this one publicly, on my stories one day. "No, I'm not making an excuse for what I eat," I said. "I owe no one an explanation for what I eat. None of you do. As I always say, what's right for me might not be right for you. We're all different, and that's the beauty of being balanced and healthy—there's no one right way."

I remember feeling so exposed in that moment. *Busted.* Because that follower had actually hit the nail on the head. I was trying to convince my followers that I eat pasta every week like a "normal" person, and that it's possible to do that and still be skinny. Maybe some people can, but not me. The thing with bulimia, in my case, is that it's a totally hidden disease. The results of my disease don't appear in emaciation. For me, my bulimia is about weight *maintenance*, not weight loss. I binge and purge, but I probably don't purge everything out, so I end up absorbing *some* of the calories I inhale. And then some meals I don't throw up at all. But in general, things like pasta don't stay down long in my system. Not the "bad" foods. "I'm just trying to show you guys that even though my whole lifestyle is about being my healthiest self, that sometimes includes pasta! And beer! And gummy bears! So, friends, enjoy yourself. It's okay to indulge once in a while!" The responses to that rant were a broad spectrum. Some followers responded with words of encouragement: "Thanks for sharing that, queen! You're so right about balance!" Or, "I love seeing a healthy girl eat pizza! We need more of that in our culture!" But then there were others who saw through me. "Yeah right. LOL." Or, "Bitch please, you're not eating that pizza." I suppose all the responses were right, in a sense.

My phone chimes, and I brace myself for a response from Ben. I feel calmer now, having eaten one of the bagels and chugged half of a Gatorade. I allow myself to feel a little bit of hope as I reach for my phone—hope that Ben will have responded with compassion, understanding, saying that he wants to be there for me. That we can get through this.

> Sounds like you've got a lot to figure out. I'm sorry, Ava. I just don't think I'm equipped to handle that right now. Good luck to you, though, really.

I stare at the message for a few seconds, trying to decipher some other meaning from it besides total and utter rejection. What could I possibly respond to that? Even in my lowest state, having endured the worst humiliation I could imagine last night, I have too much pride to try to argue with him, to try to convince him to give me another chance. He's told me everything I need to know with that text: that he's seen me, for real this time, and he doesn't want to be with me. My phone dings again, and I roll my eyes instinctively, expecting a follow-up apology from Ben, something to assuage his guilt for just brutally dumping me after I opened up to him.

But there's no new text from Ben. Instead, it's an email:

> Welcome to Island Wellness! Just Three Days Until Your Escape!

I almost delete it, assuming it's spam, but something about that name—*Island Wellness*—sounds familiar, somewhere in the back of my mind. As I bite into my second bagel, I open the email and read:

Dear Ava,

Our hearts and souls are overjoyed that you have chosen to join us for six weeks of holistic wellness here on Martha's Vineyard. Island Wellness prides itself on being a leader in the field of inner and outer wellness, through our unique mixture of yoga, breath work, meditation, organic nourishment, and what we like to call mindful connection through personalized therapy. Martha's Vineyard, the home of our sanctuary, is quite literally made up of healing elements said to have magical powers: clay, salt water, medicinal herbs, and other wildlife that will all be ingredients in the recipe of your best self. Included with this email is a suggested packing list along with a reading guide that we recommend our guests review before embarking on their journey, as well as a copy of your receipt.

Mindful connection, mindful humans.

With love and compassion,

Island Wellness

I put the bagel down, and suddenly the memory hits me. Last night, in my dizzying wine-and-Doritos-fueled spiral, I made a terrible mistake. I start to remember now, in bits and pieces, that I'd been scrolling the internet, chugging a second bottle of wine, when I'd seen an article somewhere about a wellness retreat that had liberated the writer from a life of disordered eating and body dysmorphia. A wave of dread starts to wash over me as the image of me in Ben's bathroom comes into my mind.

*This is it,* I remember muttering to myself in my haze as I ferociously tapped in my credit card number like a woman possessed. *This is it.*

I click on the attached invoice in the email, and my mouth falls open. The retreat is *thousands and thousands* of dollars, and it's *six weeks* long. *And* it's across the country, on Martha's Vineyard, of all places. There's no way I'm going there, spending that kind of money, walking away from my life for basically an entire summer just to sit through some hippie-dippie therapy on an island. Luckily, I made the reservation only a handful of hours ago, so I'm sure I can cancel and get out of it without penalty. I pick up the phone and dial, feeling a sense of relief as I anticipate my money being returned to my credit card just as quickly as I made the charge. A cheerful voice answers after a few rings.

"Island Wellness, it's a beautiful day to connect with you. This is Sarah, how can I help you?"

The way she answers the phone—*a beautiful day to connect with you*—is enough to further validate my decision to back out of this.

"Yeah, hi." I clear my throat. "My name is Ava Maloney. Last night I booked one of your retreats by accident, and I need to cancel it and get refunded. Sorry about that . . . I'm assuming you have a twenty-four-hour cancellation policy, right?"

"Life," the woman on the phone coos in a breathy voice.

"Excuse me?"

"Your name. Ava. It means *life*. I'm sure you knew that, though." I can practically smell the woman's patchouli through the phone and see her defined clavicle poking through some embroidered tunic.

"Right, well, yes, so, anyway, is it possible to just cancel everything and refund it back to my card? Sorry for the inconvenience." My stomach growls and my annoyance spikes.

"Let me see, Ava, let me see . . ." The feeling of dread starts to escalate. Something about Sarah's tone makes me feel like she's going to fight me on this. "Okay, I see your reservation right here. You booked the six-week retreat with us starting next week. And I see that you're a wellness advocate." My ears perk at that; did I indicate somewhere what I did for a living? How would she know? "That's wonderful. We're so excited to meet you."

"Well, that's the thing," I say, trying to remain calm. "I can't come. I booked it by accident. I need to cancel it."

"Sure, we can cancel your reservation, Ava, no problem. But I'm afraid we cannot give you a refund. It states very clearly on our booking website that refunds can only be granted when a medical or family emergency is the cause of the cancellation. Did you say that there was an emergency? I'll just need proof of that."

"But this is insane—I just booked it a few *hours* ago. It was a technical accident. I hit 'Yes' when I meant to hit 'No.' I didn't even know I paid for it until this morning. I can't even afford this."

"Oh, *Ava*, it's hard to believe that you did this by accident. Our registration process is somewhat lengthy. You even filled out a five-page questionnaire about your health history, your eating and sleeping habits, your room preferences . . . and your, well, your eating disorder and your business, how you don't feel honest anymore in what you're doing. And . . . everything about your mother that you're working through. The issues she had, I mean." She pauses, and I wait for her to say something else, because I'm truly at a loss for words. I can't believe that I would have written any of those things in the application, exposed myself so blatantly. She continues. "I just don't see how this could have been done by accident. You also electronically signed our waiver." My jaw begins to clench, and my head starts to throb.

24

"Can I speak to your manager, please? Someone else there needs to be able to fix this. Are you really just going to take my money if I don't come? When I just booked this *last night*? That's not exactly *ethical*." Sarah doesn't respond. I glance at my phone screen to make sure we're still connected. "Hello?"

"Ava," she says, like we're old friends—like she *knows* me, and for a moment, I think she does—"it's very normal to experience feelings of resistance before a retreat. I understand. But you signed up for this for a reason. You are clearly seeking something. There's a part of you that's in need of healing. That's what brought you to us. Don't run from it."

"Actually, I'm pretty sure that I saw an ad for this place on Instagram, and I clicked it absentmindedly when I was basically blackout drunk, and now you're taking advantage of that. What you're doing is unethical, and I demand to be refunded!"

I can feel my power slipping away. It is unethical of them, sure, but I *did* sign up. I even signed the waiver with a separate app for electronic signatures. This wasn't a mistake, even if I don't remember doing it.

"I'll give you twenty-four hours from now to decide if you're coming, how about that? I'll call you tomorrow, and you can either confirm your room or give up your spot. But unfortunately, we cannot refund you."

"Well," I say, scrambling now for some way to fix this. Maybe I can postpone my reservation, I think, or at least get a discount. "I *am* an influencer. I have over a million followers on Instagram. It's very typical for hotels and resorts to give me deals if I agree to advertise their business on my account. Would that be something we could arrange? Or maybe I could push the reservation to a later time, down the road? You can check, by the way, my Instagram handle. TheGratefulAvocado."

I hear what I'm pretty sure is a muffled chuckle on the line. "Oh," she says, "I'd love to see your work, but I don't have Instagram. Maybe you can show me when you're here. But . . . to answer your question, no, I'm sorry, we don't offer discounts for . . . what did you say?

Influencers? And, well, our schedules are very limited, our reservations fill up quickly, so unfortunately we can't change your reservation to a later time. I'm sorry, Ava."

Of course she doesn't have Instagram. I hate people like her—the ones who think they're *above* it.

"Really?" I plead. "Discounts for influencers are very standard now. I just got an entirely free weekend trip at the Miraval in Austin." The trip wasn't entirely free, okay, but it was majorly discounted.

"Well, that must have been wonderful. But we're not Miraval." Sarah pauses. I have no more weaponry tucked away to pull out to my defense. "So, like I said, why not sleep on this for twenty-four hours? You have that window to call and cancel, but no refunds."

I take a deep breath, and I wonder if this woman is someone who actually works on the ground at the resort, and interacts with the guests, or if she sits behind a computer in an office all day.

"Oh, and Ava," she says, "just remember, the only way you're going to connect with others and with the world around you is by connecting with yourself first. By being . . . *honest* with yourself."

My mouth drops open, ready to respond, but the line disconnects before I can. I sit in disbelief for a moment. What did she mean when she said *honest*? And then I remember what she said about their application process. I start to recall how I answered their questions with total recklessness, telling them how I've been suffering from bulimia, how my entire business is a lie, how I'm living two lives. And everything I said about my mom. The things I *never* speak of, not even to past therapists, not even to my dad or brother. Yes, I'd told Ben that I was still bulimic, but that was all I told him—he doesn't know that as far as my social media identity goes, I'm basically a fraud, a phony, a liar. And he's so disconnected from the world of social media that I don't think it would occur to him to ever *out* me. But I don't know the staff at the retreat. And I've confessed everything to them. It's a certainty, I think, that they've all googled me already. What if they leak my application on the internet? Surely they wouldn't. My mind reels, and I feel sick as I realize that I might actually have to go to this place, that there might be no way out.

I plug in my laptop and try to find any record of the application, to see exactly what I wrote. But it was all done through the Island Wellness website. Nothing saved on my computer. On their home page, I click on the gallery section and scroll through their photos. Moss-covered stone walls bordering rolling fields, Adirondack chairs circling a firepit, a yoga studio with a cathedral ceiling and a sliding hurricane door that opens to a view of sparkling waters. I've never been to Martha's Vineyard, but being from the East Coast, I'm vaguely familiar with it, and I've been to the Cape before. I think of the Vineyard as a place for rich, preppy people who want to appear *normal*, down-to-earth, more rustic and intellectual than their wealthy friends in the Hamptons. There seems to be a reverse snobbery to the island—and to the retreat—in its illusion of island informality.

I click on a tab for a preview of the daily schedule.

While there is no "typical" day here at Island Wellness in Chilmark, a daily schedule might resemble something like this. Keep in mind, you are not a prisoner here! We encourage you to explore the island outside our grounds.

6:00 a.m.: morning yoga and meditation in the yoga cathedral

7:30 a.m.: nourishing breakfast

8:30 a.m.–noon: personalized therapy, meditation, spa services

I pause. Therapy? Is this a rehabilitation center or a retreat? I can feel the judgment of the staff even through my laptop screen, thousands of miles away.

> Noon–2:00 p.m.: nourishing lunch and free time to enjoy the lush grounds of the property or explore the island
>
> 2:00 p.m.–4:30 p.m.: personalized therapy, meditation, spa services
>
> 4:30 p.m.–6:00 p.m.: free time to enjoy the lush grounds of the property or explore the island
>
> 6:00 p.m.: nourishing dinner

The property looks beautiful, and for a moment, I imagine myself sunbathing on the beach there, far away from Los Angeles, where no one will bother me. But as I review the schedule and other offerings, I get the impression that the retreat feels more like a cult than a spa getaway, with dull lectures, restrictive meals, stern personal trainers, and hippie-dippie brainwashing from so-called counselors. The retreat's website says that it specializes in weight loss, eating-disorder rehabilitation, and general detox, among other holistic pursuits. The hypocrisy is typical of the wellness industry in general, I think with a huff—the same hypocrisy I know I'm perpetuating. How could they possibly help guests heal from disordered eating while also instructing them on how to lose weight, or on eliminating "bad" foods from their diet? My hope that this place might offer some relaxation is quickly thwarted and replaced with visions of dry tofu bowls, scowling counselors, and hours of downward dog.

I check my reservation receipt and think through some of the logistics in my head of what it would mean to go. From a financial standpoint, the cost is a big blow to my savings. Technically, I have the money, but it wasn't money that I'd meant to spend. I've been doing well with my endorsements and finally started saving. This money was meant to be set aside for a future home, or a trip that I actually wanted to go on, not one like this. I could try to sublet my apartment to make some money back. But the real obstacle is figuring out how to make it work with my job. What will I tell my followers? I can't exactly admit to being at a wellness retreat, being treated for an *eating disorder*, when my entire business revolves around the normalcy and accessibility of my everyday life as an ED-recovered person. I suppose I could tell my followers that I'm on a summer vacation or visiting friends. Or maybe just that I'm at a spa. But for six weeks? It will look suspicious. If my followers and my sponsors found out where I really was, and *why I was there*, my entire business would be wiped out. Endorsements and sponsorships would fall through, and my followers would feel betrayed. My career would be over, and I'd have to find another job. I've worked way too hard to build my platform just to give it all up because of a drunken mistake. I'll need to come up with some kind of solution.

I start to fold laundry, and recollections of what I wrote in my application surface in drips. I told them how my online presence first started as a side job while I worked full-time at a video game development company in Venice. I'd just finished a year of therapy with an eating-disorder specialist and a nutritionist, working through my long history with bulimia, and I'd finally found a consistent pattern of eating healthily, in a way that made me feel strong and in control. For the first time in my adult life, I really did feel true freedom from my eating disorder.

What was even better was that I could finally acknowledge that I actually *loved* food. I loved cooking, I loved discovering different dishes and types of foods, I loved trying new restaurants—I loved it all. Turns out, food was my passion. But until then, I had never given myself permission to love food. Until then, food was *bad*, something that I needed to limit and to restrict. I'd been carrying around my mother's relationship with food in her absence. Letting go of that relationship was freeing, at the time, but what I didn't realize then was that it would leave behind a much bigger void within me.

At the same time that I was going through this change, there seemed to be such an abundance of twiggy girls on the internet, all documenting the same supergreen powders and shakes, multivitamins, protein bars, meal delivery services, macro bowls, and keto recipes— endless amounts of products that promised elusive thinness in exchange for money and, basically, online worship. It bothered me, because I knew firsthand that getting healthy was possible without all that. I knew that it came from turning inward and dealing with disordered eating head-on, and from doing the hard, honest work of finding balance. I wanted to show people—even if it was only a few—what it was like to be ED recovered and how I'd gotten there. I wanted to counteract the poisonous and dangerous diet culture that had dragged *me* down for so long. I genuinely wanted to help people, to be a positive influence in their lives. So, I started documenting everything I was eating and most of my workouts on an Instagram account I called TheGratefulAvocado. I told my followers that I wasn't a chef, a nutritionist, a restaurant critic, or a fitness trainer—I was just a regular ED-recovered girl in pursuit of a full life.

What differentiated me, I think, was my transparency and my relat- ability. In particular, some of the first posts I did that were *imperfect*— the ones where I talked about my former eating disorder, my anxiety, my bad days—were the ones that garnered me the most followers and positive responses. I realized that if I wanted to keep growing my base, I needed to continue this image of authenticity. So, I leaned into that, talking more frequently on my account about my anxiety and how hard it is to maintain a healthy body image and lifestyle. Quickly, I grew numb to the content of these "real" posts, and they became weekly tasks I checked off my list. My anxiety, depression, body dysmorphia— these issues morphed into talking points that I used to fill my social media feed and make myself more relatable. Somewhere along the way, I stopped acknowledging to myself that these issues were still real to me, that they still chipped away at my happiness and sense of self. I was too focused on using them as part of my platform to focus on actually getting better.

And once the responses started to come in, I knew I couldn't stop. I was truly helping people. One woman even told me that because of me, she'd finally found the courage to see an eating-disorder specialist and gain control of her life. Another told me that she'd put on a bathing suit and gone to a pool for the first time in ten years because of my encouragement. I even received a message from a seventh-grade girl telling me that she wanted to become a therapist because of how much I'd supported her through the past year.

I cared about people, and I was helping people. And in turn, my followers helped *me*. I became emotionally tethered to these strangers, or, rather, the words of these strangers, who would tell me that they *understood*, that they knew I could get through it, that they were rooting for me. The digital compassion I received in exchange became my emotional balm, my medication. My followers gave me a sense of validation and pride. They made me feel less lonely.

It wasn't long until I started making enough money through endorsement deals to quit my job at the video game company and focus on TheGratefulAvocado full-time. But as my success grew, so did the pressure, so did the real anxiety, and then, so did the bulimia.

My social media platform became something that felt bigger than myself, something that I couldn't stop. "Just go offline for a while," my brother suggested to me when I hinted to him over Christmas that I was feeling overwhelmed with my work.

I tried. But it isn't that simple. My digital world is now my real world. My followers are my lifelines. Without them—without my social media platform—I'm not sure I even exist. I can't disappoint my followers. I can't let them down.

And yet, TheGratefulAvocado has somehow become a facade, a version of me that I know *doesn't* exist, and I hate that I'm no longer entirely truthful with my followers. That's what kills me the most—I want to be honest with them, but I can't. It's gone too far. TheGratefulAvocado might have started from a place of truth, but now it's spiraled into an imaginary depiction of my life that's so far from who I actually am that I don't know how I'd even begin to explain it.

So, I live two lives: that of TheGratefulAvocado, whose motto is to "live life to the fullest," and that of Ava Maloney, whose favorite pastimes are lying, bingeing, and purging. Repeat.

I think more about how I can go on the retreat and get away with it. Logistically, I have to find a way to be there without risking the quality and consistency of my work. If I can find a way to document most of my food, using saved photos and some new ones that I take pictures of in a stealthy way, and if I can show a few snippets of workouts a week, then maybe I can sneak by being vague about it all. I just have to craft the right narrative to spin to my followers. After all, I can work from anywhere. My adventures and vacations have become job opportunities, with free hotel stays, free dinners, free vacation clothes, and more. This is slightly different, of course; all anyone has to do is google the retreat to see that it specializes in weight loss, eating-disorder rehabilitation, and general detox . . . and the questions and accusations will fire up. So I can't tell anyone exactly where I am, ever.

At least I have security knowing that my real-life friends or family won't know or care where I'm going. Ever since I left my video game job, I've sort of fallen off the social grid. I just prefer to eat at home, aside from the occasional dinner or lunch out with a fellow influencer. Most of my friends these days are other food-and-wellness bloggers, and our relationships are transactional at best. Sometimes I go weeks on end without talking to Mike or my dad, so I could come and go to the retreat and they'd never even know.

I do a search for flights online. Getting to the island is a real pain in the ass, I discover. I have to fly to Boston and then take a little puddle-jumper plane to the Vineyard. But in a stroke of luck, the flight prices aren't that bad.

I look at my phone again, really in the hope that Ben has changed his mind and apologized, that he wants to see me. But there's no message, no missed call. Even though I know that I'm probably better off without him, I nevertheless feel a deep flash of pain in my heart, a twisting of my guts, as I read his last text over again, the words burning in my mind.

I wonder what might have happened if the episode last night had played out differently. If I had purged flawlessly and carried on with the evening. Or if I hadn't felt the need to purge at all. If we had slept together, and woken up next to one another the following morning, smiling sheepishly and cuddling under the duvet. If he had made us coffee in his French press and if we had made plans to go to Palm Springs and stay at the Parker for the weekend. What if? To imagine that it could have ended any differently than it did is just a wild fantasy. Because I know that I would have messed it up, sooner or later. As Ben said: I've got a lot to *figure out*.

Out of options and out of energy, I begin to accept that in just a few days, I will be on Martha's Vineyard, starting this retreat. And while I'm mad at myself for so recklessly signing up, there's an undeniable part of me that knows that I need to go. A part of me that *wants* to go. Because even when I thought I was better, right after I'd finished that year of intense therapy and I started TheGratefulAvocado, I knew that I hadn't fully addressed all my pain—the root of my pain. I'm not healed. I've been coasting. Surviving. But not living. I still haven't grieved my mother. I still haven't acknowledged her role in all this. I haven't really moved on from that first Christmas Eve. I am still that fifteen-year-old girl with my finger down my throat, my stocking-covered knees pressed into the cold bathroom floor, desperately trying to hold on to my family, my mother, my anchor, myself. I never even left that bathroom stall. And now I'm not just stuck in time, but I'm actually tumbling backward, like a pebble ricocheting down a mountainside, out of control, on an unstoppable path to combustion. The floor is falling beneath me, and if I don't do something now to change my life—to change *myself*—I'm going to keep falling.

I pull up the flights again on my computer, and I purchase a round-trip ticket. I leave in three days.

# Chapter 5

"You're the first to arrive in your cabin," Sarah tells me with a smile—the same smug grin that I could feel through the phone when we first spoke. She's not quite as I imagined. She's about my age, maybe a few years older, with glowing, suntanned skin, bright white teeth, loose curls of brown hair with golden streaks throughout, and an annoyingly beautiful, tall, and curvy body. I don't know why, but I'd imagined her as being thin, with brittle hair and bony limbs. She's the opposite—her arms are plump but muscular, and she exudes strength and confidence. Her wholesome, makeup-free, distinctly *island* style immediately makes me feel insecure and ridiculous.

"Oh no, I booked my own private room," I say, my voice becoming curt. I'm exhausted, having done the red-eye flight, on which I didn't sleep a wink, then the terror-inducing puddle jumper on Cape Air from Boston to the Vineyard, and then a van taxi that took me through the winding roads "up island," as my taxi driver told me.

"More relaxed up here than down island," he said to me on the drive. "Less tourists, more *nature*." I didn't really understand how there could be more nature in one part of a tiny island than in another—it all seemed pretty rural to me—but I started to see what he meant as we sped past old barns with grazing cattle out front and little farm stands advertising local produce on handwritten signs. By the time he pulled into Island Wellness's pea-stone driveway on the north shore of

Chilmark, I felt like I hadn't slept in years. After the journey I've had, if Sarah tries to stick me in a room with some stranger, I might lose it on her.

"Yes, Ava, but within a cabin. All our guests stay in the cabins with other guests. Some share rooms within the cabins, while others, like you, have their own rooms." She's using the same condescending tone she used with me on the phone a few days ago: *Oh, Ava.* "We believe that cohabiting our living spaces with other humans is an essential part of this experience."

I notice that she has a tattoo of a flock of birds on her wrist, and multiple ear piercings. *Does she believe all this shit?* I wonder. I search Sarah's face for a crack, a hint at realism, a slight eye roll, but I get nothing.

"Well, do I have my own bathroom?"

"Yes, of course. You requested that on your guest form, so we made sure that you're in a cabin with your own bathroom. You have two cabinmates, and you each have your own bathroom."

"Okay." I pause, thinking about how far I want to take this. Having *cabinmates* is not something I was prepared for in the slightest. I didn't sign up for a damn *summer camp*. In my mind, I run through the possible arguments I could make here, but the thought of arguing is too exhausting. I give up. Plus, the most important thing is that I have my own bathroom. As long as I have that, I'll be okay. And, anyway, I'm in a hurry to get to my room and post a photo of a midmorning snack from my saved album. I posted something in the Boston airport of the egg-white bites I got from Starbucks and geotagged Boston (one of my favorite breakfasts when on the go!), but now I need to further articulate the narrative of where I am, what I'm doing, and what I'm eating. If I don't do it soon, the questions will start rolling in.

I decided, on the long flight to Boston, to tell my followers that I'm on vacation on Martha's Vineyard but simply not specify where or what I'm doing. I have enough saved photos to use; not everything has to be new, current content from each day. Plus, it's only six weeks. In the grand scheme of things, it's nothing. It will fly by. I'm sure I can maintain my endorsement deals and get through the summer just fine.

Sarah leads me to the cabin herself, and hands me a map of the grounds as well as a list of the week's fitness and yoga offerings. Another staff member has already taken my luggage to my room, she tells me. She smiles and waves to other staff members and guests as we walk, like she's the mayor of this place. I notice that all the staff members I see share the same *island* aesthetic as Sarah—behind their crisp, clean linen uniforms, they smile with freshly scrubbed faces free of makeup, sun-kissed skin, bright eyes, and an abundance of various ear piercings and tattoos.

A path of gray stones nestled into sprawling thyme takes me to the cottage, which, I have to admit, is definitively charming: subtle gray-green trim paint, a front porch with a swinging bench and some chairs, and the same sumptuous landscaping as the rest of the grounds—purple sage, yellow echinacea, heathery-green lavender, red heliopsis, and white peonies just finishing their early summer bloom.

"Here we are," Sarah says as we enter the cabin. It's not really a cabin at all, I see, but an elegant home in the style of a restored coastal farmhouse, with chunky exposed wood beams across the ceiling, blue-and-white furniture, and clean sisal rugs. There's no television in the shared living room, but there *is* a bookshelf full of classics and summer paperbacks. Each room has an overhead fan, Sarah explains—*we don't do AC here*—and with the windows open, the breeze from the water comes through, along with the morning chirping of birds and the gentle scent of the flowers.

But then my gaze focuses on the kitchen, which I quickly realize is more of a bare-bones kitchenette, with just a small hotel-style fridge, a toaster oven, a sink, a coffeepot, and a few cabinets with some essentials. I panic a little upon realizing that there's no microwave in which I can make instant mac and cheese or ramen. No stovetop to make pasta or grilled cheese. No oven to throw a full-size frozen pizza into at three in the morning. And even if the kitchen *were* fully equipped, it would be difficult to get away with much when I have two roommates sleeping just a few feet away.

"This is great," I say, my throat closing up.

"Your room is this way," she says, pointing through the living room. "Your cabinmate Rhoda will be here on the first floor as well, and Stephanie will be upstairs."

My room is beautiful, too, with a four-poster queen bed, curtains I can close to block out the sunlight streaming through the windows, a spacious closet, a dresser, and a little reading nook with a yellow uphol-stered chair by the window.

"Thank you so much, Sarah," I say with a tone of finality so that she'll leave me alone. My luggage has already been dropped off, as she said it would be.

"I'll leave you, then, Ava," she says, bringing her hands together in a prayer position as she smiles and walks out. I get the distinct sense from Sarah that she's stifling a laugh, as though I have something in my teeth and she won't tell me. I remember how she's seen my application and read all my confessions, and I wonder if she's looked me up on Instagram even though she told me over the phone that she didn't have Instagram. My account is public, so even if she doesn't have an account herself, she could technically still see mine.

The moment she's gone, I inspect the most important room in the house: the bathroom. *Thank god,* I think as I open the door. There's no fan, but I check the faucet, turning it on and letting the water flow, which creates a nice bubbly white noise. And the door locks, another huge plus. I can work with this.

I take a long shower, scrubbing away the germs and grease from the two flights, and change into a soft denim romper with a white T-shirt underneath. I start to unpack. I check Instagram. I resisted the urge to look at any of Ben's friends' profiles throughout the entire flight.

Full

After the first night I met him, I managed to track down one of his buddies with a public profile, and that led me to a string of other friends, whose profiles I then began to check regularly to see if Ben had been tagged in any of their pictures. I have to use my finsta, my fake Instagram account, to see their stories and go unnoticed. I created the extra account for this exact purpose: when I want to thoroughly stalk someone but don't want to be found out. My finsta is some basic wellness influencer–style account, not dissimilar to mine, but with only a handful of posts of stock images pulled from the internet. I don't see anything new on Ben, and I'm pissed at myself for caving and checking in the first place.

As I organize my things, I have to remind myself of why I came here in the first place: well, first and foremost, because I had no choice. But really, as annoying as it is to hear it from Sarah, she's not wrong in telling me that there's a reason I signed up to be here. I know, even if I don't really want to admit it, that I need to get better. That I need to move on with my life, in more ways than one. I just don't know how to not immediately fall into my habits, to instinctively treat this place like enemy territory. It's not really a matter of *habits*, is the problem. These habits are my religion, my lifestyle, my identity. I don't know any other way.

"Helloooooo?" I hear from the doorway a little while later as I continue unpacking. "Anyone home?" The voice is high-pitched but strained and slightly shaky, like it belongs to someone a hundred years old. Sarah hadn't told me anything about my *cabinmates* at all, just that we were assigned together based on meal- and exercise-time preferences.

"Hi," I say, walking into the living room. I see Sarah there with a woman who looks to be in her seventies, with silvery-white hair. She wears sensible khaki slacks, sneakers, and a white button-down shirt—the kind of outfit I assume she picked out specifically for a long flight. A male staff member silently enters with the woman's luggage and goes straight to her room with it. She shoves some cash into his palm before he leaves. He puts his hands into prayer, as Sarah had done, and backs out of the room.

"Well, this is nothing short of magical!" The woman plants her hands on her hips and gazes around the house with wide eyes. "Can you believe this place?" It takes me a moment to realize that she's talking to me.

"I know!" I say, my voice coming out like a faucet drip, forced and detached.

Sarah stands next to the woman with her hands clasped, beaming, as though her own blood, sweat, and tears are in the walls of the house.

"I'm Rhoda," the woman says to me, extending her hand. "You must be Ava. Sarah was telling me all about you."

"I'm Ava, hi." We shake hands, and I'm surprised by the firmness of her grip. I have to admit, there's something about this woman that's charming and endearing. Still, I'm pissed off that I have to spend time socializing like this, making *niceties* with strangers I don't care to know. I begin to regret not making a stink of it at the front desk when I checked in.

"Well, I'm going to let you two continue to get settled in," Sarah says. "Your other cabinmate, Stephanie, should be here soon as well. And you've got orientation at four, then dinner at six. So many blessed things await you." *Blessed things.* I stifle a snort.

Rhoda throws her hands up in the air and releases a sigh once Sarah's gone.

"Isn't this incredible?" she asks.

"It really is," I say, feeling guilty for not being more appreciative of being here. Rhoda isn't wrong; the house and the entire grounds *are* incredible. But I'm too focused on myself to appreciate it.

"I've never done anything like this," she says, taking her shoes off and sitting down on the living room couch. I wonder if she's expecting me to sit with her, to spend some time talking. I want to finish unpacking. I don't want to chat. I was about to set up a snack drawer in my dresser. "But my David just passed away a few months ago. Cancer."

"Oh, I'm so sorry," I say. Now I really can't get out of the conversation.

"Thank you, sweetheart. He lived a long life. We were married for over fifty years."

"Wow. I'm just so sorry."

"Don't be. I miss him, always will. But he'd want me to be here, enjoying myself."

"Did you always want to come here?"

"Well," she says, pausing, "I always wanted to come to Martha's Vineyard, yes. But really, I just needed to get away from everyone back home in Florida who feels *sorry* for me. They keep showing up at my doorstep with quiches and casseroles, like that's going to help anything. No one talks to me like a normal person anymore. They talk to me like I'm half-dead. *I'm fine,* I tell them all. So, that's really why I'm here. To get away from everyone who feels sorry for me."

"I know exactly how you feel," I tell her. And I do. Perhaps I misread Rhoda. "Good for you."

Just then, the door opens, and Sarah reappears with our other cabinmate.

"Hello again, ladies," she says. "This is Stephanie." Rhoda and I are speechless for a moment as we take Stephanie in. She must be six feet tall, with dark-brown skin, piercing eyes, and hair in dozens of neat, tight braids falling all the way down her back. She's stunning. "Stephanie, this is Ava and Rhoda."

"Wow," Rhoda gasps. "Are you a real-life supermodel?"

"Ha," Stephanie says, as though she's heard that before. "No, I am certainly not. Pretty much the opposite of a supermodel. Corporate lawyer. Nice to meet you both." She's wearing jean shorts, a white cashmere sweater, and suede Birkenstock sandals—the kind of outfit I wish I could wear without looking like a slob. I wonder, as I always do whenever I meet a thin woman, if she watches what she eats or if she's naturally thin.

The man who brought in Rhoda's luggage returns with Stephanie's, a set of shiny Rimowa bags.

"See you all at orientation," Sarah says.

Stephanie's phone starts ringing, and she opens her purse, a Bottega Veneta in woven caramel leather, to find it. This woman is *chic*. Even her cell phone case is glamorous. She probably takes spa vacations like this all the time.

"Hey," she answers, her voice like a jab. She pauses, listening. "Call back." She hangs up but stares at her screen and then types something with manic precision, faster than even I type. Then she tosses the phone back into the bag.

"Sorry about that," she says to us. "Work."

"That's okay," Rhoda and I mutter, both transfixed.

"I'm not even supposed to be working, really," she explains. "I *told* them that I was going to be unreachable. *Out of office.* Does that mean *nothing* anymore? Just because I have a cell phone and you *can* reach me doesn't mean you *should*. You know?" She sighs and plops her bag on the kitchen counter. "But of course, I'm having this *idiot* colleague at work cover everything for me, and what good is that going to do? I'll have to hold his hand the entire time I'm gone."

We nod. Maybe I misread Stephanie, too. And I do understand what she means. Even though my entire livelihood pretty much depends on my ability to be plugged in, connected, and accessible at all times, I hate that technology has made it impossible to ever take a break from that, even for a moment. It's impossible *to hide*.

I understand that probably even better than she does.

"So, what brought you here, then? Sounds like you need a break!" Rhoda smiles at her.

"Exactly, Rhoda—that's *exactly* what I need," Stephanie says, kicking her sandals off. "I sort of had an episode a few weeks ago, you know, a *meltdown* at work, whatever you want to call it. Too much stress, my doctor said. I thought about just doing a staycation, but I live in Manhattan, and so, you know, I just needed to get out of the city for a minute, too. It was actually my husband's idea. I'm sure he's excited to get a break from me for a few weeks. I don't exactly make it easy for him. Anyway, I signed up and here I am."

"Good for you," I chime in. "Sounds like we're all here for kind of the same reason." I wonder if Stephanie knows who I am. Maybe she even follows me. People like her—successful, smart, beautiful women who work in male-dominated corporate worlds—don't really exist in my bubble of influencers and wellness. She intimidates me.

We realize that orientation starts soon, so we split up to finish unpacking. Back in my room, with the door shut, I pull out the snacks I brought with me that were tucked at the bottom of my suitcase. My emergency rations. Whenever I've gone on a trip for the past few years, I've always brought food with me. The thought of being without food for an unknown amount of time—or, more specifically, without easy access to an *excess* of food—gives me a sense of dread. I pull out a box of Oreos, a bag of mint Milanos, a sleeve of mini powdered donuts, a box of Cheez-Its, a large bag of Cool Ranch Doritos, and three packs of Reese's peanut butter cups. Then I unfold a few sweaters, and they roll open to reveal a medium-size bottle of Ketel One vodka and two bottles of Cannonball cabernet sauvignon, my go-to red wine. I open the bottom drawer of my dresser and place the stash in there, neatly hidden beneath the sweaters. I feel calmer already knowing that I have my safety net in place.

I also pull out my influencer supplies: my mini ring light, my tripod, and my selfie stick. I didn't bring my soft box, diffusion fabric, or my full-size ring light with me, and I start to regret that choice as I realize that I'm going to have to take some photos and videos at some point while I'm here. I take out three empty containers of flavored oat-based creamers that I'd been sent back in LA as part of my sponsorship deal.

I didn't have time to take enough stock videos and photos with them before I left. They taste like shit, and I couldn't fly with full containers of them, anyway, so I plan to just photograph the empties or fill them with some milk or something if I make a video of myself pouring it into my coffee. Next are some collagen gummies I've been promoting for over a year, a new serum from an organic skin-care line that I just partnered with, a bag of downright disgusting probiotic mushroom powder that I pretend to add to my coffee or oatmeal, some trendy athletic apparel that I'm actually excited to try out, and a hideous tote bag that I say I use for my grocery shopping or for "running errands around the city."

As I shut the drawer, I hear a noise outside my window, and I jump upon seeing Sarah right there, almost pressed against the pane. I'm so startled that I let out a tiny shriek and feel a rush of fear go up my spine. Was she spying on me? Sarah quickly averts her eyes, and I see that she has a cluster of freshly picked flowers in her hand and a pair of pruning scissors in the other. Seems like an odd thing for her to be doing, cutting flowers right outside my window, of all places. Maybe that's normal around here, but I could swear that she was watching me. I glance back at my drawer of snacks and wonder if she could see clearly enough through the window to observe all the junk food and booze before I'd covered it up. When I look out the window again, Sarah has disappeared. I pull the curtains shut.

My paranoia and curiosity about the guest application flood back in. I wish I could remember all of it and what I said. But I've remembered only bits and pieces here and there. It was lengthy, I remember that, with sections about my medical history, health and weight goals, eating habits, even a question about regrets and mistakes. I remember that I wrote something about how I want to be clear that I'm not anorexic, that I'm bulimic, and that there's a big difference.

*Everyone loves an anorexic girl,* I wrote, *but no one likes a bulimic. Anorexic girls are romanticized in the media as being delicate, tortured, complicated—like they're all ballerinas. But we bulimics are gross and have no restraint or discipline. We're puffy. We stink if we don't cover up our tracks. Our skin is dried out from dehydration, our eyes are bloodshot, and our teeth can even fall out. We stuff ourselves like grotesque medieval kings. There's nothing cute about a bulimic girl.*

The recollection of my own biting words hurts me and fills me with shame. I know that there's nothing glamorous about anorexia. It's a terrible disease. It can be invisible. It can be fatal. I *know* this, and yet the truth is that I've always harbored a sick kind of admiration for anyone who possesses the discipline to say no to food, something I've never been able to do. I also know that bulimia is a disease, too, and I'm disgusted with myself for describing it in such a terrible way.

But what I wrote isn't about anyone else, or eating disorders in general. It's about me. My entire life is about creating content preaching self-love and acceptance, when really, I'm the one who needs to hear it, not the one who should be preaching it. Whoever has read my application must think that I'm devoid of any compassion and full of hatred. And I wouldn't blame them. I just wish they knew that the hatred is only directed toward myself.

# Chapter 6

Stephanie, Rhoda, and I congregate a few minutes later in the living room and then head out to the lawn for orientation. I hope it's not going to be this way the whole time, traveling together like a pack of animals. I want to be able to come and go as I please and not be tethered to these women, or to a schedule. Though as we approach the lawn and I see the other guests, I feel a strange kinship with Stephanie and Rhoda, almost like it's us against them.

The retreat has a total of twenty guests, Sarah told me at check-in, all spread out in different cabins on the property. I notice a few men, some couples, but mostly women of various ages. Two identical twins—young women with broad shoulders and pronounced calf muscles protruding from their basketball shorts—shuffle forward. Three extremely fit, tiny women I estimate to be in their late thirties, all dressed in lululemon workout clothes and Nike sneakers, chat loudly with another guest about how the retreat lined up perfectly with their kids' summer-camp schedules. A shy, overweight-looking man in his sixties, with glasses and a button-down short-sleeve shirt and khaki shorts, fiddles with his hands. An impeccably dressed and shockingly young couple who could pass for teenagers whisper to one another as they glance at the other guests. Sarah stands on a flat rock nestled into the grass in the middle of the lawn and waits for us to gather.

"Welcome to Island Wellness," she declares, her arms open wide, as we gather around. The sun is hot, and I wish I were tanning on the lawn instead of going on the tour. "Welcome to our sanctuary. Over the next six weeks, you will all be challenged. That's right, you will be *challenged*. Because wellness is just that: a challenge. It's not easy to prioritize oneself. It's not easy to make healthy choices. We live in a society that is constantly presenting us with obstacles on the pathway to our healthiest selves. But here at Island Wellness, we are going to equip you with the tools you need to have a life of mindful choices, mindful connections—with one another, with your bodies, with your health, and with your food—so that you become more mindful humans. That's what this is all about."

I look around at the other guests, hoping to find someone with whom I can share a silent laugh, a quick glance of understanding, but I don't get the sense that they share my skepticism. I wonder if this is the first time they've ever really thought about food consumption, about physical wellness. I can't remember a time, at least not in my adult life, when I *haven't* been thinking about it. I've tried it all—every diet, every fad, every "expert" in nutrition, even in holistic healing. I find it hard to believe that this place could offer me anything new.

We follow her, in line like a flock of geese, on a tour of the grounds. First is the property's garden, where the majority of the produce we will eat is grown.

"Various lettuce, kale, arugula, zucchini, tomatoes, herbs, and so much more," Sarah says. "Quite literally the earth's bounty, right here." A handsome young gardener wipes his brow with his forearm and then returns to weeding—it's something straight out of a Danielle Steel novel. A few people ooh and aah.

Next is the yoga studio—or the "chapel," as Sarah calls it. The building used to be an actual private chapel, built in the late 1800s, she says, but the center reconstructed it to be a yoga studio. It's just one large room, enough to comfortably fit everyone for a yoga class, with high ceilings and stained-glass windows on the two top sides, and a massive sliding hurricane door that opens out to an expansive wood porch. The light streams in and paints the wide floorboards in all colors. I hate yoga, despite having tried it dozens of times in LA. I need distraction when I work out: loud music, interval training, breathlessness. In yoga classes, I find myself too much in my own head, unable to focus on anything but whatever is depressing me that day. I've never left a yoga class feeling better. Physically more relaxed, maybe, but not mentally better. But the space truly is so beautiful that, even through my lens of skepticism, I think, just for a moment, that it might be a nice place to do it.

The main building is referred to as the "farmhouse." It's where most of our meals will take place and where our therapy sessions will be. Sarah introduces everyone to the center's two therapists, Leon and Wanda, who stand on the farmhouse's front porch, both holding clipboards and pens. They're dressed casually, in jeans and T-shirts, and I wonder if they're a couple. "Though Leon and Wanda are both doctors—licensed psychiatrists—of course, around here we just call them Leon and Wanda," Sarah says. "We don't believe in hierarchical identifiers here. Now, most everything on the schedule of activities is open to all guests without advanced sign-up. The only things that will be scheduled for you are your healing sessions with Leon or Wanda. You'll all have your first appointments sometime in the next few days, and our staff will notify you in advance. After that, you'll meet with them with a frequency that depends on your specific needs. Some guests find it helpful to meet daily. Others, weekly. It's your journey, so it will be up to you—with their advice and professional input, of course." *Yeah*, I think, *I'm sure they give the professional advice to seek* daily *treatment so that guests are paying out of the ass.* I decide then and there to limit my appointments as much as I can. As we continue the tour, I glance back at the so-called doctors, who are watching us like we're rare species trapped in a zoo.

Even though I've gone through several therapists myself, and in general I do believe in the power of good therapy, I bristle at the thought of enduring it here. There's no way either of these therapists could actually help me—let alone all *twenty* of us—in just six weeks. One thing I've learned is that you can't exactly unravel years of grief and disordered eating with a few hours of heartfelt and introspective chatter. I start to feel like I would have been better off just paying the cost of the whole thing and not coming at all.

We glide through the farmhouse, which includes a library full of books for us to borrow anytime, a large living room with double doors leading out to the lawn, a screened-in porch with rocking chairs, and several offices where therapy will take place.

There's also the kitchen, which Sarah takes us by, briefly, and we nod and smile toward the kitchen staff. I peer farther into the kitchen, trying to see what they're making, and I'm momentarily distracted enough to forget about the foreboding group work. One chef is filleting an entire bluefin tuna, slicing into its dark-pink meat like a conductor of an orchestra. Another chef is cleaning and sorting basil leaves off several dozen stalks, and the smell is so potent and bright that I find myself sniffing audibly with my eyes closed for a second. On one of the counters are baskets filled high with fresh produce—peaches, nectarines, plums, corn, peppers, spiky cucumbers, hothouse tomatoes bursting with the colors of the sunset. For just a brief moment, I feel relaxed and comforted by these smells and sights. Sarah and the rest of the group have moved on to the farmhouse living room, but I remain fixed in the kitchen doorway, watching.

"You coming?" Rhoda asks me. She and Stephanie have waited for me.

"Oh, sorry," I say, and I hurry along.

"Are you into cooking?" Stephanie asks. "You seemed pretty engrossed back there."

"I guess so," I say. "I mean, yes. I love cooking. Food is sort of . . . my passion." The words slip from my mouth like an experiment, unsure and wobbly. But it's true.

"Well, I love eating, but I don't love cooking," she says.

"Me too!" Rhoda agrees.

Once we're all in the living room, Sarah hands us itineraries, and I scan my eyes over the list of activities and spa offerings. At first glance, it looks amazing—options to go on sunrise hikes, an abundance of natural outdoor space to explore, bikes to rent, buffet breakfasts with a custom omelet bar, a different midafternoon fresh smoothie option every day. But tucked into the facade of relaxation and indulgence is a regimen of forced self-reflection, conversation with strangers, *workshopping*. "You might think you came here to get away," Sarah tells us, "but maybe you came here to turn inward, to *return* to yourself. And that brings me back to what I said at the start of this tour: this is going to be a *challenge*. But I know that you're all up for it."

"How many ellipticals does the gym have?" one of the women in leggings asks.

"Do you have a Peloton?" another one chirps.

As Sarah answers, I decide to take a few minutes to check my phone. My stories have gotten a pretty solid number of views, and no red flags seem to have been raised yet. I skim through some of my DMs. In the usual slew of responses—heart emojis, smiley faces, and a question about what I like to wear on flights—I notice one message from an account named mermaid1985:

**I know where you are on Martha's Vineyard. And why. Does everyone else?**

I hit the profile. It's public, but shows only a handful of posts—mostly close-ups of flowers, a sunset, a manicured and suntanned set of toes in the sand—but none of the photos are geotagged. The account has only a few followers, all of which seem like bots, and the only accounts it follows are all blue-checked celebrities in the wellness, fitness, food, or beauty space: Angela Manuel-Davis, Paloma Elsesser, Gwyneth Paltrow, the Minimalist Baker. All signs indicate that this is a finsta account. Someone real is behind it, but whoever it is, they're using this account just to troll people like me. Normally, I don't let these things rattle me. It comes with the territory—the haters, the doubters, the messages that were clearly sent to me by accident and meant to have been forwarded to a friend ("this bitch is so annoying"). But the specificity of this message is different. It scares me. I tuck my phone back in my pocket, deciding that the best course of action is to just not respond. At least for now.

In the main foyer, Sarah waves toward a table of refreshments.

"That concludes our tour," she says. "Please help yourself here to a selection of our freshly brewed iced teas and just-out-of-the-oven honey-lavender cookies, gluten-free." She pauses. "And just one more thing. If you choose to leave the grounds at any point, that is your choice, but we ask that you simply sign out on the clipboard at the front desk and sign in again when you return."

"Well," Stephanie says to me and Rhoda as we stand in the living room, waiting for the crowd around the refreshment table to thin out. "I don't know about you ladies, but I'm tired. I might go back to the cabin and get some work done before dinner."

"I thought you just said you were tired," Rhoda responds. "Why not take a nap? You strike me as someone who doesn't do that. Ever. Am I right?"

"Guilty," Stephanie says. "I did come here to unplug, but my phone has been blowing up with emails and I just . . . I guess I don't know *how* to unplug."

"I can help you," I say. "Give me your phone." Skeptically, Stephanie hands me her phone. I pull up her email settings and draft an out-of-office auto response, surprised that she doesn't already have one. "Here, look," I say, showing her the screen before confirming the setting.

"I don't know," Stephanie says. "I feel irresponsible doing that."

"Do the men in your office do that when *they* go on vacation?" Rhoda asks.

"Well, now that I think about it, *yes*, they do." Stephanie considers this, then turns to me. "Okay, screw it." I hit "Confirm," and she sighs with relief. "Thanks," she says. I'm impressed with myself that I was able to offer Stephanie any kind of advice at all, let alone advice that she actually took.

"Well, I *am* going to take a nap before dinner," Rhoda says.

"Me too," Stephanie says.

"I'm going to explore a bit more." Really, I want some of the cookies that have been put out, and I need to scan the grounds a bit, take a few photos, find some spots for potential video content. When they've left, I hang back from the refreshment table, testing myself to see how long I can wait to get a cookie. The rest of the guests mingle around, drinking iced tea and chatting. I notice Sarah standing back as well, watching the guests. I wonder what everyone else wrote on their applications, and who here gets to read them.

Just as I take a step toward the table, I notice a young staff member looking over at me. She couldn't be older than twenty, I think. She's sweet looking, with big eyes and full brows. She's clearly watching me, her hands nervously clenched together. I smile and wave, and she approaches.

"Hi," she says, her cheeks blushing. "I'm Naomi. I work here." She points to her name tag. "Obviously!"

"Hi, I'm Ava," I say. I can tell right away that she recognizes me. She's a follower. Honestly, I hate these moments of recognition just as much as I appreciate them. It's not that I'm not grateful for their support—I absolutely am. It's that I'm always nervous I'm going to let them down in person. That I'm going to be a disappointing departure from the person they've gotten to know online.

"I know," she gushes. "I'm actually a really big fan. Like, a huge fan. Since the early days." She leans closer. "Don't worry, though, I would never tell anyone you're here. We all have to sign NDAs or whatever so we can't talk about guests. Promise." I'm immediately reminded of the strange DM I received earlier. But from Naomi's eager and sincere tone, I can't imagine it was from her.

"Thank you so much, Naomi. That means a lot to me," I say. "And that's good to know, about confidentiality, I mean. I'm not exactly sharing with my followers that I'm here. Sometimes we just need time for *ourselves*, you know?"

"Oh, definitely!" she practically shrieks.

"So, what do you do here?"

"I'm just working here for the summer, helping with all kinds of things," she says.

"Cool. Must be a great place to spend the summer. Are you in school?"

"Yeah, I'm in school in Boston studying nutrition . . . Actually, what I really want to do is be an influencer like you, in wellness. I'm just getting started, but . . . I used to have an eating disorder, too, and your account really helped me. So, thank you, I guess."

For a moment, I forget that I've been lying to her—to all my followers. I forget that I filter and edit almost all my photos to make myself look like an unrealistic, best version of myself, smoothing out my skin, narrowing my nose, and widening my eyes. Or that even in my makeup and skin-care tutorials, I tell my followers that I'm barefaced and fresh when really, I've got some concealer and bronzer on. Or that I frequently binge on fast food and takeout for a family of six and then violently purge and do it all over again. Or that I often photograph healthy, nourishing, *expensive* meals only to throw them out in the garbage, untouched. Or that my right index finger is always somewhat puckered and carries the faint, acidic odor of puke no matter how much I wash it. Or that the only reason I'm not fat is that I rarely let myself digest an actual meal. For a fleeting moment, I forget all of this, and I don't hate myself. I'm proud of the connections I've made with young women like Naomi, and the help I've given them.

"Thank you for sharing that with me. And wow, good for you. That's an amazing journey you've had." As soon as I say the words, I remember who I really am, and I feel terrible. This innocent girl has chosen to believe in me, of all people. If only she knew.

"I'd probably get in trouble for asking this," Naomi whispers then, "and I, um, I don't want to be unprofessional, but maybe we could talk sometime while you're here? I'd just love to know more about how you built your business, how you create content . . . basically just like, everything!"

"Sure, I'd love to," I tell her. There's something endearing about Naomi, and it's a reminder of why I started doing what I do in the first place.

"Wow, thank you! Okay!" She smiles and starts to turn away, almost tripping.

"Hey, Naomi, can I, uh, ask you a question?"

"Of course."

"You know how all the guests had to fill out applications before coming here?" She nods. "Well, who reads those, do you know? I'm just wondering."

"Oh yeah, those are like, super confidential. Only Leon, Wanda, and Sarah read them. I mean, technically they're all in the office filing cabinets, so I guess any staff could access them if they wanted to, but it's not allowed. I think the staff here takes it pretty seriously. We'd get in major trouble."

I feel a tiny bit of relief, but not enough. Even if only the three of them read the applications, anyone with access to the office *could* read the files. I scan Naomi's face quickly but don't see a trace of anything but genuine admiration for me, which she definitely wouldn't have if she'd read my application.

"Cool, thanks," I say. "That's what I thought. I just wanted to be sure."

"Totally, I get it. Well, I should get back to work."

"Oh, Naomi? Just one more thing, really quickly. Maybe you can help me?"

"Anything you need."

"Well, you see, like I said before, I'm not really telling my followers that I'm here," I say, a plan forming in my mind. "This is really a personal trip for me. It's not like one of my sponsored vacations where I get to stay for free if I advertise the hotel, you know? So basically, I'm going to tell my followers that I'm on vacation but not say where or what I'm doing. The truth is, I don't want my followers to know I'm here just because, well, frankly, this place is so nice, and costs so much, and I like to give my followers realistic and accessible expectations for being healthy. I don't want anyone to think that they need to be here and spend this kind of money to be healthy."

Naomi nods. "Absolutely," she says. "I totally get that."

"So, anyway, sometimes I might take pictures of food, and I'm just not really going to specify who made it or where it's from." I search her face for any sign of skepticism or mistrust, but she's locked into me, ready to take orders. I'm not even entirely sure where I'm going with this plan, but I know that if I can't reason with Sarah and I'm forced to stay here, I'm going to need an inside source to help me take some photos and make my content seem realistic by supplying me with food to document. "So, once in a while, maybe you can help me out by giving me some basic things like fruit or salads, yogurt or whatever, so

I can plate it in the kitchen in my cabin and sort of make it look like I'm cooking for myself? I mean, I don't really consider it a lie when it's something I *could* have made myself, or if it's just like fruit I'm cutting up. Right?" I start to cringe at the sound of my own voice, at this stupid plan I'm mapping out. But at the same time, I know that it's the price I have to pay if I want to uphold my public persona and maintain my platform while I'm here.

Naomi stops nodding and just stares at me for a moment, and I'm worried I've lost her. She's a fan—a *pure* fan—and within two minutes of knowing me, I've asked her to help me *lie*. But then she nods, and she returns to me.

"Of course, yes, you got it. Absolutely."

"Thanks, Naomi, I knew you'd get it. So maybe you can bring some fruit or berries or something like that to my room after this? That would really be a lifesaver."

"Oh yes, of course, no problem." She beams. I thank her, and she whisks herself away toward the kitchen. I pour myself a ginger iced tea but decide not to take a cookie. Sarah is looking away, but I'm sure she caught the tail end of my interaction with Naomi. I smile at her, feeling smug for refusing the cookies.

My plan isn't perfect, that's for sure. But it's also rooted in the truth. I don't want to tell my followers that I'm here for the reasons I explained to Naomi. This place is *luxe*—it's out of reach for the average person. It's even out of reach for me. And my whole platform has been based on the belief that anyone, anywhere, can be healthy and balanced with the right choices. *Right.* But my belief in that is real—or it was at one point. Telling my followers that I'm here, at a wellness retreat, would just be confusing. Why would I need to go to a wellness retreat for *six weeks*, one that specializes in helping guests heal from eating disorders, trauma, anxiety, and depression, if I had already achieved the healthy life that I was *selling*? It would basically dismantle my entire business. But I'm allowed to have a private life, so telling my followers that I'm simply on vacation somewhere fabulous on the East Coast is fine—in fact, a certain level of mystique is a good thing, I've always believed. I just have to walk the perilous tightrope of truth and omission.

Feeling my stress level rise, I decide to take a cookie after all. I'm surprised by how delicious it is, despite being gluten-free. And, of course, right as I eat, Sarah approaches.

"Everything okay so far, Ava?" she asks.

"Oh yes, everything is great." I remember our phone call in which she flat out refused to refund me, and my anger at her floods back.

"You seemed a little upset earlier. I saw you, on your phone? Did something happen?"

"No, everything's fine. Just have a bunch of work stuff to deal with. So I better get going, actually. Thank you."

"We have a workshop next week about digital detoxing that might interest you."

The suggestion feels like a blatant insult toward me. Sarah knows exactly what I do for a living, so it somehow seems like she's implying that my entire career is something I need to detox out of my life. Or maybe I'm reading too much into it.

"I'll think about it. Thanks."

As I walk, I think about how Sarah had first told me that she didn't even have Instagram. Sometimes I think that if social media wasn't the fundamental platform of my entire business, if it was just something I used like a regular person, I wouldn't want to have it, either. But I know I *would* have it. I know I wouldn't be able to resist it. I'm envious of Sarah's restraint. I meet plenty of young women who claim to live their lives as naturally as possible, as free from all toxins—both literal and figurative—as possible, and this includes toxic social media. And yet there they are, *talking about it on social media*. But Sarah is really living it, while I only wish I were. I'm not just envious of her restraint; I'm envious of her apparent authenticity.

I return to the cabin to find that Naomi has already stealthily delivered a luscious fruit plate that sits on the kitchen counter for me—a delicious spread of raspberries, sliced kiwi, mango, and clementine sections, along with a note: *Anything you need, just let me know! Xo Naomi.* She's also put a basket of whole fruit out, and she's stocked the fridge with yogurt, LaCroix, and a crudités-and-hummus platter. Naomi is going to be my way through this thing. It's been hours since I last posted, so I need to get something up quickly and figure out what my narrative is going to be. I scan my surroundings, deciding to do a video, but triple-checking that the background of the kitchen cabinets is generic enough to be anywhere. I could be at a friend's home, or a nice Airbnb. I fluff the hair around my face and brush my eyebrows up with my fingertips, and then I lick my lips. I select the Retrocam filter and start to record an Instagram story.

"Hi, friends," I begin. "Sorry it's been a minute. I'm here on Martha's Vineyard. I can't even remember the last time I took a vacation! It's my first time on the island. I'm mostly planning to lay low and just relax, but if you've got any tips for me, please let me know! Right now, it's about five o'clock and I'm feeling a little hungry, so I just sliced up some beautiful fruit." I hit the reverse-lens button on my phone and simultaneously pan the phone down toward the fruit plate, which I've rearranged slightly to look a little less perfect. "Some kiwi, a little mango, clementine, and some raspberries," I say. I return the camera to my face. "You know how sometimes after a long plane ride you just want something *superfresh*? I mean, how *amazing* does this look? I'm not adding honey or anything—you guys know sometimes I love to do that with fruit. But honestly this is all so good it doesn't even need anything. Anyway, I hope you guys are having a beautiful Monday and are being kind to yourselves today. You deserve that."

I muster one last smile and then end the recording. I watch it a few times before posting.

Alone in the kitchen, I nibble on a bit of the fruit but decide that it would be better to save it for after a binge, when I actually want to keep something down. I rarely eat healthy food and then binge it; what's the point?

I go to my room and lock the door. For the first time since I arrived, a feeling of loneliness sets in. I wish I had someone to talk to about the retreat, the mysterious DM I received, the mix of conflicting emotions I have about being here. I consider calling Becky, an LA friend I met after attending the same Saturday spin class for a year. We always rode next to one another in the front row, so after a while we decided to get a juice next door after class. Our friendship has since remained within those parameters: weekly spin class followed by a green juice or smoothie. She's a manager at a boutique Beverly Hills management company where she helps groom B-list reality stars into brand-endorsement kings and queens. She understands my work, and I appreciate that. I can use a shorthand with her, and sometimes I run endorsement offers by her for her opinion. Despite the somewhat transactional nature of our friendship, hers is pretty much the only one I've maintained in LA, or anywhere.

Instead of calling, I text her:

You're not gonna see me at spin on Sat. Last minute summer trip to Martha's Vineyard. See you in six weeks!

Becky responds right away. She's always on her phone, even more than I am.

Whaaaat? Need more info, call this weekend. Get a suntan for me.

I don't know what else I had expected from her, but the interaction doesn't do anything to squelch my emptiness, my loneliness. I'm homesick for my apartment, or for something I can't quite put my finger on. Maybe for our old house in Cherry Hill. Or maybe I just miss my mom. I pour myself a glass of water from the bathroom sink and chug it, then open some of my snack supplies, starting with Oreos, inhaling them two at a time. I have another glass of water and then a few mini powdered donuts, until I eventually feel my stomach expand like a balloon and my anxiety begins to dissipate, knowing what will come next and how good it will feel. I go to the bathroom, curl into position in front of the toilet, and puke.

This time, it's somewhat of a struggle, because I'm actually hungry, so my body tries to resist the purge. A therapist once explained this to me like it was obvious: "Right, Ava," she said, "your body actually *wants* that food. It's telling you, *'Please, let me have it! Let me* keep *it!'*"

I rolled my eyes at her. "Just because my body *wants* something doesn't mean it should *have* it," I said. I didn't go back to that therapist again.

When I'm done, I sigh with relief, and I don't exactly feel *better*, or less lonely, but I feel like I've done something, accomplished something, *felt* something other than what I was feeling before. I'm calmer. I wash my hands, brush my teeth, and splash my face with cold water—the usual routine. I dab some cream onto the bags under my eyes, noticing how tired I look. I return to my bed, where I sit and check my email. I need to post something soon for Skin Beams, an organic skin serum that's paying me *a lot* for a partnership. The rep has emailed me with a "friendly reminder." But I check my face in the camera of my phone. I'm bloated and puffy, dried out, like I've aged ten years since before the Oreo purge. Even the best editing won't fix it. I decide I'll wait until tomorrow to post, when I hopefully don't hate my reflection as much as I do right now.

I start to get ready for dinner, applying a little highlighter and brushing my brows. It's been three days now since I've heard from Ben. The first few days, back in LA, were sort of bearable. I was in such a daze preparing to leave that I had managed to suppress my feelings about what had happened. I almost found a way to deny it entirely. But now, as I look at myself in the mirror, I feel the heavy silence of my room, the carefully curated beauty of the cabin, the manicured landscape of the property, the perfumed East Coast salt air, and I don't think that I could ever be fixed here. Or anywhere.

# Chapter 7

The indoor dining room of the farmhouse, which we'd somehow skipped on the tour, is cavernous, like a banquet hall, with exposed wooden ceiling beams and large windows that give the room an indoor/outdoor feel. It's not a room in which one can hide and eat alone, in peace, as I'd like to do. It's well lit and meant for communal dining, with several large tables throughout the room and only a few small two-seaters. My worst nightmare. Rhoda, Stephanie, and I approach and claim three chairs at an empty table. The three of us have barely gotten to know one another, but it's unspoken that we'll eat dinner together, at least this first meal, and in a way, I'm glad to have them.

"Well, hello," says one of the three leggings-clad women I'd noticed earlier at orientation. They trot up to the table in unison, in their black spandex and form-fitting zip-up jackets, like a group of slick and rubbery underfed seals. "Mind if we join you?" I examine their faces. Not a forehead line or crow's-foot in sight, and their skin is so plumped with filler that it's hard to know what their natural facial structure is. I'm all for some injections here and there, absolutely, but these women—the *leggings*—I think they've gone a little too far. Now that I see them up close, I can't tell if they're actually twenty-five or fifty-five years old. They could be either, or anything in between.

"Sure," I say, though I get the sense that Stephanie and Rhoda share my apprehension at the prospect of dining with the leggings. As we mark our seats with our sweaters and napkins, the leggings introduce themselves as Bronwyn, Eliza, and Hadley.

"We're from Wellesley," Eliza tells us, as though that should mean something to us.

"Ah. Wellesley College," Rhoda says proudly. "Class of 1971. Spent some time in Boston after. But now I live in Florida." The leggings nod.

"Are you ladies all here together?" Hadley asks, eyeing us. I can tell that she's trying to figure out how the three of us could possibly know one another.

"We're cabinmates. We just met," I say. "I live in LA." Bronwyn is staring at me, and I'm almost positive that she knows who I am. I wait for her to say something, but she doesn't.

"Manhattan," Stephanie says. The leggings nod again.

"Well, shall we?" Rhoda suggests, looking toward the buffet set up on a long banquet table to the side of the room. I'm grateful to her for moving it along; I'm not in the mood to chitchat with them any longer than I have to. The buffet spread looks and smells delicious, and my stomach growls in response. There are two different kinds of green salads, sesame-crusted local tuna, grilled steak with herb chimichurri sauce, roasted red potatoes, charred corn on the cob, freshly baked rolls, and, for dessert, local blueberry pie and homemade ginger ice cream. As we wait in line, I scan the room and notice that the tables all have pitchers of water on them and that staff members float around offering what looks like the signature iced tea that was served earlier. But there's one thing that I notice is conspicuously missing, and my stomach drops.

"Hey," I say to Stephanie as she takes a plate in the line, "where do you think the alcohol is?"

"Are you joking?" She looks at me with what I think is a mix of amusement and pity. "This place is *dry*. Like, bone dry. It's a wellness retreat. You seriously didn't know that?"

"I guess . . . I didn't think about it. I mean, we're paying so much, and it's not like this is rehab."

Stephanie shakes her head. "Yeah, well, I guess we're paying the big bucks so that we *don't* drink." She spoons one of the green salads onto her plate. "So that we load up on all this instead." She rolls her eyes just slightly at me, the first sign yet that someone else here might be on the same page.

I take a plate behind Stephanie and walk through the buffet line, piling on some salads and a slice of tuna. There's too much pressure for me to treat this dinner as a potential binge, too many unfamiliar people, too much judgment. But I start to worry. I had stupidly thought that alcohol would be offered here, and now I don't know why I ever would have thought that. I'd figured that the right amount of sauvignon blanc might make these group meals okay—*fun*, even. I do a mental inventory of the alcohol I brought with me and decide that I'm going to need a lot more, and soon.

I reach the end of the buffet line and feel a painful flash of nostalgia for the Christmas Eve buffet with my family, and I wonder if anyone else here is triggered by something as mundane as a warming plate.

At the table, I begin to pick away at my greens, and I decide that I'm going to leave the property tonight. After all, I'm not a prisoner here. Sarah said we can come and go as we please. And this is my *vacation*, sort of. I'm going to find some food, a dark bar, somewhere I can disappear. I researched the island a little bit before my arrival. There are six towns, I learned, but only three of them really offered a selection of restaurants, bars, and shops: Edgartown, Vineyard Haven, and Oak Bluffs. Edgartown was the farthest away, and Vineyard Haven seemed a little too sleepy. Oak Bluffs, I read, was where I could find late-night food and dive bars, crowded streets of tourists licking ice-cream cones, maybe even some live music. That's exactly what I need.

The leggings talk throughout the entire meal, finishing one another's sentences, yammering away, and inhaling bites of food in between. I try not to notice what everyone else is eating and compare my own intake, but it's become a force of habit. Particularly when it comes to other women. None of the leggings selected rolls or potatoes—nothing starchy. Rhoda and Stephanie did, though. I wonder if the leggings are competitive with one another, the type of friends who feign unconditional support but who actually get off on being *just* a little bit thinner, or *just* a little bit better at Pilates, or *just* a little bit more restrained with the group order of french fries.

The leggings explain that their husbands all went to college together, their kids all go to the same elementary school, and now all the kids are at sleepaway camp together in Maine.

"Do any of you have kids?" Eliza asks.

"No," I say. "I mean, I'm only twenty-eight and pretty focused on my work." I'm not sure why, but I feel the need to justify myself to them.

"Not yet," says Stephanie. "Though my husband, Ralph, keeps pushing it. *Let's just do it, Steph!* he keeps saying. I tell him, honey, if you want to take time off from work to take care of the baby so I can go back to work and keep my career intact, then okay, you've got a deal. Or if you want our baby to be raised by a nanny and not know us at all, sure. And then he shuts right up. The truth is, I do want kids—I just don't know how I can have my career, too. This idea that women can do both . . . I don't know. Maybe some women can. I'm not sure I could." Stephanie stares off, and Rhoda and I look at each other, sharing a fleeting glance of concern for her. The leggings shout in agreement, a little too eagerly.

"I've got four kids," Rhoda says. "And nine grandchildren, if you can believe it!" She turns to Stephanie. "Life is full of compromises, honey. With or without kids. Trust me on that."

Luckily, one of the leggings chimes in, so I avoid having to say whether I want kids myself. I might, someday, but it just doesn't seem like an option for me yet, or even something I want to seriously think about. The age and career things aren't the real reasons. It's that I still feel more like someone's daughter than I do someone's potential mother. Plus, I'm sure I'd manage to mess up a kid really fast with all my issues, especially a girl. How could I take care of someone else when I can barely take care of myself?

Dinner moves along quickly, and then it's time for dessert. Even the leggings each help themselves to a small sliver of blueberry pie and some ice cream. I snap a picture of my plate and quickly post it with a simple caption: Sweet, sweet summer. #marthasvineyard #handpicked #eatlocal. When I look up, Bronwyn is eyeing me.

"I *thought* so!" she barks. "You're the blogger," she says, "or Instagrammer, influencer, whatever you call it. Right? TheGratefulAvocado?"

So, she did know who I was, after all. "Yes, that's me. TheGratefulAvocado." I hold my hands up and shrug my shoulders.

"Eliza, Hadley, here, look," Bronwyn says, jabbing at her phone screen to pull up my account and thrusting it in their faces. "There she is!" The leggings look from the screen and then over to me, as though searching for cracks in my facade that I'd hidden online.

"Oh yeah," Eliza chimes in, "I know you!"

"Is the retreat paying for you to be here?" Hadley asks, cutting to the chase. Rhoda and Stephanie look confused.

"No, I'm not being paid. I wanted to come here on my own, just like all of you. To . . . reset, get away."

"I'm sorry. What's an influencer?" Rhoda asks.

"Well, it's sort of like a blogger. I have an online platform where I document my eating and wellness habits. I make a living through companies that pay me to advertise their products or partner with them on endorsement campaigns, things like that."

Stephanie has pulled up her phone to look. "Whoa, a million followers?" She raises her eyebrows.

"Yeah, I mean, I've been at it for a while."

An arm suddenly reaches out in front of me, and I see that it's Sarah, extending a pitcher of iced tea to fill my glass. "Don't mind me," she says. "Just keeping you ladies hydrated."

"Wow," Hadley says, still looking at Bronwyn's phone, "I bet my daughter knows who you are."

"Well, I'm trying to keep a low profile. Not really telling anyone that I'm here. And I know I can trust you all to keep it that way."

The leggings nod, appreciative to be on the inside.

"Don't worry," Bronwyn says. "We won't out you."

Sarah has been making her way around the table. She fills up the last glass and then cascades away. I catch the side of her face and am sure she's got a snide smile plastered on there, like she knows that *I* know she's got the power, the information. Or maybe I'm just paranoid.

After dinner, back at the cabin, I tell Stephanie and Rhoda that I'm going to meet a girlfriend who lives here in town for a cocktail. I considered not saying anything at all—just leaving—but we've now developed a kind of buddy system, whether I want it or not.

"Good for you," Rhoda says.

I change my outfit and call myself a cab from Stagecoach Taxi, the same service that dropped me off earlier. I head out as soon as I place the call, even though they tell me it will be about fifteen minutes. I want to meet the taxi at the start of the road, not all the way up by the farmhouse. The last thing I need is Sarah's judgmental questioning.

"Downtown Oak Bluffs, please," I tell the driver when he arrives in a van cab. "Circuit Ave." He laughs.

"Breaking out, huh?"

"I guess you could say that." As we drive, I realize that I never signed out, like Sarah told us to, but I don't let it worry me. What difference could it really make? I gaze out onto the winding roads, now dark aside from the moonlight in the clear night sky.

As we drive, I can't shake the memory of my family's last Christmas together. Even though Mike and I still spend the holiday at my dad's each year, we never went back to the steak house after Mom died, like we used to do every Christmas Eve. We never discussed this; it was just silently agreed upon.

One year when I was home from college, I woke early on Christmas morning and was sitting alone in the kitchen drinking coffee when my dad came in carrying a cardboard box. He placed it on the table.

"Ava," he said, "you should have this."

My dad was, and still is, the silent type. He never showed much emotion or gave us long-winded speeches. After sports games when we were kids, he'd congratulate us with a pat on the back and a simple *Well done*. Or, later, when we were teenagers, he'd scold us for breaking curfew with the succinct *I'm disappointed in you*, and that was that. Even today, his words carry more weight with me because there are so few of them. I knew that this box contained something important; if it didn't, he wouldn't have said anything at all.

I opened it, and inside was a folded stack of some of Mom's favorite clothes, her red Christmas blazer on top. I touched the material, rubbing it gently between two of my fingers, wishing that it would somehow conjure her back to life.

"Thanks, Dad." He gave my shoulder a quick squeeze and then turned away.

I waited until I was alone in my room later that day to go through the box. I tried on her clothing—a sparkly blue dress, a mohair sweater, a gold pleated skirt, a printed blouse. Everything still smelled like her, felt like her. And it all fit me perfectly. But looking in the mirror, I still felt bigger than her, somehow. It didn't make sense. My mother had been perfect to me. I couldn't possibly be the same size that she was. I stared at myself, and then I felt a deep, burning resentment toward her. I ripped off the clothes and shoved them back in the box. I hated that when she looked in the mirror, I knew that she had felt the same thing I did. I knew that she had struggled to feel good about herself, struggled to not be consumed by food and dieting, the constant hum of calorie counting in the back of her mind. I had idolized her, and yet I also knew that she'd been just as susceptible to it all as I was. I hated that she had passed that struggle along to me, that she didn't do more to help me, that she didn't set a different example for me. I hated that I spent so much time during her last few months alone in the bathroom, making myself sick. None of it made sense.

I still hate it so much, and yet the only comfort I can find—when my longing for her is so profound and painful that my entire body feels like one big bruise—is on the cold tile of the bathroom floor.

# Chapter 8

As we approach Oak Bluffs, I immediately perk up at the sight of lights and crowds, which promise anonymity and greasy food. We drive past a row of small, brightly painted homes with wooden trim so detailed that it looks like lace.

"The gingerbread houses," the driver says, glancing back in the mirror. It's clear he's given this unofficial tour many times. We drive by the harbor, packed with powerboats illuminating the water with neon hues. A large patio outside a restaurant called Nancy's overflows with customers sipping drinks from plastic cups and glass beer bottles, eating plates of fried clams and burgers.

It's about nine o'clock. Life back at the retreat is over until dawn, but life here in Oak Bluffs is just beginning.

"And up there is the Flying Horses," the driver says as we approach downtown. "Oldest carousel in America." The crowds are eclectic and diverse, I notice. Families with little kids, couples out on dates, teenagers looking for cigarettes and trouble, and all walks of life. We pull over to the side of the road, outside a movie theater. "Here we go. Circuit Ave. Nightlife central," he says. I pay him the forty-dollar flat rate in cash and throw in an extra ten. In LA, the ride would have been a fifteen-dollar Uber ride, but tonight, I'd pay almost anything to just get away. "Thanks," I say as I slam the van door and begin the ascent up Circuit Ave.

I'd changed my clothes back at the cabin right before I left, and I'm glad I did. Oak Bluffs is *fun*, and my retreat-chic outfit before wouldn't have matched the energy here. I readjust the straps of my black bodysuit and yank up my high-waist Levi's, taking my sweater off and draping it over my arm with my clutch. The air here feels warmer, and the night sky somewhat brighter. Everything is still open—even clothing stores. Doors are open to the street, and people spill in and out, buzzed and happy after dinner. I walk by a fudge store and am overcome with the sweet, sugary scent of warm chocolate: Murdick's Fudge, I note, reminding myself to go back there and load up at some point. I scan the street with my phone and post a story, geotagging Oak Bluffs.

Just diagonally across the street from where I'd been dropped off, I see a bar called the Ritz. I can hear live music from inside, and there's a grizzled bouncer on a stool outside. I google it on my phone quickly. *They serve food. Bingo.* I hand the bouncer my ID, and he gives it a discerning look, which gives me a nice boost of confidence. "All set," he says.

Inside, the bar smells of chili and old beer, and I love it right away. A rock band led by a blonde woman who reminds me of young Courtney Love plays to a packed crowd. Some people sit at high-top tables and eat food, some sit at the bar, and others just stand around holding their drinks and dancing to the music. As though it's fate, a seat opens up at the end of the bar, and I snag it. A pretty bartender slides up to the counter.

"What'll it be, babe?"

"I'll have a Corona, please, and"—I quickly scan the paper menu tucked into the condiment basket—"the burger, medium rare, with bacon, and an order of cheesy tots." I like to drink beer when I'm bingeing. I like the way beer fills me up. It makes the release later on so much more satisfying.

"Right on," she says. This is where I need to be; I've found my place. My seat is on the edge of the bar, right against the wall, so I can lean back and listen to the band while remaining hidden away by the shadows and crowds. For a moment, I relish the knowledge that no one here knows me. Maybe someone recognizes me, or might, if they looked closely, but it doesn't seem like the kind of crowd that would care. The bar is populated by a few men who look like regulars, old and leather-skinned with tattoos and missing teeth, and the dancing crowd is young and hip. A woman with her hair in two tight buns atop her head squeezes up next to me to get the bartender's attention. "Hey, Jenny, can we get two pickle backs? Tequila, please! Thanks." The bartender places my Corona in front of me with a smile and then pours two tequila shots and two shots of bright-green pickle juice. The woman winks at Jenny as she slaps down a wad of bills on the bar and scoops up the drinks in her hands, haphazardly carrying them back through the crowd.

I ask for a glass of water, too, which Jenny delivers to me within seconds, like magic, and I make myself chug half of it right away. Then I sit back, leaning against the wall behind me, and watch and listen, sipping my beer. For the first time all day, I feel a sense of peace. As much as I want to just ignore it all, I know I need to check my phone and do a little bit of work. I need to get something up for Skin Beams, and I had the sense to throw a little bottle of it in my clutch for a potential photo opportunity tonight. Those are the things I'm always anticipating. I turn my camera on to see what I'd look like right now in a selfie. Multicolored twinkle lights dangle around the bar, giving the room a dim glow. I look around. No one here is snapping selfies, that's for sure, but I also don't think anyone here gives a shit. I hold up the serum next to my face, as though putting it on an imaginary pedestal, and take a few pictures, the haziness of the bar behind me. It looks like I'm somewhere fun, enjoying myself. Being normal. I edit quickly—blot out the grease on my forehead, smooth out a red patch on my cheek, and add a filter that gives me a subtle radiance. Then I post: Sometimes you just need a night out in a dark bar with a cold beer, am I right?! You guys know I always say that everything is about balance.

And with Skin Beams, I know that even the craziest night out won't leave my skin suffering the next day. I'm obsessed with their new Silk Serum. It makes my skin feel sooooo plumped and hydrated all night long. Party on, my friends! #ad #skinbeams #skinbeamspartner. Normally I'd add more hashtags, and probably more creative copy, but I just don't care enough. This will do—it's fun, I look cute, it's creative, and it feels honest. My followers love it when I show this side of me—the one that lets loose, the one that indulges, enjoys alcohol, acts *normal*. It's shameful, really, what I'm doing, but there's a code among influencers and their followers, even if it's rarely acknowledged out loud: If *I* can drink beer and eat greasy food, so can they. If *I* can be "bad," they can, too. Who am I to give anyone *permission* to do or not do anything? No one. I have no right, whatsoever. But that's the transactional nature of my relationship with my followers. Whatever I do, say, or post ends up bouncing off themselves, forcing them to reevaluate their own actions.

I hit "Post" and geotag the bar, but I turn off commenting. I don't want anyone questioning me, especially not anyone at the retreat. As I'm finishing up, a guy in a faded white T-shirt splattered in paint slides onto the stool beside me.

"Internet more exciting than the real world?" he says to me. I've heard this kind of judgment before—from both men and women, ones who assume that because I'm on my phone, I'm not interesting. Or that because my job is in social media, my work lacks meaning. Usually, I'm able to mutter some strong retort, but tonight, I don't have it in me. Tonight, I just don't care enough.

"Sometimes it is, yeah," I say as I finish my post. I put my phone down on the bar and return to my beer, looking straight ahead, not willing to make eye contact.

"I hear you," he says. "Sometimes reality sucks." His response isn't what I had expected, and that almost never happens. I look over at him. He looks like he's in his late thirties, and I notice that his jeans are covered in paint, too, in splashes of bright blue and green. He orders a Guinness, and from the way the bartender knowingly nods at him, I get the sense that he's a regular here. I can tell that he's tall, over six feet, with long arms and hands to match. A messy head of brown hair falls toward his eyes.

My food arrives just then, on two giant plates. The burger comes with a generous pile of fries, and I've got an entire separate plate of cheesy tots. Paint guy has to move his forearm away to make room.

"Another Corona?" Jenny asks, and I nod gratefully.

"And one of those pickle back things. With tequila," I add. *Fuck it.* Paint guy looks over at me, and we make eye contact for the first time.

"You know what," he says, turning toward the bartender. "Make that two. But mine with whiskey." Paint guy swivels his body on the stool toward me. He's cute, that's for sure, but at the moment, all I really care about is digging in to this food. I'm genuinely hungry, having barely touched my dinner at the retreat, and once I start settling into a binge, it's like I've got blinders on. I don't want to be interrupted. I want the total engrossment of the experience. So I simply raise my eyebrows and nod at paint guy, acknowledging his order but not giving him anything more than that.

I dig in to my burger first. It's not the best I've ever had, but it's exactly what I want right now. I can feel paint guy watching me. And really, this is one of the best parts, one of the secret highs of being bulimic. The ugly truth, I think, is that guys *say* they love it when a girl actually eats, at least they do in LA, as if seeing a skinny girl eat a cheeseburger is such a foreign, outrageous, audacious act that it's positively sexy and wild. But I'm not sure they actually mean it. And that's the thing about bulimia: it allows me to pretend to be someone I'm not. I can pretend to be that carefree, high-metabolic, naturally thin girl who doesn't count calories like those *other* girls but who instead just lives her life to the fullest. If only they knew. I wait for paint guy to comment, to say something like, *Wow, you can really put it away,* or

*That burger is bigger than you are.* But he doesn't say anything. Does he think this is *normal?*

Jenny returns with the pickle shots. "Have fun," she says to us with a smile.

"I'm Carter," paint guy finally says. "And you're a visitor."

"Ava," I say, swallowing a bite. "And yeah, how'd you know?"

"A local would never come to the Ritz to hide. And I kind of get the sense that you're hiding from something, or someone."

I take a bite of the cheesy tots before responding. They burst with delicious grease, and I stab my fork into another. *Hiding?*

"You're right," I say. "I'm not from here. But I'm not hiding. Just because I want to be left alone doesn't mean I'm hiding. And some might say that by focusing on me, you're really just deflecting attention away from yourself . . . as if to, you know, *hide?*" I take a swig of beer.

"Touché," he says. He takes his shot and holds it up, waiting for me. "And in case you weren't sure, you take the shot first, then the pickle juice. It's a house specialty."

"Here goes nothing," I say, and knock back the shot. I scrunch up my face, feeling the burn of the tequila rage down my throat, and I quickly inhale the briny pickle juice, which is surprisingly cool and refreshing. "That was shockingly good," I say, returning to my burger and fries.

"I haven't done one of those in maybe ten years," he says. "I guess you inspired me." He sips his Guinness.

"How come you're covered in paint?" I ask. I want him to do the talking so I can keep eating. As cute as he is, and as fun as the prospect of a harmless flirtation might be, I didn't come here for that. I came here to self-medicate.

"I'm an artist. Paint is my medium." I finish my burger and stuff myself with a few more tots. Jenny returns with another round of beers, even though we hadn't asked for them yet.

"Figured you'd want these," she says. Fair enough. My stomach is now starting to really expand, and the waistline of my Levi's is digging into my skin, causing that familiar pinching feeling. I haven't yet examined the bathroom here, but I don't need to—I know what I'm in for. In dive bars like this, the bathrooms are usually so gross and the bar is so loud that you can do anything in them, and no one will suspect a thing. I still have some fries I want to eat before, though, so I tuck in to those.

"What kind of paintings?" I ask in between bites. I wish I weren't, but I'm genuinely curious. In LA, I've met plenty of guys who describe themselves as artists, when really it just means that they throw some globs of paint on a canvas or glue some shards of broken glass together, display it in a warehouse downtown, and call it an installation.

"Oil paintings," he says. "Landscapes, mostly. The occasional person, too. I've got a gallery in West Tisbury. You should come check it out."

"Yeah, maybe I will sometime." I push my plates away. "Hey, do you mind saving my seat for me? Just running to the bathroom."

"Sure thing," he says.

I shove past the crowds and to the restroom in back, down a dimly lit hall covered in stickers. The bathroom is just as I had imagined it—small, tight, cramped, stinky, but drowned out by the sounds of the music and people. I'm done in just a few minutes, and I'm instantly soothed. I wash my hands, rinse my mouth out, and brush my teeth, then apply a few spots of concealer and fluff my hair. I check my phone briefly. My post has already gotten over ten thousand likes, and it hasn't even been an hour. Not bad, but not great. I check my DMs to see if I've received any more weird messages; I'm still a little rattled by the mysterious one from earlier, but nothing else from them has come in, so I decide to brush it off as a onetime fluke, meaning nothing.

I practically bound my way to the bar when I'm done. Carter is still there, but Jenny has whisked away my plates. Even though I've puked, I still feel the effects of the alcohol I've consumed, and it feels good. Just a light buzz, giving me a feeling of looseness and ease.

"I can't believe I'm suggesting this," I say as I sit back down, "but what about another round of pickle backs?" High from my purge, I'm ready to get wasted.

Carter looks at me suspiciously, like I'm an alien.

"Why not?" He motions to Jenny for another round.

This time, the tequila goes down smooth, and the pickle juice is not only refreshing but downright delicious. I've still got half a beer left, and now I'm definitely feeling buzzed. The music suddenly sounds sharper and more energizing, the crowd seems to vibrate around me, and just for a moment, I forget the reason that I came to this island in the first place: because I hit rock bottom.

"So, Ava, right?" I nod. "I've been trying all night not to ask, but you've gotta tell me. What are you doing here, at the Ritz, eating a burger and drinking alone on a Monday night?" I sip my beer, taking my time to respond, and I mentally run through a few different things I could tell him—that I'm here for a wedding, that I'm here with family, that I'm just passing through on my way to Nantucket.

"I checked myself into a fucking wellness retreat." The unplanned explanation pours out of me, and maybe it's because I'm simply too tired to spin another lie, but it feels surprisingly good to just tell the truth. "I'm a wellness influencer in LA. But I guess, lately, you could say that I've been *unwell*. So, here I am. But it's only night one, and I've already ditched the place to drink my feelings, so clearly it's not going well. Cheers." I knock my bottle against his glass.

"Island Wellness?" he asks. *Oh god*, I think, *this island is so damn small. He's probably married to Sarah or something.* I should have kept my mouth shut.

"That's the one," I say with hesitation, straightening my posture.

"Yeah, they bought one of my paintings a while back. One of my favorites, actually, a really nice one of Lake Tashmoo."

"I'll look for it." I did notice that the retreat has some beautiful and tasteful artwork around the property. I wait for him to say something more.

"You don't seem unwell to me," he says. "But if you want my advice, that place won't get you better. You know what will, though? A swim."

"A swim? It's that easy, huh?" I ask with a laugh. "It's just gonna solve all my problems? And this expensive retreat won't?"

"Well, I don't really know much about Island Wellness besides what's on their walls," he says, taking a sip. "I just know that a swim in the ocean can fix most things, at least in my experience."

"That would be pretty nice if it were true," I respond.

"Try it," he says. "The place where you're staying is right on the water and near some of the best beaches on the island. Have you gone in yet?"

"No, I haven't even been down to the beach yet." I'm embarrassed to admit it, now that I say it out loud. Pretty much the first thing I did after arriving there was leave. "But I've got six weeks, so I think I'll find the time."

*"Six weeks?"* My embarrassment increases. "Well, I don't mean to pry, but you must have been feeling *really* unwell if you're here for that long. But hey, seriously, good for you. If this island can't heal you, nothing can. I bet you anything that after six weeks here, you won't even want to leave."

As I finish my beer, I wonder if he's right. I feel wistful for *something*, but not necessarily LA. And not my life there.

"I grew up here," Carter continues. "Trust me, I never thought I'd end up back here. I lived in New York for a while, almost ten years, did that whole thing. But something about this place will pull you right back, I'll tell you. And now here I am. Back for good, I think."

"I can understand that. I mean, I literally just got here today, but I can see how this place is . . . special." I wonder what Carter's life is like here, and if it's so great, why *he's* at the bar alone on a Monday night. But I know better than to ask, at least not yet, not directly.

He finishes his beer and takes out his wallet, fishing out a few bills and then putting them on the bar beneath the edge of his glass. "The pickle backs were on me," he says, and I raise my hand to protest. "I insist."

"Thanks." I wasn't expecting him to leave. I was sure he was hitting on me. It's only ten thirty, but then again, it is a Monday night. Not everyone is on a twisted version of a vacation, like I am. He probably has a life to live, a beautiful girlfriend to go home to. And yet, something tells me otherwise. "Wait," I blurt out. Maybe it's the pickle backs, maybe it's the feeling that I've literally got nothing to lose, but something compels me to do something I almost never do. "Want to go for a swim together sometime, then?"

Carter is now standing, and I can see his real height. He's slender and lean but muscular, with a sharp jaw and serious eyes.

"Huh, I didn't see that coming." I see just the hint of a smile cross his face, but enough to know that he's glad I asked.

"Oh, relax. I'm just suggesting a friendly swim. Really, it was *your* idea, in a way."

"That's true. Do they even let you out of that place during the day, or are we gonna have to go night swimming?"

"I think I can get away for a few hours here and there."

Carter fishes out an old receipt from his pocket. "Here, why don't you give me your number. And I'll, uh, make a reservation at the island's best swimming spot."

I try to play it cool as I jot down my number. I wish Ben could see me now, setting up a date with a tall, handsome artist.

"All right, then. See you soon, Ava," he says before turning to leave. He says goodbye to a few other people on his way out. Everyone seems to know everyone here, and I wonder if they noticed Carter and me flirting. While I'm not even sure I'm going to hear from him, and I'm not even sure I care, I feel liberated by my boldness. It's a reminder that it might actually be possible for me to start fresh with someone. Maybe if I'd been honest with Ben up front and not tried so hard to cultivate a certain image of myself for him, things would have turned out differently. I might not have even liked him so much in the first place. After all, anyone who makes me feel the need to be *perfect* all the time probably isn't right for me.

I order another round—a shot and a beer—from Jenny, who, this time, gives me just the quickest look as if to ask, *Are you sure?* But she returns dutifully with a cold one. I drink it quickly, and after that, I definitely feel drunk and know that it's time to go. I pay, leaving Jenny a nice 30 percent tip—I'm sure I'll be back here—and put my sweater on.

Outside on Circuit Ave, the town is still wide awake, though things have quieted down a bit since I first arrived. I decide to walk up the street to see what else there is in town. The fudge store is closed, *dammit*, but I continue on. My stomach, empty aside from booze, rumbles, and I feel a gentle wave of dizziness. A few stores up the street, I notice a line of people waiting outside for something. I crane my head to see what it is and realize I've found exactly what I need: a bakery called Back Door Donuts. I get in line, smelling the freshly baked glazed confections just a few feet away. When it's my turn, I'm greeted by a quick-talking teenager, and I have to make my decision fast. They've got so many choices—chocolate donuts, coconut donuts, french crullers, and giant apple fritters.

"One of everything," I say. I expect the order to shock her, but the teenager doesn't even flinch, and just starts grabbing at the various pastries with a paper-covered hand and placing them into a brown box. Once I pay, I leave with the confections like they're pure contraband, hidden treasure found just for me. I'm tempted to stuff them in my face right there on the sidewalk, but I decide to wait until I'm back at the retreat to dive in. I duck into a corner convenience store next door and buy several large bottles of water, some tabloid magazines, and some cheap tanning oil. I'm bleary-eyed as I pay at the counter, jamming my credit card into the chip reader, avoiding the stare of the cashier. With all my goods safely tucked under my arms and hanging in bags on my wrists, I feel armed and ready to return to the retreat, so I stumble back down the road to the taxi stand where I was first dropped. I hop into one of the van cabs, and we cruise back up island, the crisp night wind whipping my face, the stars shining brightly overhead.

"Thanks," I say as I slam the van door shut. Even in my drunken state, I have the sense to be dropped off at the start of the quarter-mile driveway so as not to attract any attention. My sandals crunch against the pea-stone road. My cabin is down the sloping lawn, away from the farmhouse, which is situated right at the front of the property, so I have to walk through the farmhouse or edge myself around the side of it along the hedges. With everything I'm carrying, it's easier to just tiptoe right through the main entrance. I can see as I approach that inside, all the lights are out, aside from the main foyer, where the reception desk is. I remember Sarah saying that though there might not actually be someone at the desk, there would always be a phone number that guests could call should they need anything, and a staff member available during the night shift. I also remember her saying something about the staff living upstairs on the second floor of the farmhouse, and I wonder who's up there right now, who's sleeping with whom, and what their rooms are like.

I tiptoe up onto the porch and start to creep toward one of the windows to look inside. I don't see anyone, just a framed sign on the reception desk with an after-hours number. I carefully open the door, my giant paper box of donuts cumbersome in my arms, and I step inside. I shut the door behind me and begin my walk to the other side, ever so gently. Past the reception desk, it's just a quick walk into the sunken living room and then out the other side. But as I descend the stairs, my sandal snags beneath me, somehow, and before I know it, I'm lurching forward, my donuts and water bottles and magazines all flying out of my grip and onto the living room carpet. I land with a thud, in an awkward bend, most of the weight going onto my chest and one shoulder. "Shit!" I scream in as much of a whisper as I can manage.

I pick myself up and just wait for a moment, standing still in the silence, hoping that no one heard. I don't move, and I wait. No one comes, and thankful that the coast is clear, I hastily begin to clean up as best I can. All my donuts have landed on the rug, and the greased brown box has ripped. I'm determined to salvage them, anyway, so I pick them up and carefully place them in one of the convenience-store plastic bags along with the other junk I bought. The carpet is now covered in jelly, powdered sugar, bits of baked apple fritter, and coconut flakes. I try to scrape up as much of it as I can with the sleeve of my sweater, but in the darkness and in my inebriated panic, with the impending threat that anyone could appear at any moment, I call it quits after a minute and sneak back outside, running to my cabin. Once there, I again tiptoe to my own room, finally closing the door and exhaling. I made it.

# Chapter 9

I'm so parched in the morning that my thirst wakes me up. It's nearly ten when I open my eyes in search of water. I binged and purged the entire box of donuts the night before, and finally fell asleep having pushed my stomach muscles to the point of exhaustion.

The three-hour time difference between here and LA feels particularly painful this morning. I rub my eyes, visions of pickle back shots and donuts flooding my mind. After chugging a glass of water, I check my phone—the first thing I do every morning. My Skin Beams post has gotten strong feedback, so at least I have that intact. I go through my DMs, taking some time to actually respond to most of the messages, something I try to do each day. It's important to me to have as much direct communication with my followers as I can so that they feel authentically connected to me. I don't like that I'm not being honest with them right now, especially the ones who've responded to my being on vacation by telling me that I deserve it and that they hope I have the best time ever.

Nothing new has come in from mermaid1985. I could just block them entirely, and I consider it, but something tells me not to. What if, I think, this person really *does* know where I am? Wouldn't blocking them give them more juice to come after me?

I peer into the common area of the house; the cabin is quiet. Stephanie and Rhoda are gone, probably having been up since early this morning. Even though I'm a guest at the retreat and how I spend my time is up to me, I nevertheless feel guilty for not partaking in whatever they've gone to attend today. On the kitchen counter is an itinerary of the daily offered activities. I missed breakfast, which ended at nine, and lunch doesn't start until noon. I've already missed several morning yoga and workout classes. There's a basket weaving class happening right now and a tai chi introductory class on the lawn, neither of which I'd go to if someone paid me. And I haven't gotten any indication yet as to when my first therapy appointment will be. So, really, even though I feel like there's something I *should* be doing, there's nowhere I have to be. I plan to spend the rest of the morning filming some content and then check out the beach before lunch.

I don't consider myself a big workout person, but I do include fitness as part of my overall brand. It's become a chore more than anything else, though. Sometimes I just want to go for a walk or a hike, or attend a spin class, but I started filming myself doing at-home workouts about a year ago, and now I feel like there's an expectation for me to keep them up. It's a lot of effort just to get a quick workout in; I spend almost as much, sometimes more, time prepping for it as actually doing it. This morning, I decide that I'll do a quick half-hour barre class. I pick my outfit first, deciding on a block-print Outdoor Voices set, and then spend about twenty minutes finding the right space, ultimately landing on the living room in a spot where the light floods in behind me in a flattering way. I apply a little bit of light makeup and perfect my messy bun, and then I'm ready. The class is a welcome distraction from the shame I still feel from my sloppy night, and when I finish, I'm glad I did it. I've recorded it on my phone, so I set it in fast motion and then upload it to my stories with a link to the workout, adding a caption: It's amazing what even a quick workout will do for my mental and emotional sanity! Get your movement in today, guys, you won't regret it!

Most of the responses I get from my daily workouts are positive—"You go, girl" types of things. But some of them are resentful:

"Not everyone has time to do this every day!" or "You set unrealistic expectations" or sometimes just an eye-roll emoji. And really, I don't blame the people who send these responses. It *is* annoying to see some-one else working out every day, especially someone who's already in good shape. But this is where I struggle with feeling like my role is to motivate and inspire but also to remain somewhat aloof, somewhat aspirational.

When I finish posting the class, I turn the camera on myself for some more personal footage.

"Good morning, friends," I say. "It's a beautiful day here. I just did a really energizing thirty-minute barre class with one of my favorite instructors—I'll tag her so you can check out her classes. I just wanted a quick workout to wake up, you know? I was *not* in the mood to do it at first, but when I finished, I felt so much better. So just a reminder to move your bodies. It's the best therapy! Let me know what you're doing to stay active today!"

After, I toss my phone on the bed and take off my workout clothes, changing into a bikini and cover-up dress. I pack up a beach bag with my magazines, AirPods, the latest Elin Hilderbrand novel, and a few other essentials. I can't find the tanning oil I bought last night at the convenience store. I must have dropped it in the farmhouse along with the donuts.

Outside, the sun is bright, and the air is warm and smells clean. I walk through the main lawn, toward the woods, where a path is marked TO THE BEACH! After just a few paces through the woods, the trees and brush give way to an expansive, open view of the north shore waters. It's an impossibly clear day, not a cloud in the sky, and the calm water is a deep shade of blue, rising and falling gently like the belly of a sleeping cat. The path ends in a steep wooden staircase down a cliff and onto the beach, which is sandy but peppered with smooth beach stones of all colors.

A few other guests have decided on a beach day as well. I wave and walk down the beach to pick a spot. I spread out my towel and start to arrange my things so I can relax, and I lie down, propping myself up on my forearms behind me and examining my body, scanning my eyes from my chest to my toes. In the three days between booking the retreat and arriving, I got a Brazilian bikini wax, a gel manicure and pedicure, and an eyelash tint and curl, and I bought a few new bikinis and other summer clothing. I look down at my body, in my new cranberry-red bikini. I'm slender, thin by most people's standards. But it's not easy to be this way, and that's where the bulimia really holds me prisoner. After that first year of truly feeling healthy and redefining my relationship with food, I lost the weight that I wanted to and was finally at my goal. It was the *maintenance* that I found difficult. I worked so hard to reach that goal, that anytime I even slightly slipped off a healthy diet, I felt like I needed to compensate for it. I didn't think I deserved to ever indulge, or else it would destroy everything I'd worked for. It would destroy *me*. Once in a while, I let myself splurge—a nice dinner out with friends, or a big brunch on a Sunday, or late-night fries after going out. But every time I did this, even though I told myself that it was all part of a *balanced* lifestyle, I nevertheless regretted it. This regret is what the bulimia sank its claws into. It was too easy for it not to come back. The problem with bulimia is that once you know how to do it, once you know how *easy* it is to do it, it's basically impossible not to do it whenever you're tempted. How do you ever *move on* from that?

At first, the purges were occasional, and what I would describe as accidental, meaning that I didn't plan to purge. I didn't binge with the intention of purging. It was more subtle. I would eat a slice of cake at a coworker's birthday party with the full intention of keeping it down, but I just couldn't. So I purged.

And even just those first few sporadic purges were enough to send me right back into the clutches of full-blown bulimia. Before I knew it, I was bingeing and purging regularly, to the point that my life, my schedule, my plans, my relationships, and my emotional stability were centered around my bingeing and purging.

I lie back on my towel and take a few deep breaths. Only seconds later, my phone chimes with a text, interrupting my serenity. I remember Carter and how daring I was with him last night, asking him to go for a swim. Maybe it's him.

Ava, it's Sarah here at the front desk. Please come by before lunch today. I have a few things to discuss with you. Thank you. Hope you're having a blessed morning.

Well, definitely not Carter. Sarah must want to talk to me about scheduling my first therapy appointment—or whatever they call it here. *Healing sessions.* That's the logical assumption, but something about Sarah's message makes me feel like I'm being called to the principal's office, like I've done something wrong and am going to get scolded.

Before I head back for lunch, I decide to take a few beach selfies and post the best one after editing it by brightening my skin and slightly thinning out my thighs and butt that poke out behind me in the photo. After I finish, I quickly scroll through Instagram again. I have more good responses from my Skin Beams post and good feedback and views from my morning stories. I'm about to toss my phone in my bag and head to lunch when I notice, in my DMs, another message from mermaid1985:

Six weeks is a long time to hide.

Startled, I look around at the other guests. The man in his sixties sits alone in a beach chair, reading a thick hardcover book. The young, impeccably dressed couple walks hand in hand along the shoreline. I'd seen the two stocky sisters on my way down—they were returning from the beach with wet hair and towels around their necks, like they'd been doing laps in the ocean. I suppose one of the leggings could be behind these messages, but I just didn't get the sense from any of them yesterday that they'd do this. And there's no way a staff member could, not even Sarah, at least based on what Naomi told me about how strict they are with client confidentiality. But it has to be someone with knowledge of the retreat and the length of my stay.

I call Becky, the only other person outside the retreat who even knows where I am. She answers immediately.

"Ava. Whaaat? Tell me everything."

"I know, I know. It was sort of a last-minute decision."

"Well, I'm here for it. A summer of self-care. Go you! Wait, what about Ben? Did you break it off?"

I obviously hadn't *forgotten* about Ben, but I'd managed to distract myself enough that I actually hadn't even thought about him at all that morning.

"Um, not exactly. I mean, yeah, we're over. But it didn't end well. I'll tell you about it another time."

"Eesh, okay. Sorry, girl."

"Hey, listen, so I'm just wondering. Did you mention to anyone else where I am?" As I say the words out loud, I realize how ridiculous and self-absorbed they sound. Why would she have told anyone where I am, and why would anyone care? "It's just that, I've gotten some weird messages from someone on Instagram basically being like, 'I know where you are.' And I mean, it's not like I'm at *rehab*. But for me, for my business, you know, I don't think it would look that good if people knew I was at a fancy retreat for six weeks that specializes in helping people recover from eating disorders. You know?"

"Messages? Huh?"

"Yeah, these weird cryptic messages. It's . . . Never mind, it's probably nothing."

"Well, no, of course I haven't told anyone where you are, and I won't. But listen, I say this to my clients all the time: It's the price you pay for being an influencer. For having a big following. You know that. You're always gonna have trolls. Just ignore them."

When I hang up, I don't feel any better. I don't entirely trust Becky, but I also don't think that she'd be the one sending me the messages. I do, however, think that she could have let it slip to someone else. And Becky's world is full of opportunists who would jump at the chance to exploit me. She probably did it accidentally—told some publicist over cocktails how her influencer friend is at a fancy eating-disorder rehab and then begged them not to tell anyone else. But still . . . I'm not certain. There's something about whoever is sending the messages that feels much closer than that.

Hungry for lunch, I pack up my things and make my way up the stairs toward the farmhouse to find Sarah. I dump my towels in a basket, with a sign reminding us to please only have washed what we really need washed: WE ARE AN ECO-CONSCIOUS RESORT.

As I step into the main living room of the farmhouse, I'm reminded again of my late-night donut fiasco. But to my relief, there's no sticky evidence on the carpet. It's like I was never there. In the light of day, I glance around the ceiling beams for hidden cameras, but don't see any. Sarah stands behind the front desk, focused on her computer screen.

"Good afternoon, Ava," she says when she sees me approaching. Today she wears a beige, fitted tank top tucked into light jeans, accentuating her hourglass shape. I notice her excellent posture and straighten my spine, pushing my shoulders back but still feeling small and disheveled around her.

"Hi," I say, fidgeting with my tote bag. "I figure you want to see me about scheduling my therapy sessions?"

"Yes, we can do that now," she says, "but actually that's not why I wanted to see you." She crouches down and disappears for a moment. I look over the desktop, at my chest level, and see that she's reaching for something inside a cabinet down below. She pops back up, holding my bottle of tanning oil. "I think you dropped this last night," she says, handing it to me with no expression.

"Oh, right, thanks," I say, my face starting to burn. How does she know that the tanning oil is mine?

"We also had a little bit of a mess to clean up, you see, and I'm not assuming that the mess was *your* doing, or rather, I'm not *blaming* you, but there are several signs that indicate to me that it was, in fact, you who caused the mess." I wait for her to give me some kind of punch line, but she just stares at me as though I'm on trial. "Do you know what I'm referring to?"

I search Sarah's face, though I'm not sure what I'm looking for. A sign of recognition, perhaps, that this conversation is absurd, that people make mistakes and it's okay, that I am an *adult* paying to be here, that I'm a guest here. But her face is resolute. Annoyingly relaxed and wrinkle-free, but resolute.

"No, I'm sorry," I decide to say. "I don't have any idea. But thanks for finding this for me, I was wondering where it went," I say, waving the tanning-oil bottle and then dropping it in my bag. I do feel bad that the cleaning staff had to deal with my mess. But besides that, I don't want to give Sarah the satisfaction of hearing an apology from me. It's obviously clear that she—or someone else—must have seen me last night. So, there's no point in my denying it, but I'm going to, anyway. I give her my corniest, fakest smile and shrug my shoulders.

"No problem, Ava," she says. She returns to her computer screen. "Now, how about tomorrow at ten o'clock for your first appointment with Wanda? Her office is just down the hall from here. First sessions are usually ninety minutes."

"Sounds great!" I exclaim. "Thanks so much."

"Namaste," she says as I turn to leave.

I rush to claim the only single-seat table in the dining room and immediately take out my book so the other guests know not to even try to talk to me. Once again, the food looks delicious. Today, there is freshly barbecued local chicken, grilled shrimp-and-vegetable skewers, a watermelon-and-feta salad, a farro-and-herb salad, and some farm vegetables on the side. For dessert, fruit salad and molasses-ginger cookies. I pile a little bit of everything onto my plate and eat slowly while reading.

When I'm done, I feel . . . *good*. Full but not uncomfortable. I don't need to throw up this meal, I tell myself. I don't *want* to. I decide to go for an afternoon hike on one of the property trails after lunch. If I get some more exercise in, I won't feel as bad about not purging.

Back in the cabin, Rhoda rests on the living room couch.

"Oh, don't mind me," she says as I enter.

"Hi, Rhoda," I say. "How's your day been?"

"Just fabulous, let me tell you. I got up early and did one of those yoga meditation classes. You know, I thought it was going to be a bunch of bull crap, hippie stuff. But it was really amazing! I felt calmer than maybe I have in my whole life. You oughta try it, I can tell you that."

"You're right, I probably should. Not sure I can do the sunrise thing, though."

"Well, not after a night like the one you had last night, sweetheart," she says, and I worry for a moment that I woke her. She sits up from her reclined position. "Don't worry," she says, as though reading my mind. "No judgment from me. You're a young, beautiful woman. You're allowed to go out and have fun, stay up late. And, anyway, you didn't wake me up. I have to get up and pee about a hundred times during the night, anyway, so I was already up when I heard you come in. Did you have fun?"

"I did, actually," I say. "Thanks." Rhoda gives me a thumbs-up and rests her head back down on the sofa pillow.

"As long as you're taking care of yourself," she adds. "I didn't do that enough at your age."

"Me too. That's good advice," chimes Stephanie, who has surfaced from her room.

"That's why I'm here, I guess." Both women nod and smile at me, and while I'm grateful for their advice and support, I'm starting to feel awkwardly *mothered* by them. "Well, I'm going to change and go for a hike," I say. "See you later, at dinner."

"Sounds fabulous," Rhoda says. Stephanie gives a thumbs-up.

In my room, I put on my sneakers and the same workout clothes from before and grab my phone and AirPods. I walk toward the trail, which the retreat map says winds through the woods for almost two miles before reaching the beach farther down the shore. I try to resist, but I log in to my finsta account and check to see if Ben's been posted in anything. This time, he *has* been tagged in a photo, by one of his guy friends. It's a photo of a group having drinks on the rooftop of E.P. & L.P. on La Cienega, the twinkling lights of West Hollywood and Beverly Hills glistening in the background. I click onto the friend's profile, which is public, and hit his story icon. More scenes from last night appear, videos of Ben and a sleek brunette drinking tropical cocktails with the pulsating thump of electronic music filling the air. The girl is tagged. I click her profile, which is public. I scroll through, wishing that it proved her to be tacky or not that pretty after all, but it doesn't. She's beautiful and seems annoyingly cool. There's even a photo of her volunteering at a food drive, which really pushes me over the edge.

I know better than anyone that what's posted online is just a snippet of reality, and usually the best part. It's not the whole story, not even close. And yet I find myself seething with jealousy and insecurity over this girl I don't even know, because of a guy who didn't want me. Here at the retreat, I suddenly feel like I'm missing out on something else, excluded, not good enough to make the cut. I continue looking at the girl's profile until I land on a photo of her with her mom, smiling together on a Hawaiian beach, fruity drinks in hand. I'll never know what that kind of closeness is like, and it's not fair. Even though I'm all alone on the trail, my face burns with sadness and shame.

I put on a workout playlist and jam my phone into the waistband of my leggings. My sadness begins to turn into anger. I'm angry at Ben. How could he just turn his back on me after I revealed to him something so personal, something that made me so vulnerable? I know I'm the one who ran out on him, but shouldn't he have known that it was out of deep embarrassment? That I was paralyzed by fear? If Ben had ever cared about me, he would have been there for me. I realize, then, that just because Ben doesn't have social media and didn't know who I was from Instagram doesn't mean he didn't create an image of me in his mind. He wanted me to be a certain type of person, and when I didn't live up to that standard, or when I revealed a different side of myself—the *real* side—it wasn't what he wanted.

*All men are the same,* I think to myself as I pick up my pace. *They say they want one kind of woman, but when they're actually shown her true self, they can't accept it.*

My phone rings suddenly, interrupting my music, and in my blind rage, I answer without even bothering to look who it is.

"He-Hello?" I sputter. "Hello?"

"Bad time, avocado girl?"

"Excuse me? Who is this?"

"Jeez, you already forgot about me. I see how it is."

*Carter.* Paint guy. Calling at the absolute worst time, when the last thing I want to do is engage in a flirtatious conversation with someone. In that moment, I hate all men, even the handsome ones like Carter.

"Sorry, right, hi," I say, continuing to walk at a brisk pace. "I'm out for a hike. What's up?"

"Well, I don't mean to interrupt, just wondering if you're free later this week? Thought maybe I could show you around the island a little. Go for that swim or something." I vaguely recall Carter saying something about the ocean having the power to cure anything.

"Listen, I'm not sure," I say. "I mean, I'm not here to date, or whatever." I'm emboldened by my anger. And as cute as I remember him being, I'm not interested in putting myself out there.

"Who said it was a date?"

"I just mean . . . I don't know." I stumble over my words, pissed at myself for jumping the gun and not being quick enough to come back with a witty response.

"I just thought you could use a friend outside the walls of Island Wellness," he says. "How about Saturday? It's supposed to be nice. Pick you up around noon?"

"Sure, okay." I decide that I'll just cancel on him beforehand. *Or he'll cancel on me,* I think to myself. "Sounds good." I'm about to hang up when I realize he had called me *avocado girl.* Had he looked me up? "Wait, why did you call me *avocado girl?*"

Carter laughs. "You showed me your account last night. And you know, I've got one of those things, too, the *gram* or whatever the kids call it. I was told I have to have one for my art. I friended you, so don't leave me hanging."

"That's for Facebook," I say. "Friending." The image of Carter—tall and long limbed, with intense eyes—pops into my mind, and I suddenly feel flustered. "But I know what you mean. Right. I remember now. Anyway, I have to go. Bye."

"See you Saturday, then," he says, hanging up, and I swear I can hear him chuckling as he does.

I put my music back on and continue walking. If Carter doesn't flake on me, I plan to flake on him. What's even the point of getting to know someone here, in that way? I'm only here temporarily, and if I have to be here, I might as well focus on *why* I'm here and not get distracted. The last thing I need is some local guy to wine and dine me only to end up dropping me and making me feel worse about myself than I did before meeting him in the first place. I increase my speed again, pumping my arms by my sides.

My phone chimes again and I decide to silence it. But when I look at the screen, I see a notification that my *Los Angeles* Magazine profile is out. I turn off my music and stop my walk, and I click the link to the article. *Meet the People Redefining Modern Wellness.* I scroll past the other profiles and find my picture, in ripped jeans and a white T-shirt, with a purposely messy-looking blowout; glowing, tan skin; and a big, shiny smile.

*Ava Maloney starts her day by writing in her gratitude journal.* I cringe, having forgotten that I'd said that. I haven't written in my gratitude journal in months. If I even had the patience to keep a journal anymore, most entries would just be me lamenting the previous night's binge and purge. *"This morning," she tells us, "I wrote that I was grateful for my mom, who died when I was fifteen. I know she's still watching over me."* I can barely get through the rest of it, which goes on to say that my popularity is rooted in what the article describes as my "girl-next-door normalcy." *Ava's followers,* it says, *trust her like a best friend.*

The person in the profile is a good person, a loving person, a *truthful* person. But that person isn't me. Even the part about my mom isn't true. I miss her, and I'm grateful for her in so many ways, but I'm not grateful for her every day. I'm mad at her on many days. And if she was really watching over me, why would she be making things so hard?

I put my phone away and continue to walk. I can hear the ocean waves and the slight movement of the leaves in the breeze, the gentle chirping of birds. I feel hollow, sad, and alone, but too empty to cry. The beach appears suddenly, and all at once the ocean is before me, vast and welcoming. The shore shaped like a semicircle, with natural jetties poking out on either side and large boulders dotting each corner, creating a sense of total privacy and peace. I look around. The beach is totally empty, and all I can hear are the waves.

I think about what Carter had said, about how a swim could cure anything. At this point, I'm willing to try whatever it takes.

I strip off all my clothes and leave them in a pile on the sand. And then, with a big breath, I run into the water, lifting my arms up overhead and bringing my hands together in a diving position, catapulting myself forward and into the waves, my toes trailing behind. I stay under for a few seconds, pushing through the water, swimming out, feeling like I'm shedding something with each stroke. When I emerge, I think I've gone a hundred yards from shore, but when I look back, it's only a few paces away. The water feels slippery on my skin, and the sensation of it against my breasts and between my legs is at once natural and shocking. I float on my back and let my hair fan out around my face.

When I was little, maybe six years old, I walked in on my mom taking a bath. My parents' bathroom had a giant tub, and baths were one of the things she loved more than anything else. She'd light a candle and play a Chopin CD. I remember that this time, when I came into her bathroom and saw her, she was lying there in the tub, her eyes closed, the water line creeping up just around her lips and corners of her eyes, her hair fanned out just like mine is now. I'd seen her take baths many times before. I'd taken them with her. But something about that time made me scared. I thought she was dead. I screamed out but couldn't move. I was unable to go to her, so I just stood there and released a blood-curdling scream.

She popped up, the water nearly spilling out over the side of the tub.

"Sweetie, what's wrong?" she asked, wiping her eyes and giving me a smile. "Come here."

I went to her, tears streaming. "I thought you had drowned!" I cried. She reached her arms out, and I let her embrace me with her wet body. I pushed my head against her chest.

"No, sweetheart," she said. "I'm right here. I'll always be right here."

I remember not wanting to let go of her. I remember the smell of her shampoo and the soap on her skin, the way her chest felt warm and wet against my face, the way she held me so tight that I could feel the curved edges of her clavicle, the sharp line of her jaw. She was strong then, and I was small.

I suddenly feel a piece of seaweed graze my leg and am snapped out of my memory as I kick it away. I dip under the surface of the water one last time before trudging back to shore. I rest on a warm rock for a few minutes to dry off, naked, exposed, feeling outrageously brash as the sun warms my skin, and then I put my sticky clothes back on and ascend the trail back to the retreat.

The swim might not have cured me, but I do feel better. And I wonder if maybe Carter is onto something after all.

# Chapter 10

I run into Naomi on my way back to my cabin, and she agrees to bring me more supplies. She nods like an enthusiastic puppy each time I make a request, which I preface with *If you really don't mind* or *If it's not too much to ask.* Avocados? No problem. A few slices of twelve-grain bread? Of course. Another fruit-and-berry plate? Sure thing. She's becoming my secret weapon, and with her help, I think I've got a handle on my food-content plan while I'm here. I'll document occasional meals that the retreat is serving, maybe every other day or so, and then I'll document the snacks and mini meals I make myself in the cabin with Naomi's supplies, most of which I won't actually eat. Plus, I've got a good amount of my old stock photos to choose from. If I spread them out the right way, I think they can get me through to the end. This balance allows me to spin a narrative to my followers that I'm on vacation somewhere on the island, but not necessarily at a retreat like this. I could definitely just be renting a house with some friends and fixing most of my meals myself. As long as mermaid1985 keeps their distance, I can get through the summer.

I've just stepped out of the shower when I hear a knock on the door. I wrap a towel around my body and dash through the cabin, opening the front door to find Naomi there with an Island Wellness tote bag full of the items I asked for, as well as a fruit-and-veggie plate.

"Oh, I'm sorry," she says when she sees me in the towel. "I can just leave this stuff here."

"Please, it's fine," I tell her. "Come on in." I hold the door open for her. "Thank you so much, Naomi. This is awesome."

"It was seriously no problem," she says. She puts everything down on the kitchen counter. "Anything else I can get for you? Have you had a good day so far?"

"Yes, I've had a great day, actually. I hiked one of the trails down to the beach and went for a swim. It was awesome."

"Oh yeah," she says, nodding. "It's gorgeous down there."

I sense that she's nervous around me, fidgeting her hands together and shifting on her feet. She's probably gone through my entire feed several times since she met me. I know the feeling, having met many of the influencers I also follow, and it's disorienting and strange, to feel like you already know someone intimately from the internet, when in real life, you don't know them at all.

"And actually," I add, "maybe I could get your help taking some photos of me a few times here and there? You know, I actually totally suck at taking my own photo."

Naomi predictably agrees, with glee, and she agrees to help me at the end of the week with a little photo shoot in some activewear I was sent. In return, I assure her that we'll talk about her own career and goals, and that I'll help her however I can.

"Whatever I can do to help," I say before she leaves.

Later, I'm assembling some sliced avocado with sea salt and olive oil to photograph when Stephanie and Rhoda return.

"Oh," coos Rhoda, looking over the counter, "is that for your blog?"

"Instagram, Rhoda. For her *Instagram*," Stephanie says, tossing her beach bag onto the couch and checking her phone.

"Yeah, just wanted a little snack, and this is the kind of thing I document." Stephanie isn't paying attention. Rhoda nods, but I'm not sure she really gets it. I take a couple of photos but wrap up the avocado and stick it in the fridge. If my cabinmates weren't there, I'd just throw it out completely.

"You're not gonna eat that?" Rhoda asks.

"You know, I just realized when you guys came back that it's almost dinnertime. And um, I just don't want to spoil my appetite."

"Okay," Rhoda says. Stephanie glances up from her phone, and she and Rhoda share a look.

"Listen," Stephanie says, "we just want you to know that what you eat, when you eat, all of that—that's your business. We care about you, but we're not gonna judge you. After all, everyone at this retreat is here for some reason, something relating to their health and wellness. We've all got issues."

"Yeah," adds Rhoda, "and not to downplay how serious eating disorders are, but who doesn't have some kind of issue with their body or with food, right? I mean, I feel like I've been dieting for a hundred years! You don't have to be self-conscious about your battle with us, honey."

I can't tell if they're being genuinely supportive of me or if they're fishing for something. Maybe they heard me puking last night, or maybe they're suspicious of all the food that Naomi has stocked for me in the house.

"Thank you both," I say, treading lightly. "I appreciate that. And . . . you're not wrong, I mean, I definitely am here to work on myself. My . . . relationship with food, I guess." I realize, as I say it, how foreign it is to me to feel actual support from other women without the veil of competition, or without the instinct to distrust it. But it feels nice.

"We understand," Rhoda says. "And if you do need anything, or want to talk, just let us know. Okay? Anyway, I'm going to take a shower and get ready for dinner." We make a plan to head to the farmhouse together in half an hour.

I'm not sure if it's because I'm simply too tired to resist, but I decide that I'm going to just eat what I want for dinner tonight and not purge. That's the goal, anyway. Tonight's meal is an Asian-inspired feast: fresh local black bass in a light miso sauce, bok choy with ginger, purplish-black forbidden rice, tempeh and vegetable dumplings with chili dipping sauce, and a coconut-curry soup. This time, the three of us sit alone at a small table off to the side. Without saying it, we all share a silent sense of relief when we smile and wave at the leggings, knowing that we don't have to endure another meal of chatter with them.

"Well, I had my first therapy session today. I got Leon," Stephanie says. "You know, I was skeptical. I'm not a therapy person. I actually told Sarah when I first got here that I might not partake at all in the therapy stuff. Ralph has told me for years to try it, but I don't know, I'm sort of a 'pull yourself up by your bootstraps' kind of person."

"And?" Rhoda asks.

"I have to admit . . . I liked it. It was actually *helpful*."

"That's great," I say.

"Yeah, I mean I came here just to take a break. Work's been crazy, to say the least." Stephanie reveals to us that she's the in-house counsel for a film production company based in New York. Not a little indie company, but a major one, it seems, a high-profile one with a lot of financing and a lot of awards. And, perhaps unsurprisingly, a lot of controversy right now with its CEO, who's been accused of giving a young actress a plum role in exchange for sex.

"Well, did he do it? Is he guilty?" Rhoda asks. I love her for being so blunt. I was wondering the same thing: What does Stephanie think?

"Listen, I really shouldn't even be talking about it. But I'll say this: sometimes I wonder if I'm spending my time *on the wrong side of history*. I didn't become a lawyer to work with men like *that* . . ." She cuts herself off, as though she's said too much. "But it's my job. Or at least it is for now."

"Well," Rhoda says, "it doesn't have to be, though, does it?"

Stephanie looks at Rhoda like it's a question she's never considered before.

"I guess not . . . but it's the job I always wanted. It's what I worked my entire life for. I'm not ready to just throw that away."

"I understand." Rhoda nods.

"I do, too." And I do, very much. I know exactly how it feels to have built something from nothing and to *finally* achieve the thing you'd always thought you wanted, only for it to be a disappointment.

"Anyway, Ralph has been telling me for years to try therapy. And I guess I have to say . . . he was right. I'm actually looking forward to my next session."

"That's wonderful," Rhoda says. "I'm seeing Wanda tomorrow."

"Me too," I add.

"Have either of you done therapy before?" Stephanie asks.

I don't even know where to begin in answering that question. Not only did I go through a myriad of therapists and eating-disorder specialists in my early twenties, including the one who I thought had actually *healed* me, but I also saw several family therapists when Mom got sick. There was the first round of therapy we did together—the four of us as a family—right after she was diagnosed. It was her idea.

"I want you all to have the tools to grieve. I want you to know how to talk to one another," she'd told us. I was so angry at her for that. She had barely started her treatments, and it felt like she was already giving up. I mostly sat through those sessions stone-faced and bitter. Sometimes we would go out to dinner afterward, as a family.

And then there was the therapy when she actually did die, first with that same therapist and later with someone else. We couldn't go back to the same therapist as before. It always felt like there was an empty seat in her office, and it only made our sadness more acute. My dad started cutting out of the therapy pretty quick, saying that it was better for me and Mike to have our own process without him. Those sessions went away after a few months, too, when Mike and I both decided that there was no point. The therapist would probe us about our mother, as if trying to get us to state the absolutely obvious: Yes, we miss her. Yes, we're upset that she's gone. Yes, life is unfair, and now we've learned that the hard way. What else do you want us to say?

And then, of course, there was the eating-disorder specialist I saw twice during my sophomore year of high school, when Mom was still alive. She'd caught on to what I was doing and whisked me away one afternoon to a suburban doctor's office with peach-colored walls. She sat outside in the waiting room both times, and after the second time, she went into the doctor's office herself and spoke alone with him for twenty minutes. After that, I never went back. I had told the doctor that my puking was a onetime phase, that I was fine, that I had just experimented with it to deal with the stress of Mom's cancer. He bought it, and so did my mom. She knew that she wasn't going to be around much longer, and I think it gave her some comfort to tell herself that I was okay, that I was better.

I really don't know why I kept dabbling in different kinds of therapy later on in Los Angeles. There was a wacky new age therapist in Eagle Rock I'd see once a month, mostly to get my Adderall prescription, which she still fills. There was the Beverly Hills boutique therapist whose office had a juice bar in the front, the Santa Monica shaman who worked out of his patchouli-scented house, the emaciated diet coach in West Hollywood who recommended I add protein powder to pretty much everything. The one I stuck with for a year, who helped me lose weight and gain control of my relationship with food, was probably more of a drill sergeant in retrospect. I had to email her everything I ate every single day.

"A little bit, here and there," I say. "Not much."

"I think therapy is just fantastic," Rhoda says. "Everyone should do it, if you ask me. David and I went to couples therapy when we became empty nesters. It really helped us."

We keep talking throughout dinner, about the pressure of Stephanie's job and her uncertainty about having children, and about Rhoda's new life now that she's a widow. For once, I just sit and listen.

I don't make it about me. When we finish dinner, I realize that I've eaten what I wanted without really thinking about it that much. We return to the cabin and I feel . . . *okay*. I feel full, but not too full. I drink some more water, brush my teeth, wash my face, and consider the contents of my emergency snack drawer. It would be so easy to binge and purge right now; it's almost like I have to do it even if I don't want to. But tonight, I make the decision to just go to bed. I tell myself that if I can't fall asleep within the hour, I can change my mind. But once I get under the covers and shut my eyes, I'm lulled into a deep sleep almost immediately.

The next morning, I wake feeling immensely victorious. My hangover is gone, and I feel light and refreshed, well rested. I didn't fall asleep to the glow of my phone like I normally do, and I even slept with the windows open, letting the sea breeze in. I slept later than Stephanie and Rhoda, who are already up and about when I emerge from my room. I eat breakfast alone, choosing a Greek yogurt bowl with fresh berries, homemade granola, and honey. I take a boomerang of it for my stories. Then it's time for my appointment with Wanda.

I use the farmhouse's bathroom after breakfast. And despite the instinct I always have to purge, even after a light meal like the one I just had, I don't do it. I don't even seriously consider it, not really. I like the way I feel, and I decide to try to hold on to that.

The doctors' offices are in a wing at the far end of the farmhouse, overlooking the vegetable garden. I enter the waiting area, where a staff member I've never seen before sits behind a desk.

"Good morning," the woman says. "Ava?"

"Yes, good morning." The woman sits at a desk that's neatly organized, not a pen out of place.

"Fantastic. I'm Beth, Leon and Wanda's assistant." She unearths a file with my name on it from a stack of folders on the desk, as though pulling a card from a deck. Behind her is a large black filing cabinet, and I imagine that every single guest at the retreat has their own file in there, filled with their secrets. My folder is thin, but I can see that there are a few pages of paper in there. *My application.* All my secrets, wrapped up in a tidy little folder. "You can wait here, make yourself comfortable. Just one moment." She gives me a wide smile as she rises and waves her arm out toward the leather loveseat and chairs. I sit on the loveseat and watch her walk to one of the offices, where she knocks and opens the door, just a crack, and whispers. She enters the office with the folder and shuts the door. I feel exposed, sitting out there in the waiting room, like I'm being watched. A moment later, she emerges without the folder. "Wanda is ready for you," she says.

"Thanks," I say, suddenly regretting being here entirely. Beth gives me a smile of encouragement as I push open the door.

Wanda's office is painted a bright yellow, and the walls are covered in framed posters from art museums and exhibitions, mostly postmodern with bold shapes, crude brushstrokes, and citrusy colors. Her furniture is sleek and mid-century modern: two cowhide Le Corbusier chairs, a white leather chaise lounge, a minimalist blue-velvet sofa. It's a stark departure from the updated farmhouse style of the rest of the retreat, and I'm pleasantly surprised by the eccentricity of it; even though it's a bit garish, I appreciate the unapologetic nature of it. I'd never have suspected it from this petite woman who seems to wear the same T-shirt and jeans every day.

"Ava," Wanda says. "Hello!" She rises from her desk, and I shut the door behind me. "Have a seat, wherever you like. The chaise is more comfortable than you think. Usually, people wait until the third session for that, though I say, why not just go for it, if that's where you'll be most relaxed." Wanda is slight, a small woman with delicate features, pearly-white skin, and jet-black hair. Though she seems to be in her sixties, I don't see a gray hair or a wrinkle on her face.

I sit on the velvet sofa and place my hands on my knees, releasing an exhale.

"Well, nice to meet you," I say. "Just so you know, I've been in therapy before, many times. So, I know how this works."

"Okay," she says, moving from behind her desk to one of the cowhide chairs across from me. "How does it work?"

"I just mean that I'm comfortable in therapy. I'm comfortable talking about my issues. You're not going to have to pry anything out of me. I'm pretty aware of my problems. It's not like I'm one of those people who's in denial, you know?"

Wanda crosses one of her legs over the other. "Do you want a coffee or anything? I should have offered. Twenty-five years doing this, and I always forget."

"No, thanks, I'm good."

"Okay, then. You were saying?"

I know exactly what she's doing. She's letting me *lead*. This is what they all do. They ask open-ended questions to put a figurative mirror in front of me, which they want to result in a big "aha" moment of discovery at the end, so that they can say, *I didn't do anything, I just listened.*

"I just mean that I'm here for very clear reasons. I used to be severely bulimic, and I worked very hard to overcome that. I went to therapy, I worked with a nutritionist, I totally changed my life and my lifestyle to get better. And lately I feel like I'm slipping a little bit. But that's normal. It's a day-to-day struggle. And I know that. So, it's definitely helpful to talk about it, sure, but I mean, I *know* what I need to do to get better. I've done it before."

"Okay," she says. "So, are you doing those things? The things you know that you need to do to get better? Are you doing them?"

"Yes," I lie. "I'm trying to."

Wanda doesn't say anything. She picks up my file and skims through it for a moment but then closes it and tosses it behind her onto her desk.

"Tell me about your family. About your childhood. Where are you from? I'm from Cohasset, not too far from here, on the south shore. Hated my childhood. Loved my parents, but hated growing up in Cohasset. Didn't have any friends who were Asian, like me. Thought I'd live in New York or San Francisco, somewhere I'd fit in. But here I am, on this island. Been here almost two decades. And it's even whiter than Cohasset. And yet, I love it here."

I nod, feeling some relief that she's taken time to share her own story, so I don't have to immediately dive into mine. Though I know that it's just a tactic she's using to get me to open up.

"I'm from New Jersey," I say. "Cherry Hill." Whenever I tell someone I'm from Cherry Hill, if they know the East Coast, they assume I'm nouveau riche. And they're not wrong. But I hate telling people that, at least my followers. I don't want them to know I grew up with any money. I hate the other influencers who pretend like the income they get from endorsements or a fluffy cookbook has actually paid for the Soho apartment they just bought. Sure, I lie to my followers about some things, but I don't want to lie about that. So, I try to leave that out from the narrative completely. That's another reason why I don't want to admit to being at the retreat. "I had a good childhood, I really did. I have an older brother, Mike. We're pretty close. He and my dad still live in Jersey, near one another, so they see each other a lot. I moved to LA after college and stayed there ever since, so I only see them like once a year now over the holidays."

"Okay," Wanda says. "What about Mom?"

I hate when therapists do this. Obviously, I didn't mention my mom on purpose. And obviously, she's seen in my file that my mom is dead. And yet she's going to make me spell it out for her. But I suppose that what Wanda does isn't really therapy, not really. It takes years to even break the surface of a healing process. She's on a limited time schedule with us, so she has to fast-track it all. What could she possibly do to truly help someone in a matter of weeks?

"She died when I was fifteen. Breast cancer. It happened really quickly. So, it was definitely a tough time for me, for my whole family. I miss her a lot. But it was a long time ago now."

"Okay." Wanda switches her legs. I don't like the way her eyes stay locked on mine. "But you were close?"

"Yes," I say. It's starting to feel like she's interrogating me in an investigation. "Very close."

"Now, what was *her* relationship with her body like? Did she suffer from bulimia as well?"

I feel a pang of anger toward her for asking me this, so bluntly, right off the bat. It somehow feels like a violation against my mother, an insult to her. I'm tempted to get up and leave. But I feel glued to my chair and am compelled to answer.

"I mean, she had issues just like most women do, I guess," I say definitively, as though trying to really say to her, *Don't act like you're above it, either, Wanda.*

"What kind of issues?"

"Look, if you're trying to get me to, like, villainize my mom, that's not going to happen. That's not what this is. She had body insecurities just like everyone else. She took care of herself, she cared about what she looked like, she watched her figure, or whatever. But my stuff isn't about her."

"Okay," Wanda says. She lets us sit in silence for a few seconds. "You know, you're allowed to be mad at someone who's no longer with us. It doesn't mean you don't love them."

"Okay," I respond.

"So, Ava, I understand that you're in the wellness industry. Can you tell me about that?" She's shifting gears, and I feel smug that I forced her off her path.

"Yes. I'm an influencer. I used to work in video game development. But that was a few years ago when I was feeling really unhealthy and unmotivated. I basically made a pact with myself to get in shape, to get healthy—back on track, you know. And I took it really seriously and started kind of documenting the process. So, like, documenting what

I was eating and what workouts I was doing. And people were pretty into it. So now I do that full-time."

"You do what full-time?" Wanda's expression hasn't changed, I realize, this entire time. She's got a warm, friendly face, but it doesn't shift in expression.

"I'm an influencer. I document my wellness habits, I guess you can say, and I get paid to promote and endorse different products I use."

"Okay. Interesting." She crosses her legs again, as though trying to fill the silence with movement.

I explain in more detail how my business works. I'm used to doing that, and I'm comfortable doing it. I can easily fill the time talking about it. I wait for Wanda to give a typical reaction, with follow-up questions. She just nods for a few seconds.

"And do you love your job? Do you like your work?"

"I mean, yeah, it gives me a lot of freedom," I say, on the defensive. "I can work from anywhere, I dictate my own hours, I get lots of free stuff through partnerships. It's really good."

"But the work itself," she says. "Is it fulfilling? Are you passionate about it?"

"Not everyone can be *passionate* about their job. I mean, it's a job, after all."

Wanda ponders this, tilting her head to one side.

"That's true," she says. "But you quit a job you didn't like so that you could pursue this instead, right? There must have been something about it, at least initially, that you did love."

I think about it. She's absolutely right.

"Well, I love food," I say. "I guess that's the problem. I love food, but food is also my problem."

"It's possible to love and hate something at the same time," Wanda tells me. "That's something we're going to work through." She clasps her hands in her lap with a sigh. "For next time," she says, "I'm going to give you an assignment. I want you to recall a moment—*the* moment, perhaps—in your life when you first became aware of your own body, as it appears to others, and to yourself. When did you first become self-conscious?" I had not used the word *self-conscious* with Wanda in our conversation. And I don't like the way she says *body* again. It feels invasive and violating, somehow. Not sexual, but somehow too intimate for this room. "And I'd like you to be prepared to talk about it next time." She rises from the chair. "Beth will schedule your next visit on your way out. Ava, I very much look forward to working together."

"Yes, thanks," I say, shuffling backward to leave. "Bye."

Beth pulls up the schedule on her computer. I wonder if she has read all the files, too, and if she talks to Wanda about her patients after the sessions. She books me for another session in a few days.

As I leave the farmhouse, I feel a sense of relief at having done the first therapy session. Now I know what's coming. She's going to push me to talk about my mom. As if it's never occurred to me before that my eating and body issues are connected to hers. I know all this already. But what Wanda doesn't understand is that I can't go down that road. It's not an option for me. I'm scared that if I do, the memories I have of her will be replaced with nothing but anger.

# Chapter 11

A few days later, I wake up early and realize that I'm overdue to post one of my weekly "What I eat in a day" posts. They're some of the most popular ones I do. I show every single thing I eat in a typical day, plus an exact schedule of when I eat, as well as my daily workout. I try to portray it as an "average" day for me so that my followers have a good sense of what I do to stay balanced and maintain a healthy weight. I'm always clear with my followers that this is just what works for me, but that it might not work for them. I'm not *telling* them they can only eat fifteen hundred calories in a day or that they have to work out for an hour. I'm just telling them what *I* do. Or what I want them to think I do.

In bed, I scroll through my saved photos, thoughtfully selecting what I'm going to use and being careful to only choose photos that don't show my nails or any signs of seasons or location. I choose a pretty typical day: overnight oats with a hearty spoonful of almond butter, sprinkled with raspberries, hemp hearts, and pepitas for crunch, plus a homemade matcha latte with the collagen powder I'm sponsored to advertise; sliced celery and cucumbers with hummus for a midmorning snack; a salad bowl with chopped kale, chickpeas, tomatoes, golden beets, and roasted tofu, drizzled with a vegan salad dressing sent to me for free; an afternoon snack of turmeric tea, some sliced watermelon, and a refrigerated protein bar from another sponsorship; and for dinner, broiled salmon, brown rice, and steamed broccoli; dessert is a home-made cashew brownie that I tell my followers I'm working on perfecting. Once I load them to my post, I immediately move them from my saved photos to a separate folder of used photos. That way, I'll never accidentally use a photo twice. These are the things the trolls look for, the ones who hope you'll trip up and be shown to be a fraud.

WHAT I EAT IN A DAY, I post at the top of the caption. Good morning, friends! Sorry I am a bit late in posting this. If you're new here, welcome! Once in a while, I post an example of what I eat in a "typical" day. Though, of course, life is crazy, and no day is the same. But this gives you a pretty good idea of what I try to eat when I'm feeling my best. I want to be clear that what works for me might not work for you! We're all different! I am not a nutritionist or a doctor, and I will never, ever tell you what you SHOULD eat or shouldn't eat. I don't believe in that! I just want to give you guys a sense of what works for me. This is the kind of food that fuels me and makes me feel strong and healthy. The breakdown is below! Have a great day, friends ☺

Then, I painstakingly type out a description of all the foods and the brands used in each meal, and I make sure to tag them in the photos as well. The whole thing takes over an hour.

When I'm done, I get dressed and head out the door with Stephanie and Rhoda to a morning vinyasa flow yoga class before breakfast. I begrudgingly went with them the day before, and I was surprised by how much I enjoyed it. It didn't feel competitive, like the classes in LA that I'd been to. Right before the first class, I received another weird DM from mermaid1985:

**???**

I was sure I wouldn't be able to focus during the class, that I'd be too panicked and anxious. But somehow, just a few minutes in, I found myself letting go of that worry. And by the end of class, I had decided to just relinquish control, to not let myself get consumed by something that someone else was doing.

We're a little bit late to yoga this morning, and we sheepishly enter the chapel and quickly put down our mats. The instructor, Samantha—a glowing woman with long, beachy hair—greets us with a radiant smile, anyway. I get into child's pose and focus on my breathing, something Samantha always reminds us to do during challenging moments. Four counts in, four counts out. Gentle acoustic music plays through the sound system. We move into downward dog, then to warrior two, then into a standing series, and finally back to the mat, landing in Savasana, the ninety minutes having flown by. We close our eyes, and Samantha comes around to give us personal adjustments. She squats behind me and cradles my head in her hands, and I let the full weight of it collapse into her palms, sparking within me an odd desire to cry. Not because I am reminded of something in my mind that makes me sad, but because the specific physicality does something to my body that feels like a kind of unlocking, a clicking, a release. But I hold back the tears.

Later, on my way to the beach, I hear my name being called across the lawn. I turn to see Naomi waving and walking briskly toward me.

"Hi, Ava!" she says. She looks around, as though she's not allowed to be approaching me.

"Hey, Naomi, how are you?" I remember that she'd asked to sit down and talk sometime, about her career, about my path in wellness. I feel bad that I haven't followed up yet, especially since she's agreed to help me take some photos tomorrow.

"Great, thanks! How are you? I was just wondering if you need anything." Naomi has been a loyal friend, bringing me my requested supplies with the utmost subtlety. Most of what she brings is straight from the kitchen, and I wonder if Sarah or anyone else has suspected anything.

"No, but thank you." I readjust my beach towel on my arm. "Hey, if you're still willing to help me with those photos tomorrow, maybe we can have some tea together after and talk? About your career and stuff? If you want."

"That would be amazing! Thank you." She smiles, but then her face grows serious, and she leans closer. "But we just have to keep it quiet, I mean the whole thing. I'm not really allowed to become friends with guests or spend time with them. I have a long break tomorrow right after lunch, so I'll just come by your cabin then. But if you don't mind, don't tell anyone. Especially not Sarah. It's just not allowed, you know, to interact with guests like this."

"Right, I get it. Don't worry." I understand that there should absolutely be boundaries between staff and guests, but I'm the one asking her to do me a favor, and it's not as if it's something that feels violating or offensive. "See you then." I smile and walk to the beach.

I lie back and shut my eyes, the sun warming me like a blanket. With my next therapy session looming just a few days ahead, I think about the assignment Wanda had given me, to try to identify the first time I became aware of my body.

I'm reminded of all the times that my mom took me back-to-school shopping. It was always a day I looked forward to. We were squarely middle class, not rich, but my mom made me feel like we were royalty on those annual excursions. She let me buy the *cool* stuff—the platform slides, the square-neck spaghetti-strap tank tops, the plaid miniskirts, the retro-style puffy vests. She sat patiently in the dressing rooms of Gap Kids and Limited Too, a stack of clothing on her lap.

"You *have* to have it," she said when she thought something looked great on me. "That doesn't do you justice," she said if something looked terrible. She made two piles of clothes—buy or not, and she'd hang each piece that we weren't taking back up on the hangers the way they were when we picked them out.

In between stores, when we needed a break, we went to the bakery. Mom got a coffee and I got a cookie, a special treat. Then we sat by the mall's fountain, the floor of which was carpeted in shiny pennies, tossed in by children making wishes. I loved to stare at the coins, wondering if any of those wishes ever came true.

When I was little, she would hand me a penny from her purse.

"Here you go, Ava," she would say to me, smiling into my eyes, like she was handing me the keys to the universe. "Make a wish."

The thought was always overwhelming. I wanted to be able to fly, to breathe underwater, to land the lead role in the fourth-grade play. My mother watched me as I contemplated, rubbing the penny between my little fingers.

"You can do anything you want to do, Ava. Anything in the whole world."

"Anything?"

"That's right, anything."

"Can I be anything I want to be?"

My mom looked down at me and waited a moment before responding. "Yes, you can be anything you want to be, too. But you know you're already perfect, just the way you are. All you have to do is be *you*, Ava."

I tossed the penny into the fountain, though my wish didn't really matter, and I knew it, even then. With my mom by my side, the wish was unnecessary. I had everything I needed right there. As long as I had her, I knew that I'd be okay.

Somewhere along the way, when I became a teenager, we stopped going to the bakery, and she stopped giving me pennies for the fountain, or maybe I started rolling my eyes and refusing them. Our shopping trips became more perfunctory, more about necessity than joy. The fun and pleasure of the experience diminished each year, and I could feel our relationship evolving. I still needed her, but I began to see her differently.

As I got older, the dressing rooms seemed to shrink. I quickly became more self-conscious standing in front of the three-way mirror with my mom sitting right behind me as I pulled a pair of low-rise corduroys over my thighs and butt. We used to agree on almost everything when it came to clothes, but we started to get into more arguments about what looked good and what didn't when I turned fourteen, just as my growth spurt was starting.

"See how this makes your waist look bigger than it is?" she asked, reaching out her hands to adjust a boxy sweater.

"This is the *style*, Mom," I insisted. But I paused and took a closer look at my waistline than I would have otherwise. I'm not sure I would have thought my waist looked big if she hadn't said anything, but once she said it, I agreed.

"Well, sometimes it's better to forget trends and just do what works for your body," she said.

I never thought about my mom's own personal habits when it came to food or exercise until I was that age. I never thought about how my brother and my dad and I ate dinners she prepared, but she rarely ate any of it herself. I mostly saw her snacking on rice cakes and drinking hot tea. She never seemed to have time to eat. She was always *moving*: organizing a school event, planning one of our birthday parties, cleaning the kitchen, folding laundry, driving us to school or basketball practice. Before she had Mike and me, she was an interior designer, with her own small but consistent business. She kept it going as much as she could, with the occasional jobs here and there, but before Mike and I were out of elementary school, her business fell away almost completely.

"My most important job in the world is being your mom," she said to us. And I knew she meant it; there was no detail she ever overlooked as our mom. But sometimes I wondered, when I got older, if she had lost some of who she was in her role as a mother. She devoted herself to us every single day. Each morning, she drove us to school, dressed in her workout clothes—cropped leggings, sneakers, a zip-up fleece, and a fanny pack—and she met other moms for speed walks around one of the local reservoirs after school drop-off. Sometimes, at home, she did workout videos—Jane Fonda ones early on, Buns of Steel, and later, Tae Bo. Sometimes, when I was little, I did them with her, and I laughed at how silly some of the movements looked. She laughed a little, too, but then she returned to the video with a focus and an intensity that I otherwise didn't see from her, as if she *had* to push herself to the brink.

And yet I still never really thought about any of this in a critical way until the following year's shopping trip, just before I turned fifteen. By then, we could buy clothes from some of the same places. Once, at one of the adult stores, we were both trying on some dresses. I was looking for something to wear to the fall formal dance at school, and she was looking for cocktail dresses for the holiday season. I begged her to let me pick something from the juniors section of the department store instead, but she was adamant that this place would offer more tasteful options for my body.

The saleswoman let us use one of the large corner dressing rooms so that we could try things on together. I combed through our rack of dresses, and I remember looking at the sizes she picked for herself and then looking at mine. She was a size 2 across the board, and I was a 6. It didn't make sense. In my mind, she was bigger than I was, stronger than I was, capable of carrying me or holding me in her lap. After all, she had *birthed me*. Somehow, the fact that she was my mother simply made her *bigger* than I was in my mind. How was it possible that I still wanted to be comforted by her, held by her, protected by her, if I was bigger and stronger than she was?

I tried on a pink strapless dress with a corset-style waist. It reminded me of a princess dress, and I loved it immediately.

"Mom, what do you think?" I asked, doing a twirl.

"It's nice," she said, bringing her hand to her chin, something she did when she was pondering how to be diplomatic. "But are you *comfortable* in it?"

The truth was, I wasn't really comfortable in it, no. It was a little bit too tight on the hips, and the fat between my new breasts and armpits burst out from the top of the neckline. But I still loved it.

"Because it doesn't look that comfortable," she added. "What about this instead?" She pulled out a navy shift dress with a boat neck: drab, shapeless, boring. "This might be more flattering."

Knowing it was a futile fight, I pulled the pink dress off and stepped into the navy one.

"See?" she said, standing behind me, adjusting the neckline. "This shows off your nice legs and hides the waist."

I looked at her in the mirror, and then I looked at myself. That was the day I felt a fundamental shift in how I viewed myself. Until then, I'd only viewed myself as *me*, not me *compared to* someone else. But after that, my self-image became forever connected to how I looked in respect to someone else, or some standard, some ideal, some *goal*.

Maybe this was body dysmorphia, as one therapist had suggested years ago. Maybe it was just common teenage-girl insecurities. Or maybe it was really only about comparing myself to my mother, not to anyone else. She bought me the blue dress, but I still longed for the pink one.

After that, it took some time for my disease to develop. It grew on its own, like a parasite that had latched on to me, out of my control. I never thought I generated it myself, and I never thought that the seeds of it could have originated there, in the harsh lighting of a shopping-mall dressing room. I wanted to believe that it had to be from some external force that had worked its way inside of me. And so, I did believe that.

I flip over onto my stomach and untie the straps of my top, lying flat on my towel to avoid flashing anyone. I flip through Instagram. Becky does a boomerang of a blueberry smoothie after a hot Pilates class. Another influencer is doing a Whole Foods shopping trip and snaps a picture of everything in her cart, noting some of her staples as well as new things she's trying. And another one posts a then-and-now shot of when she was anorexic and underweight, versus now, free from the shackles of restricted eating: Forty pounds heavier but never been happier, she says. Another does a tour of her newly designed baby nursery with two walk-in closets and a full bath, in her six-bedroom house in Salt Lake City. Really, all this content is identical. It's all promising viewers the same lie: if you do this, you can have that.

I doze off to sleep soon after, and wake only when my stomach rumbles, signaling me that it's time for lunch.

I eat lunch alone, but the leggings spot me as I make myself a bowl of berries for dessert.

"We all follow you now, on the Insta," Hadley says to me. The trio are wearing their usual spandex and tank tops.

"Does that collagen-powder stuff really work?" Eliza asks. "We were wondering about that."

"Yeah, I swear by it," I tell them, though the truth is that no collagen powder will make their skin look ten years younger. "I can get you ladies a sample."

Impressed, they thank me and return to their table. I wonder for a moment if any of them could be behind the cryptic DMs, but it just doesn't feel like they could be.

Later, Stephanie, Rhoda, and I have dinner together, and I make the same decision to try to just go to sleep and not binge and purge. But when we return to the cabin, I remember that I have a bag of pastries from the Scottish Bakehouse that I'd picked up the other day on a bike ride. They'll be stale after tonight, so it's as good a time as ever. And I have one more bottle of wine left. The urge starts to set in as I begin to say good night to my cabinmates.

"Hey, you ladies want to have a drink before bed?" Stephanie asks us just as we're all about to retire. I wait for Rhoda to respond. I don't, really. It will interfere with my binge. But I also have a hard time saying no to a drink, and I tell myself that I could binge afterward. "I actually have a few bottles of wine," Stephanie says. "Got them earlier today when I was shopping in Edgartown." She opens the fridge, and I see that there are two bottles of white wine chilling on the door.

"God," Rhoda says. "Wine never sounded so good. I think this is the longest I've gone without drinking since I was eighteen!"

"Sounds good to me, too," I say. Stephanie takes out the bottles and pours us each a glass. It's a crisp, dry sauvignon blanc, and I immediately feel soothed by its familiar zing as it trickles down my throat. We sit in the living room, me on one of the chairs, Stephanie and Rhoda on the couch.

"So, do you guys feel *well*? I mean, now that we've been here for almost a week?" Stephanie continues. "I personally find it hard to put my stress aside, you know? My body feels good, I guess. We're eating well and exercising, and I'm sleeping more than usual, but I'm not sure I'm feeling more centered." Rhoda and I nod. I'm already halfway through my glass of wine.

"Listen," Rhoda says, "you need to remind yourself that your life— your husband and your job and everything else—is going to be right there for you when this is over. It's not often that you get to hit pause on things and just focus on yourself." She takes a sip of her wine. "As a woman, our whole lives are about taking care of others. That's just the truth. We're always thinking about other people but rarely ourselves."

Stephanie leans forward with the wine bottle and refills my glass, then Rhoda's and her own.

"Well, I don't know," Stephanie says reluctantly. "I mean, I'm pretty nice to myself. I buy what I want and take good care of myself. I'm here, after all, aren't I?"

"Yes, but *why* are you here?" Rhoda asks, turning her body toward Stephanie. "You said you had a breakdown, right?"

"Well, yes," Stephanie says. "I guess it just feels so indulgent to admit that I need time just for myself. That's just such a greedy thing to say. My mother didn't think about *self-care*. It's a bullshit thing that our society has just made up so people buy stuff or have something to talk about on social media."

The second the words *social media* come out of Stephanie's mouth, I can tell she regrets saying them. She's really talking about *me*, my world, my business. She tries to backpedal.

"That's not what I meant," she stammers before I've even responded. "I didn't mean to insult what you do. I just meant that this whole culture of self-care has gotten a little out of control, don't you think? Older generations didn't think that a facial would cure their depression, right? I mean, they barely even acknowledged depression. They were too busy focusing on getting dinner on the table and keeping the lights on. *Real* life."

"No, I agree," I say, and Stephanie's face relaxes. "And you're right. The self-care culture has gotten out of control. Now people are told they need to buy certain things or look a certain way, live a certain way, to be happy, to be healthy." I pause. "And it's totally backfired, spiraled into something totally antithetical to self-care, actually. Now women are just competing with other women on social media. We present this bullshit, fake image of perfection to the world, but it's totally unattainable. And it's dangerous." I'm getting heated as I talk. I hadn't realized until now how badly I needed to say all of this. I'm not even sure I knew that I felt it. "The craziest part of it all, though, is that even though social media has completely pitted all these women against one another, it's actually all rooted in the patriarchy, I think. Fucking men are the ones who have created these impossible standards for women to uphold."

"Amen to that. Fuck the patriarchy!" Rhoda says.

"Well, if you feel that way, why do you do it? I mean, why are you part of it?" Stephanie asks me. I don't think she's judging me, but I wouldn't blame her if she did.

"Because . . . it didn't start out this way. It started out from a good place. And it just turned into something else. *I* turned into something else."

"What do you mean?" Stephanie asks as she goes to the fridge to get the second bottle of wine.

"I just mean that when I first started my account, I did it because I really loved and believed in this healthy way of life that I'd found." I hesitate before saying more. I feel like I can trust Stephanie and Rhoda, but I'm still not sure I want to open up to them about my history. Because there's only one place that it will lead, and that's to where I am now, and the lies I've been telling. "I loved food, I loved cooking, I loved finding ways to enjoy food and feel good about myself. And before that, I'd had an eating disorder for a long time. I'm, uh, I'm better now, but it's just been a struggle lately, that's all."

"We all have setbacks, honey," Rhoda says.

"Yeah. And if you really love food, cooking, and all that, you need to find a way to get back to it."

"Hmm," I say into my glass. If only it were that easy. The notion of being able to love and appreciate food—to savor it, to relish in it, to treat the act of eating as a sensual one—now feels foreign to me, impossible, even. I think about the person I was when I could enjoy food, and I'm not sure that was even me. How could I ever get that back?

"Ava," Rhoda says, "it's okay to admit that you're struggling." I start to wonder if maybe the two of them have heard me bingeing and purging, or if they've been checking my Instagram and comparing it to what I'm actually doing and eating here. "We're here for you."

"I'm really okay," I say. "Seriously."

We work our way through the second bottle as we discuss why we each came here and how we want to feel when we leave, but now our inhibitions are stripped away due to the wine and a few days of getting comfortable with one another. Stephanie is leaning toward leaving her current job, but she's petrified of what it will cost her and where she would work instead. Rhoda wants to reinvent herself, to start fresh after her husband's death.

"I never got the chance to really be who I wanted to be," she says, almost as though she's telling us a cautionary tale.

Soon after, we say good night and go to our rooms. I think about what Rhoda said—about not getting the chance to be who she wanted to be. And I feel guilty, because I have every opportunity to be who I want to be, to pursue the life I want to have. I just don't know who that person is or what that looks like, not anymore.

I open one of my own bottles of wine and tuck in to my binge supplies, catapulting myself into a deep, bottomless tunnel of regret and desire, angst and longing. My vomit comes out in agitated mouthfuls, sour and pungent and purple, and even after I brush my teeth twice, I still feel the acidity of the wine and bile burning the back of my throat like it's a freshly sliced wound.

# Chapter 12

The next day, I prepare for my photo shoot with Naomi. I purposely eat a light breakfast and lunch so that I look less bloated. A few weeks ago, I landed a pretty great sponsorship deal with an LA-based workout apparel company called Urban Sweat. The founder is a young Silicon Valley ingenue who says that she got tired of spending more than she wanted to on workout clothes.

"Plus, everything was boring," she said in an interview I read when I first got the deal. "What about bright pink? Neon green? Funky patterns? Biker shorts? When did workout clothes stop being *fun*?" My deal with Urban Sweat is really just preliminary for now, like a test run. They've agreed to send me some free outfits over the next couple of months to see how the response is, and I received a package just before I left LA. Today's pile includes sports bras with crisscross backs, metallic leggings, and crop tops with holes purposefully slashed throughout the fabric. My deal with them is pretty standard: I have a discount code just for me that I share with my followers, and then the company sees how many new customers and purchases there are using my code. This is where I really excel. I've always been great at convincing other people that they *need* something. I'm even better at convincing myself of it.

I'm wearing fire-engine-red ribbed leggings and a matching bra when Naomi arrives, and I've got my "no makeup" makeup on. I blew out my hair but added some beachy texture with a few products, so it looks like I could have just finished a light workout and let my hair out of a ponytail or bun.

"Come on in," I say when Naomi arrives. "Thanks so much for helping me out with this. Seriously, I really appreciate it."

"Of course," Naomi says. "I'm excited to see what your process is like. It's cool."

I've got three outfits to photograph, and I decide that we should do some indoors and some out. In the red outfit, I suggest going to the kitchen, where I envision a scene of me cutting some fruit or pouring coffee, evoking a serene morning routine either before or after a workout.

I give Naomi my phone and show her how to use the ring light, how to use the wide-angle lens, what the most flattering angles are, what to include in the frame and what not to. I move around the kitchen, looking down, away, and occasionally toward the camera, fake-laughing here and there. And when I think we have enough, I quickly look through what she's taken and decide that they'll work fine after I edit them. I change into outfit number two, a set of short-shorts and a strappy bra in a camo print in various shades of blue.

"This outfit is really better for yoga," I say as I tug on the shorts and get the waistband exactly right on my hips. "Something chill." The shorts cover my butt only when I'm standing. I'd never wear these for yoga. They'd give me an immediate wedgie. But we move into the living room, with the windows behind me, the translucent curtains pulled closed to create a feeling of tranquility, and I unroll my yoga mat. I bend into a few standing poses, the ones that I know are the most flattering and create the illusion of thinner thighs and a thinner waist. They're the same poses all the influencers use.

"Ugh," I say when I review the photos. "I look so fat here." I'm quick to correct myself, realizing immediately what kind of message that sends to Naomi, and what it says about everything I stand for. "Sorry,

I don't mean that. It's just, you know, even I can be critical of myself sometimes. These are great, though, really."

"I think you look awesome. I don't think you look fat at all," Naomi says. "You're not fat."

I'm ashamed that suddenly she's the one having to console me, so I quickly pivot the conversation by suggesting we move on to the last outfit and take a few photos outside.

I change once more and pose outside, running in place, the retreat's lawn behind me. I ask Naomi to take these in portrait mode, so the background is fuzzy and unidentifiable. When I look them over, I know I'll have to edit them heavily as well, but I can make it work.

"Thanks so much, Naomi," I tell her when we finish. We sit down on the front stoop of the cabin. "This has been a lifesaver. You don't even know."

"Really, I was happy to," she says. "I have another half hour until I have to go back. But I probably shouldn't be sitting here. I'd get in trouble." We move inside, and I pour us both glasses of water. "So, can I ask, like, how did you get so many followers? I mean, I'd love to have my own business someday where I do something in wellness. But I'm just not sure what that is yet or, like, how to make it work."

"I sort of got lucky," I say. "I started blogging and Instagramming before it became really popular. I was one of the early ones. Now, there are so many wellness influencers out there. I think the key to success these days is finding a way to stand out. Finding a way to be different."

"Right," she says. "Makes sense."

"You're in school for nutrition, right?"

"Yeah, I have one year left."

"Well, you know, you could definitely work as a licensed nutritionist and build your business online as an influencer at the same time."

Naomi looks skeptical. "I guess that's not really my issue. My issue is, like, being authentic. I mean, I know who I am, I think, but what if who I am isn't that different? I'm not saying I'm not special, I'm just saying that I'm not sure I'm different enough to stand out."

I wonder what Naomi's parents are like—whether she has close friends, a boyfriend, a girlfriend, someone in her life to tell her that she matters.

"You don't have to be extraordinary to be special," I tell her. "I know that probably doesn't make much sense, but it's true. In fact, there's so much bullshit content out there that's fake, edited, just not real, that what people really want is something and someone *normal*. Being *normal* is what's special. Being . . . you. That's what will make you stand out." I pause, remembering where my words came from, and feel a lump in my throat. "All you have to do is be you."

Naomi nods. "You know, I think I'm just going to start now. I'm going to start documenting some things, nutrition tips I've learned in school, stuff like that."

"You should!" I tell her. "Oh, before you go, do you like any of these outfits?" I show her the rest of what Urban Sweat has sent me. "If you like any, please, I want you to have it."

"Seriously?" She picks up a pair of cream-colored cropped leggings and a matching bralette. I know immediately that it's not the best choice for her; she's got a long torso and shorter legs, and the outfit will just cut her off and make her look wider than she is. "I love this set," she says.

"What about this one instead?" I hold up full-length silver leggings and a matching hoodie. "I just feel like this one will be much more flattering on you."

"Yeah, okay," she says. And I realize, with absolute horror, that I just did the exact same thing that my mother did to me in the dressing room when I was fourteen. Who the hell am I to tell Naomi what looks good on her or how she should dress? I try to think of something to say to remedy the damage I've done, but nothing comes out. "You're right," Naomi says before I can speak, anyway. "This is probably better for my body type."

"That's not what I-I meant," I stammer. "You'd look amazing in anything, truly," I add, hating myself.

"No, really, I like the silver," she says. "Thank you. Are you sure I can have it?"

"I'm sure. It's the least I can do for your help."

When Naomi leaves, my stomach drops. Naomi represents all my followers, really; she believes in me, she believes what I'm selling, she looks up to me. And I've completely betrayed her.

I feel like scum. I wonder what Naomi is thinking now. She probably hates me, and I wouldn't blame her.

And what's worse is that I'm about to edit, alter, and manipulate the photos she took so that I look better. Everything I told her about being authentic is bullshit. And I know it—I know it's wrong. I *do* believe what I told her, or I want to, anyway. But I'm not brave enough to be who I really am on social media. I can't. I start my editing process and just hope that maybe Naomi didn't really internalize my comment to her. Maybe she isn't going to overthink it.

I choose one of the photos of me running in place outside and decide that I'll prepare it to be posted tomorrow. The rest I'll save. The photo itself is a joke. My sneakers are bright and clean, clearly never been used to run outside, and my hair is down, flowing in the breeze. Who runs with their long hair down? But what matters is that the photo is good. I use the Skinny Pics app to gently finesse the edges of my body, making it smaller and tighter, longer and leaner. I slenderize my jawline and my cheeks and ever so slightly smooth out my greasy forehead. And then I play with the brightness levels and tones until I get it just right. There, much better. I write out my caption:

Happy summer, friends! I love taking my workouts outdoors when it's nice out. There's something about the fresh air and sunshine that makes me feel my best. But I really struggle with finding workout clothes that not only look great but FEEL great, especially when it's hot. What I'm looking for in my summer workout gear is something that feels amazing for a jog but that's cute enough to take me right to brunch. I'm telling you guys, I have found this in Urban Sweat! They have the chicest matching sets, and I'm obsessed with the way they fit—supportive and snug but not restrictive. Check them out and use my code AvaUS20 for 20 percent off your first purchase! You will never want to wear anything else! #ad #sponsored #urbansweatpartner

I read it over a few times and then edit it so that my hashtags are several lines below the actual copy—another common trick.

After, I head out for my afternoon hike to the beach. I listen to a podcast episode about the forest fires in California and the inmate firefighters sent to the front lines with minimal equipment and training, where they risk their lives all day and then return to their cells at night.

I've seen tons of posts over the last two days about the air quality in LA, which is a hundred miles away from the fires, but the air there is nevertheless a thick fog of ash and smoke. Another wellness influencer I know in LA has posted a ten-minute series of stories about her anxiety because of the fires. "I can't go outside," she tells the camera. "I mean, the world is *literally burning*, you guys. My anxiety is really at an all-time high." I wait for her next comment, thinking she's going to say something about ways to help, organizations where people can donate, the typical suggestions of privileged bloggers. "So, it's times like these that I really love these CBD gummies," she says, holding a package of them in front of the camera. "They're not THC, guys, like, they won't get you *high* or whatever; they just give you that nice feeling of calm. I've found that they've really helped with my anxiety. You can use my code here for a discount if you swipe up . . ."

I click out of Instagram. The world is absolutely burning, she's right. But where does she get off suggesting some overpriced CBD gummies as a way to deal with the stress of it all? Which she gets *paid* to post, no less. As soon as I think this, I realize it's almost exactly the same as what I'm doing. Who am I to judge?

I get a text from Carter just as I reach the beach:

Pick you up tomorrow at 3. Wear shoes for the forest. No swim. Better plan.

Shoes for the forest? I immediately envision Carter leading me out into the middle of a secluded, wooded grove, where he will chop me up with an old ax and bury me beneath dirt and leaves. As if reading my mind, he sends a follow-up:

Thinking we'll go for a walk at Fulling Mill Brook.

I google it and, to my relief, find that Fulling Mill Brook is a public walking trail through the woods only a few minutes away.

Sounds good, I respond.

Whenever I had made plans with Ben, even after dating for a few months, I was hyperaware of my tone, my level of enthusiasm, and of course my suggestions. I thought that this was because of how much I liked him and how much I wanted him to like me in return. I don't even know if this walk with Carter is a date, but I already feel a level of comfort with him that I never felt with Ben. Maybe it's because Carter has already seen me at my worst—drunk, sloppy, ranting and raving about my job, admitting that I checked myself into Island Wellness at rock bottom—or maybe it's because I know I'm only here on this island temporarily. Either way, it feels good not to *care* so much. It doesn't even occur to me to plot out what I'm going to wear, or how many issues of the *New Yorker* or the *Atlantic* I'll need to skim before seeing him. With Ben, everything had to be planned. Curated.

Stephanie, Rhoda, and I have signed up for a sound bath in the chapel just before dinner, even though it's not something I particularly want to do. I did a sound bath once in Tulum, but all I felt the whole time was that I had to pee. According to today's itinerary, this sound-bath experience promises breakthroughs of clarity, healing epiphanies, and a dialogue with one's inner self.

The chapel is filling up with other guests as we walk in, and a woman stands at the head of the room.

"Welcome, everyone," the woman says. "I'm Ophelia, your sound therapist today. Has anyone here ever participated in a sound-bath experience before?" I tepidly raise my hand, along with a few others, including one of the leggings, Bronwyn.

"Canyon Ranch, last Christmas," she says to Eliza and Hadley, who nod.

"Well, for anyone who is brand new, I am honored to lead you through this transformative journey. Now, I'm going to ask each of you to lie back on your mat in a comfortable position. You can also sit upright. What's most comfortable might be different for each of you. Play around with your legs and your arms until you feel centered and peaceful, connected to the mat, and start to focus on your breathing." She plays some gentle, rhythmic music in the background and coaches us through some breathing exercises. I squint my eyes open slightly after a few minutes. Stephanie and Rhoda seem to be deeply engrossed in the process, their bellies rising and falling with Ophelia's instruction. Ophelia then begins to tap her array of glass jars and vessels with two different mallets. The sound is soothing, even I have to admit, and I start to dip in and out of sleep. The sound seems to travel closer and closer to me, until it's right up next to me, somehow smoothing itself over my body. I open my eyes slightly, thinking that Ophelia has moved around the room and is closer to me now. But she's still exactly where she was, up front. I shut my eyes again. I have no idea if it's been five minutes or an hour. My mouth feels dry and my body is rubbery.

The session ends what feels like only moments later. Ophelia opens the doors to the chapel, and I feel the crisp evening air pour in. She tells us to remain still, and in silence. I notice the hum of the wind in the leaves of the giant beech trees right outside, the singing of birds, the distant sway of water on the shore. The air itself has a sound, it seems, and it's like I've never noticed it until now.

But when I open my eyes, it's as though all that peacefulness evaporates in a split second. It's gone, and my head is instead filled with the familiar virtual greetings of DMs, sent messages, likes, texts, and the chatter of voices barking through a fluorescent screen. Everyone around me exclaims to one another in dazed whispers how much more relaxed they feel, how transformative that was, how they've never experienced anything like it in their entire lives. But I feel the same as I did. I feel nothing.

"Amazing, right?" Rhoda asks me as we leave. "I feel so much calmer."

"Yeah. Me too," I lie. There must be something wrong with me.

At dinner, my numbness in the wake of the sound bath grows into a desire to binge and purge. I rush through the meal and tell Stephanie and Rhoda that I'm going to meet my friend for drinks after. Then I take a cab to Oak Bluffs, where I stumble upon a Thai restaurant at the end of Circuit Ave. Alone, with my elbows on the sticky floral tablecloth, I gorge myself on crab rangoon, pad Thai, spring rolls, and fried rice. I return to the retreat with a protruding belly, my fingers and toes swollen with salt, my eyes glazed over, my skin puffy. And I bring myself to my knees once again. I feel more emotion in that position than I did during the sound bath, the yoga classes, my therapy session—*anything*. How could something that makes me feel like my truest self be bad for me?

*All you have to do is be you, Ava.*

If only it were that simple.

# Chapter 13

Carter waits at the beginning of the driveway in a 1980s Toyota Land Cruiser. The kind that has boxy edges, Coke-bottle headlights, and those distinct capitalized TOYOTA letters on the front. The windows are down, and in the passenger seat is a yellow-haired dog with its tongue out that looks like a cross between a corgi and a beagle. The blue of the car pops against the cream-colored gravel on the road and the lush greenery of the trees. The image is like some wholesome painting of American nostalgia—or, I think to myself, a really fantastic Instagram post.

I give him a wave as I approach, and he smiles and waves back. He'd told me to wear shoes "for the woods," but the only thing I had was an older pair of Nikes, my go-to for my runs and walks. I'm dressed casually in black leggings and a gray cropped tank top, with my hair in a messy bun. Just in case, I decided to bring my small leather backpack with some essentials: a change of shirt, a bikini, some makeup, a hairbrush, and my wallet.

"Well, I would be worried that you might be a serial killer," I say as I hop into the car, his dog jumping into the back seat, tongue still wagging. "But I googled you extensively this morning."

It's true—I had researched him. But I hadn't found anything incriminating. Mostly local articles about his artwork and various gallery openings, a donation he made to the local high school's art program, a junior fishing derby award he won when he was thirteen, his grandfather's obituary, and a few photos from his time in New York in the art scene. I found him on Instagram, too: *vineyardpainter*. He doesn't have a ton of pictures posted, but most of them are thoughtful, serene images of the island at various times of year, or photos of his work, or of his dog. And I didn't see any girlfriend pictures.

"I could say the same about you," he says. "Ava, this is Bailey. My number-one girl. Just so we're clear."

I turn toward the back seat, where Bailey sits smiling at us, her mouth agape and a string of viscous drool hanging out.

"Hi, Bailey," I say. I like Carter more now that I know he's a dog person. "What kind of dog is she?"

"I don't know for sure. She's a mutt. One of those Caribbean-island potcake dogs. I got her four years ago from a rescue group here. It was love at first sight." Bailey has moved on from looking at us and has now stuck her head out the back window, waiting for Carter to get going. As if on her cue, he shifts the car into drive and peels out onto the main road. "So, how's the spa life been treating you?" He glances over at me.

I feel embarrassed to be staying at the retreat, and it suddenly feels wildly indulgent and ridiculous.

"I don't really know what I'm doing there," I say. "I mean, it's been really wonderful at times, don't get me wrong. It's beautiful and it's a vacation. A big vacation. But it's also strange. Everyone is there for a different reason. I have these cabinmates, Stephanie and Rhoda—"

"Cabinmates?" Carter looks over at me again. "Sounds like summer camp."

"I mean, it kind of is. Summer camp for fucked-up adults," I say with a laugh. "Anyway, my cabinmates and I are so different—we each have our own issues. But it somehow . . . works." I don't know how to explain it to him without sounding overly sentimental. "Anyway, where are we going?"

"Well, I told you we were going to the woods. And we are. We're going hunting." *Hunting?* I look Carter over; he's wearing jeans and a paint-splattered white T-shirt again, maybe the same one he wore when we first met. "Don't worry," he adds, seeing my distressed face. "Mushroom hunting."

"Ah," I sigh with relief. "I can't say I've ever been mushroom hunting before."

"Well, it's a little bit early in the season, to be honest. But we had a really wet spring, and I've found a few chicken of the woods this time of year before, so I figure why not try."

"Chicken of the woods?" It sounds like it could be the name of an organic hipster restaurant in Silver Lake.

"Yeah. Or hen of the woods. They're similar. They're these big, glorious mushrooms that you can find around here on trees if you look hard enough. Mostly dead trees, but sometimes living ones, too. They're delicious. They taste like . . . well, chicken."

"I don't know if I'd want to eat a wild mushroom. I mean, couldn't it be poisonous?"

"Not if you know what you're doing."

The road curves, and we speed by a field in which a majestic white ox grazes.

Carter pulls off onto a somewhat hidden road that takes us slightly down a hill and then into a small parking lot covered in wood chips. There's a trail map posted on a tree trunk. I decide to leave my backpack behind, in his car, but I keep my phone tucked into a side pocket of my leggings. "We're going off trail today," he says with a smile, opening the back of the car for Bailey to hop down. She runs around the car and jumps up to greet me properly, and I rub her head, behind her ears, and her neck, before she runs off to find a spot to pee. "Follow me," he says.

"So, what exactly should I be looking for?"

Carter describes the mushrooms—golden yellow, broad and wavy like the reflection of a sunset on calm waters, with layers of warm, sunny hues like the inside of a conch shell, almost pink. "And no gills. You know how sometimes the underside of a mushroom has those gills, like folds of paper? These don't. No gills."

"Got it," I say. We walk past the entrance to the trail and cut straight into the woods. The brush is thick and comes up to midcalf, so I have to step carefully and keep my eyes sharp for branches with thorns. The trees are mostly oak and pine, peppered with highbush blueberries, magnolia trees, and abundant clouds of bittersweet bushes. The search for the elusive mushrooms is somehow engrossing enough that we barely talk, as though noise might scare them into hiding.

"Wait," Carter says. "Look there. It's not a mushroom. But something really special." He points to a slight knoll among several trees, and I notice a striking, vibrant splash of bright coral-red flowers, with perfectly pointed leaves and bright-green stems that shoot them straight up from the earth. "Wood lilies," he says. "They're very rare these days. The deer love them. I actually haven't seen one in a while."

There are only about a dozen of them, all tucked into the same knoll, gathered in a four-foot space, like a coven whispering to one another. I've never seen such beautiful flowers in the wild, only in the refrigerated cases of floral shops. "Hard to believe that something like that can just . . . *exist*," I say. "On its own, I mean. Something so perfect."

Carter glances over at me, and I think I catch the corners of his mouth turn upward. "I know."

A few minutes later, it occurs to me that we're walking deep into the woods, and I have no sense of where we are or how we'll get back to the car.

"So, do you just have an internal compass or something? You're not worried about getting lost?"

Carter laughs. "Nah," he says. "I know these woods like the back of my hand. I grew up doing exactly this, right here."

"Seems like a lot of trouble just for a mushroom. Are they even any good?"

"Well, they're delicious, of course." He pauses. "But I guess it's not really about that. It's about the satisfaction you get from finding your own food, from the time you spend searching, waiting, observing, walking. And then when you find one, it's like you've found a treasure. That might sound kind of sad. I mean, it is just a mushroom. But it's special. You'll see . . . if we're really lucky."

"Well, if we find one, you better share it with me." I wonder if he had a plan this whole time to bring me back to his place afterward and cook dinner.

"Of course. We're in this together."

Carter points out other natural wonders along the way: newly emerging hazelnuts, wrapped up in fuzzy cocoons; wild grapes, still sour and green; tiny budding raspberries, white and hard. He points to a small stream and waves his arm to beckon me. He pulls a Swiss Army knife out from his pocket and crouches down to cut away at a leafy cluster of dark purple and green. Bailey sidles up next to him and gives the murky ground a sniff.

"Wild watercress," he says, rising. "Try it."

I taste a sprig. It's peppery and sharp, fresh and wet in my mouth. "Delicious," I say. "I didn't know watercress grew like this, wild."

He gives me a side smile, and then he pulls a plastic shopping bag from his pocket. "Here," he says, giving me the knife. "Slice off a few handfuls." We load the bag and continue on our mushroom hunt.

"So," he says, "you don't know a lot about where food actually comes from even though your job is to blog about food." His tone isn't accusatory or critical, but curious. And it's actually refreshing to be called out, in this case.

"You're right. I'm a Whole Foods shopper. I don't know anything about where the food actually comes from. I've never picked anything in my whole life." As great as my obsession with food is, I haven't spent much time—if any—thinking about the source itself, or the effort required to grow food, to harvest it, to nurture it, to seek it out in the wild. I think about the piles of watercress I've seen at supermarkets. It never occurred to me to wonder where it might have come from, or whose hands ripped it from its stems. "This is . . . amazing."

"I love food," Carter says. "I mean, I'm not a big restaurant person. I guess I like to go out, for sure, and I love trying inventive things. But I really love to find my own food and cook it. There's nothing better. Catching your own fish, getting your own clams . . . and, you know, foraging your own mushrooms, with any luck."

After another half an hour of fruitless wandering, Carter turns to me. "Well, it might have been an unsuccessful hunt, at least for chicken of the woods. We're almost back at the car." I would have had no idea where we were. Somewhere along the way, I stopped trying to keep track of our proximity to the car, or the sun's position in the sky, and I just let myself walk.

"That's okay," I say. "This was really nice." But a few paces ahead, I notice a broad tree with only a few sad leaves left on its branches. It's dead. And there, on the opposite side of the tree trunk, just barely peeking out, is the tip of what I think is a mushroom, waving its soft, rounded edge at me. I run forward, to the other side of the tree.

"Holy shit!" I scream out. "Is this—is this one of them?" The mushroom looks like an art installation, glued onto the bark of this decaying tree, its colors and patterns simultaneously eccentric and wild but also balanced and perfect. I examine it. No gills, no dark colors besides the various shades of orange, yellow, and white. I've found one.

"Holy shit, indeed," Carter says, approaching. "You're a natural. This is a chicken of the woods. And a big one, too." He extends his hand out and gives me a friendly shake. "Well done, Avocado." He begins to slice the mushroom away from the tree. "I try to leave an inch or two of it still there," he says, "so that next year, it might grow back. And then the trick is just remembering where you found it." I'm watching him with an intensity and an interest that feels invigorating to me. I can't remember the last time I was so *interested* in something. Fascinated by something, in awe of something. He places the layers of mushroom gently into the bag. "Mission accomplished."

"So, what now?" I ask. I'm honestly more interested in tasting the fruits of my labor than in wondering what might happen with Carter. "I mean, I need to try that mushroom!"

"Well," he says, "I know we just met, but we could go to my place, fry some of it up, have a glass of wine? God, that sounds weird." We both laugh.

"No, it sounds great." I have the fleeting thought that I should call the retreat and let them know that I won't be back for dinner, but the thought disappears just as quickly as it entered my mind. When we get back to the car, I realize I haven't taken my phone out once the entire time. I'm regretful—it would have been incredible, unique content. But I'm also glad I didn't do it. Not because I would have cared what Carter thought—he knows my whole schtick already—but because I wouldn't have been present. I would have missed the mushroom. I don't even check my phone now. I leave it in the pocket of my leggings, and instead I just let the wind blow against my face as we cruise down North Road.

"So, where do you live?" A guy in LA at Carter's age might still have roommates and live in a condo with all-black sheets, black appliances, and black countertops, ones that are dotted with cocaine like a snowstorm on a weekend. Who knows what I could be walking into?

"On a farm," he says. "Kind of a cliché, right? It's not actually a farm, though. Right now it's really just land. And a barn that I live in." He rounds a corner in the road and glances over at me. "But soon enough, I'm going to have goats and chickens. Maybe a pig. I can't just be an artist, I don't think. Gotta find a way to live off the land."

I can't quite tell if he's joking or not.

"Yeah, my job doesn't always provide me with what I need, either," I say, deciding that maybe he wasn't joking after all. "That's why I have to do so many promotions and partnerships. It's just . . . the job."

"Well, this might be a little bit different, but I guess it's the same idea. I think it's boring to just do one thing, anyway. Plus, the farm gives me inspiration for my art. It's all connected."

We pull off the main road when a sign points us toward Lambert's Cove, and a few minutes later, we enter a driveway marked with a large, stone-flanked wooden gate. The driveway curves past a field of grazing sheep. Past that is an open meadow of wildflowers, a moss-covered stone wall bordering it to one side. A faded-red barn sits at the end of the field, simple and inviting. "Here we are," he says as we pull up front. "The barn is original to the land. 1902," he says. "But a few years ago, I renovated the inside so there could be an apartment up top."

We hop out, Bailey following, her tail wagging with the pleasure of being home. I follow Carter inside. The downstairs of the barn is a real barn, filled with musty hay and dingy windows, and it makes me feel like time moves slower here. We ascend the stairs, and Carter opens a door to a beautiful, light-filled apartment, with windows overlooking the fields. It smells like paint, fruit, and clean laundry. Bailey bolts past us and into the living room, where she attacks a squeaky toy on the floor. The living room is a little bit messy, with a few glasses and beer bottles on the coffee table, a pillow on the floor, and sketch pads and pencils everywhere. But it's incredibly cozy.

"Here we go," he says as we venture farther into the kitchen, a small room with a retro-looking fridge and a tiny four-burner gas stove. The shelves are all open and are stacked with mismatched glasses and plates. I love it. On the kitchen island are several bowls with all kinds of produce—potatoes, garlic, onions, apples, a cluster of vine tomatoes, and some oranges. By the sink is a jar of water bursting with handfuls of fresh herbs.

"You're a regular Martha Stewart," I say, looking around, hoping he doesn't take offense to it. He doesn't. He laughs.

"I told you, I like to cook. And I do live on a farm."

Carter shows me how to slice up the mushroom into palm-size slabs and then gently clean them off with a damp mushroom brush over the sink.

"Who has a *mushroom* brush?" I ask as I work.

"You'd be surprised."

I watch the dirt cascade off the mushroom's porous skin, and I'm grateful to have a task to complete with my hands. But I'm more grateful when I finish and Carter pours us each a glass of white wine, something he had opened in his fridge already. It's terrible—gone bad and way too sweet to begin with, but I drink it anyway, relieved to know that the alcohol will still relax me, whether or not it tastes good.

"What's the grand plan with this stuff?" I ask, holding up the fresh watercress that Carter had washed and put through a salad spinner.

"Something simple." He rummages through a fruit bowl and pulls out an avocado. "Here, slice this up," he says to me. Meanwhile, he puts on some water to boil. "I'm thinking pasta. With the mushrooms. Trust me on this."

When he says *pasta*, I realize that until then, I haven't been riddled with my usual anxiety of whether I'm going to need to purge. I've been surrounded by food, talking about food, preparing food, and yet I somehow haven't been obsessing about it. But the moment he suggests pasta for dinner, I'm jolted back to reality, my disease once again reminding me that I'm incapable of consuming normally. And now I kick myself, knowing that I'm going to ruin the rest of the evening because I'll be too preoccupied thinking about the pasta sitting in my stomach and how I'm going to get rid of it. I decide that I need to at least scope out my options.

"Bathroom?" I ask. He points through the hallway.

"On the left."

The bathroom is small, with a pedestal sink and rickety wooden door with a latch lock. The mirror is dingy, but it's a mirror. I take a moment to examine myself and breathe. I've gotten a little too much sun, and my face is somewhat pink. I fix my bun and decide that this is the best it will get, and that's fine. Even though I've started to appreciate how tall and strong Carter is, how romantic it would be to wake up in his barn, how much I've enjoyed spending the day with him, I still feel a funny lack of jitters over what might happen between us. I realize that I'd been confusing the pressure and nervousness I felt for so long with Ben—with *every* guy I dated in LA, really—with excitement and enthusiasm. *It's possible*, I think as I head back out, *to be into someone and* not *be nervous.*

And still, the issue of how I'll deal with dinner looms heavy over me. The bathroom isn't ideal, to say the least, and the apartment is too small for space and privacy. Purging here isn't going to be an option. I'm going to need to either bolt back to the retreat soon after dinner or just suck it up and keep it down. *Please,* I think to myself, *just keep it down. Don't ruin things again.*

There's a narrow balcony outside the living room, just wide enough for two chairs and a small table, on which we place the food and our drinks. Carter magically whipped up some spaghetti in a garlic butter sauce, sprinkled with lots of fresh parsley, and then added the mushroom, which he cut into slices and sautéed in butter until it was brown and golden. The salad is tossed, and we serve ourselves on different-colored china plates.

"Cheers," I say, looking out over the green fields, the sun now just a few inches above the horizon. I can hear birds chirping, and maybe even the sound of the ocean a mile away. "Thanks for having me. It's been a pretty great day. I've never done anything like that. In fact, I don't think I've ever eaten something that I've gotten—caught, whatever—myself. I guess if you don't count apple picking as a kid. But even then, I'm not sure we actually cooked anything with them."

"You're welcome. Cheers," he says. We clink glasses and dig in.

The food is spectacular. Impossibly fresh and simple and flavorful. The mushrooms do taste like chicken, but better. They're soft and tender but still have some chewy bite to them, and the butter has enhanced their natural, nutty flavor, rich and complex, warm and comforting. The spaghetti is perfectly al dente, and the parsley gives it a bright freshness. The watercress is intensely spicy but cooling at the same time.

"Okay," I say, between bites. "How'd you learn to cook?"

"From my dad, mostly," he says. "He loved to fish, garden, hunt. And I always helped him. There was always a fish in the smoker, meat being brined, vegetables being harvested. Always something to do with the food we grew or found ourselves. This island really has everything you need."

"Sounds amazing." I wonder, just then, why I never cooked more with my mom, but I let the thought evaporate.

As we finish our meal, Carter sits back in his chair. "So, you haven't taken your phone out once, you know. When we met, you said you *always* had to be on your phone. Is today your day off?"

I feel a prick of anger at myself for not documenting today's adventure. It would have made for excellent content. But somehow, I'm able to let it go.

"I don't get a day off, not really. I probably should be doing some work on my phone. But . . . I don't want to." And it's true. Even though I know I missed an opportunity for some unique food photos and videos, the choice to just experience it rather than document it makes it feel more special, more *mine*.

"So, Avocado," he says later as we're washing and drying dishes side by side, "tell me about your childhood. Where'd you grow up? Mom and dad, high school. I want to know everything."

"Everything? I'm not that interesting, really . . ." I'm not sure where to start. Usually I can rely on somewhat of a script on dates, focusing mostly on my work as an influencer.

"I think you're fascinating," he says, looking at me. And I don't know why, but I believe him. And so I tell him about growing up in Cherry Hill, about Mom getting sick, about my relationship with Mike and his life as a suburban dad. And he tells me about his childhood growing up here, playing ice hockey on the ponds in the winter, fishing on the jetty in Menemsha, teaching his little sister how to dig for steamers.

Though it's a possibility, I make it clear that I'm not spending the night, and Carter doesn't push it. He drives me back to the retreat. I wonder, as we pull up to the farmhouse, if he's going to try to kiss me. There's a spark between us, I know for sure, and yet it's more like a mutual respect, a curiosity, an interest—but not necessarily a sexual spark just yet. That said, in the afterglow of the sunset, behind the wheel of his old Land Cruiser, I have to admit that he looks good. Really good. Still, we don't kiss, and I reach for the door.

"Thanks again," I say. "I'll come check out your gallery this week." He'd told me to come by in the next few days for a special exhibit he was doing of some new landscapes.

"Sounds good, Avocado."

I briskly walk back to my cabin. It's been well over an hour since we ate the pasta, and normally that's too much time for me to purge it all out of my system. My body will fight me on it. What if, I ask myself, I just went to bed again—tried, once more, to let myself digest?

I try to keep it down. I wash my face and brush my teeth and get into bed. I focus on how hard I worked for that food—the way we found it and pulled it straight from the earth, cleaned it so carefully, cooked it with thought.

And it's only in the morning that I realize I've done it once more: I made it through the night. Maybe I *am* able to break my bad habits after all. *Maybe,* I think as I stretch awake, feeling rested and energized, *I can come out of this place better than when I came in.*

# Chapter 14

For my eleventh birthday, I had a sleepover with six of my closest girl-friends. Everyone came over at five o'clock, and we ate pizza and cinnamon sticks dipped in sugary syrup and then arranged our sleeping bags on the floor of the living room, turning the room into a sea of pillows and blankets, snacks, a Ouija board, nail polish, and face masks from CVS. I wanted to watch *Cruel Intentions* or *The Virgin Suicides*, but my mom said we weren't old enough yet and that they were inappropriate for the sleepover. So, we watched *Can't Hardly Wait*, which, in retrospect, was probably more inappropriate than the other two movies in some ways. The whole plot revolves around a nerd's love for the prom queen and her subsequent quest to find him after he writes her a love letter. I never understood why he was so obsessed with her. The characters had barely even spoken to one another. It was all just based on physical attraction. But then again, who could blame him? It was Jennifer Love Hewitt in 1998. She was a living, walking, brunette Barbie.

As the film ended, with the nerd and the prom queen kissing at the train station, I whined to my friend Bridgette. During the movie, we'd all inhaled freshly baked chocolate cookies and brownies my mom made, plus popcorn, Doritos, Sour Patch Kids, and peanut M&M's. "Ugh," I said, "I'm so full." And I didn't mean *fat*. I just meant stuffed, uncomfortable.

"Oh, I love going to sleep full," Bridgette said. Bridgette was tiny, a little twig with skin so pale you could see her blue veins. "It makes me feel warm and happy knowing I have all this good food in my belly."

I remember that I didn't respond to her. I only considered her words. It was a ridiculous concept to me, the idea that feeling full of food could be a good thing, a sign of safety and security and well-being. I tried to conjure up those feelings once the movie ended, after we played Light as a Feather, Stiff as a Board, as we all began to doze off, but all I felt was the uncomfortable expansion of my gut and the overwhelming desire to turn back time. I wondered if Bridgette got enough food at home. Was she naturally so tiny, or was she underfed? Was the stack of hot, greasy pizza boxes at my house more food than Bridgette had ever been exposed to at her own house? Or did she just have some internal barometer that informed her when she was sufficiently full, and an ensuing appreciation for that feeling of perfect fullness?

But when I woke up that next morning, I felt fine. The pizza had been forgotten. We all ate pancakes and bacon, and the despair of my churning gut was just a distant fever dream.

The morning after my dinner with Carter, I wake feeling similar to that morning after my eleventh birthday. My first thought as I rise from bed isn't about what I had eaten the night before. It's about what I'm going to do today. I'm hungry but not ravenous.

I double-check my Urban Sweat draft from yesterday and then post it, along with the photos on my story as well, with a link to swipe up and buy. The likes and comments immediately flood in. *Good,* I think, *the photo shoot with Naomi wasn't a total waste.*

A few minutes later, I scroll through some of the comments and notice one from *NaomiBriggs*. Of course, she already follows me, and I decide to follow her back. Curious, I look through her profile. The photos all seem happy and healthy, depicting the life of a young woman with friends, a love of the beach, family cookouts, school, and health-and-wellness tips here and there, mostly in the form of recipes. She looks like herself.

I can hear Stephanie and Rhoda in the kitchen.

"Well, good morning," Stephanie says to me when I emerge from my room. She and Rhoda are grinning at me, waiting for me to tell them about last night.

"Yes, good morning," Rhoda echoes. "So, how was your *date*?"

"It wasn't a date," I say. "He's just a friend."

"We were worried, you know. Sarah asked us at dinner where you were."

*Shoot.* I'd forgotten to sign out again. I make a mental note to seek out Sarah and explain. "I forgot," I say, pouring myself a cup of coffee. "Sorry. We went foraging for mushrooms, and I thought I'd be home for dinner, but then we ended up going back to his place to cook dinner."

"Honey, you do realize you're smiling ear to ear, right?" Rhoda says.

"Well, it was a fun night."

"So, did you *bone*?" asks Stephanie.

"No, we did not *bone*. Jeez!"

"Well, you should," Rhoda exclaims. "Do you like him?"

"I do," I tell them. "But . . . I don't know. That's not why I'm here, I guess."

I leave a few minutes early for yoga to find Sarah. I hate that I have to account for my whereabouts, like I'm a child at boarding school, but those are the rules here. *Come and go as you please, just let us know.* Where's the freedom in that?

Sarah is at the front desk, her hair up in a bun but with a few loose tendrils hanging out around her ears, framing her face. She looks up at me as though she was expecting me, like she's the principal and I'm in trouble.

"Good morning, Sarah," I say before she has a chance to scold me. "I'm really sorry I didn't sign out yesterday when I left. A friend picked me up, and I ended up staying there for dinner. Hope it didn't cause an inconvenience."

"You know, Ava," she says, her tone severe, "here at Island Wellness, we try to be as low waste as possible. That means that our chef prepares an exact amount of food for each meal based on how many people will be eating it. Of course, portions vary, but it's very important to us that we have an accurate head count for each meal so that we can do our part in taking care of our planet by generating as little waste as possible." I look at Sarah's wrist, covered in bangles of beads and metal, and her iPhone on the desk, and the subtle swipe of mascara on her eyelashes, and I wonder how much of what she preaches she actually practices.

"Yes," I say. "I understand and I'm sorry. Won't happen again."

"Well, I hope you had a lovely evening. That was Carter, right?" She gives me a straight-lipped smile.

"Uh, excuse me?"

"Sorry, it's none of my business. But, you know, it's a small community. I'd know that Land Cruiser anywhere. Carter is sort of . . . *infamous* on this island."

"Uh, okay." A thought crosses my mind: Could Sarah and Carter have dated? I could see it, absolutely. They've both got the beautiful-island-free-spirit look. I'm tempted to ask, but I don't want to risk looking like I care.

"Anyway, like I said, none of my business. Enjoy yoga. Namaste."

I shrug away the thought of Carter kissing Sarah and her perfectly voluptuous body, trying to squash the comparison I'm drawing to myself. I remind myself that I'm a paying guest at the retreat. Sarah is working for *me*. And yet I feel so exposed around her, like a fraud. And what did she mean, anyway, that Carter was *infamous* on the Vineyard? Is that supposed to be a warning to me? Could Carter have some master plan to screw the LA influencer just so he has some good stories to tell his buddies?

On my way into the chapel, I see Naomi scurrying ahead of me, carrying a tray of cucumber-and-mint water.

"Hey," I say, "let me get the door for you." I grab the handle of the chapel door and swing it open for her.

"Thanks." She doesn't look at me, and her tone feels curt. Something's definitely up. My first thought is that Sarah found out about the photo shoot and got Naomi in trouble for it.

"Naomi, is everything okay? Did something happen?" I ask her, looking around to make sure that there's no other staff in sight. I'm a few minutes early, and the only other person in the chapel is Samantha, who's busy lighting candles.

"Yeah, totally," she says, putting the tray down and avoiding my gaze. "I just, um, saw what you posted." I panic for a second, worrying that I posted something wrong or by accident. What is she talking about? She's obviously mad at me.

"What do you mean?"

"I mean, the photo you posted that I took. It just looked . . . I don't know . . ." She obviously doesn't want to say what comes next. "It looked fake. Really edited. I guess I just didn't think that was you."

So that's why she's mad at me. Because she saw how I tweaked my photo to make myself look thinner, brighter, *better*. Naomi doesn't have original copies of the photos—they're all on my phone—but she's the one who took them, so it's not hard for her to see what I posted and know that it's slightly altered. But I thought I'd been honest with her about how it works: there's nothing wrong with a little tweaking here and there.

"I mean, it's *filtered*, yeah, and I brightened it up and stuff, but that's standard. I didn't *change* my body or my appearance in the photo, if that's what you mean." *Deny, deny, deny,* I tell myself. If you do a good enough job editing a photo, no one can *prove* that you did it, unless they have the original photo, which she doesn't. "Seriously, brightening up a photo can go a long way in how it looks. I can show you some tips, if you want. But I'd never really alter a photo."

I expect Naomi to buy it, but she doesn't.

"Yeah, okay, I just . . . It doesn't look that way. I mean, I know how filters work, and it kind of seems like you did a little bit more than that."

"Look, Naomi, this is my job. We can talk about it more later, but I haven't done anything wrong."

"I guess what confuses me," she says, "is that you don't *need* to edit yourself. I mean, no one needs to, no one should, really. But you *really* don't need to. You're like, thin and fit and pretty, and I saw those photos. They were great. You looked great. It's honestly sad that you think you need to edit them that much."

I've never been called out like this, at least not face-to-face, in real life, by someone I know. I get called out constantly by followers or trolls, but it's pretty easy to just hit "Delete" and move on. I might internalize their words for a day or two, but I'm always able to move on. This is different. And I don't have my phone to hide behind, my keyboard to tap at in order to spew some argumentative response. I've got no weaponry. And deep down, I know that she's right. I wish I could say that I'm better than falling into the traps of social media, that I've got more confidence and bravery, more wisdom, but I don't. Somewhere along the way, I decided to partake in the perpetuation of the exact toxic culture that I was so strongly against in the beginning.

I want to come clean with Naomi, but I can't. There's too much on the line. I don't know her, I can't really trust her, and if I admitted to her that she's right—that I did edit the photos—then she could expose me.

"Listen," I tell her, "I know it looks like I edited the photos like that, but I really didn't." My voice comes out in a pathetic whisper.

"Uh-huh," she says. She finishes setting up the water, casting her eyes away from me.

"Do you want to talk more later?"

"I can't, actually. I have the rest of the day off. I was just helping with the morning shift. I'm going to the beach."

"Oh, great, well, have fun."

"Yep," she says, still avoiding my eyes. Then she looks up and stares at me square in the face—a look more of disappointment than judgment. It breaks my heart. "Have a great yoga class." She shuffles out the door just as Stephanie and Rhoda come in. My guts feel tied in knots.

Now that Naomi hates me, who is she going to tell about this? And then I wonder, could *Naomi* be mermaid1985?

I don't have time to dwell on it, because it's time to start class, and we hastily pick our spots, spreading out our mats. Samantha greets us and starts everyone in child's pose. During the past few days, I've been able to find some peace during yoga class—maybe not completely transformative peace, but tranquility nonetheless. But today, I'm completely distracted and find myself fidgeting. I'm angry, agitated. Not just at Naomi, but at myself—at the fact that I know she's right, and she called me out and I had zero defense. I extend my arms out in front of me and push back my hips, releasing a sigh of frustration.

By the time we finish the hour-long class, I'm starving, which only adds to the feeling that my blood is boiling. We head straight to breakfast, where I order an omelet (with real eggs, not just egg whites), with cheese and mixed vegetables, and a side of whole-wheat toast. I even add a side of chicken sausage. I eat it all like I'm on a mission to drown out my feelings with food.

Stephanie and Rhoda chat about the day's activities and decide to partake in a tour of the garden later that day.

"Sounds good," I say, agreeing to join, though I'm still checked out, unfocused. "I'm gonna go get some work done now, though. I'll see you guys later."

The encounter with Naomi has not only made me feel like a giant hypocrite, but it's made me feel out of control, like I'm losing my grip on my business, my identity. I know I'm not posting enough content. I need more stories, better videos, more personality. It's only been about a week since we've been here—I've got over a month to go—and that's plenty of time for everything I've built to just go down the drain.

Back in my room, I consider puking, but I was so hungry before breakfast that it already feels like the meal has settled into me and it would be too much of a battle. I tell myself that I'll just eat lightly for the rest of the day.

When I open Instagram, I have yet another message from mermaid1985:

**Your followers deserve the truth.**

My skin prickles with fear. I consider typing out a response: *Stop threatening me, leave me alone.* Or maybe something more in the "Kill them with kindness" vein: *I'm sorry you feel that way. Be well!* But I decide again to not reply at all. Despite my suspicions, it could still all be empty threats from a random troll, a stranger I'll never meet. And furthermore, what could this person actually *do*? They don't have a big enough platform themselves to publicize anything about me in a way that would actually make waves. I remind myself that this is just part of being internet famous. I need to let it roll off.

I skim through my feed, and then something else catches my eye: a new post from Naomi. It immediately strikes me as being different from her previous posts, though really only to a discerning eye. Someone else might not catch the subtle visual shift. In this photo, she poses in a skimpy bikini on the beach, her shins and knees nestled into the sand like a *Sports Illustrated* swimsuit model. Summer daze, she wrote beneath the picture. I zoom in and examine the photo, checking the outline of her body for giveaway signs of editing. Even for me, it's hard to tell. There's a heavy filter, that's obvious, but with the ocean background I can't be sure if she's actually altered herself in the picture. Still, that's not really what throws me. It's the content itself that's different. The picture is hypersexual, it's aggressive, it's a definitive *pose*, and one that was clearly done to make her look her thinnest, her sexiest. To someone else, it might just appear to be a fantastic but almost accidental beach photo, but I see that it shows something else. It shows Naomi's newfound effort to manufacture herself, to style herself, to *groom* herself for other people. It shows the direct impact that *I* just had on her. By revealing to her that I succumb to the pressures of social media, I realize that I gave her permission to do the same.

It's not the first time I've seen this happen. It happened within me, after all. We start by criticizing someone else for enhancing their content, doing whatever it takes to appear a certain way on social media, to curate their brand, their image, their every little detail. And we're jealous, because when we look at them, even though we *know* it's not real, we still long for that appearance of perfection. For a while, we hold a grudge and tell ourselves that we're above it, that we're better than they are. But then we see how easy it is to make those alterations—little edits here and there, a filter once in a while, and then it's a slippery slope into full-blown deceit. The question is whether or not Naomi will be able to come out of it.

The guilty pit in my stomach growls, and I instinctively open my snack drawer in pursuit of comfort. I devour the sad contents that I have left—some crackers, chips, cookies, and a Snapple iced tea.

I can't blame myself for Naomi, not really, I tell myself as I eat. It's not like I invented the Instagram game, the influencer tricks, or the editing tools. Everyone does it, not just me. Everyone finesses their photos. *Everyone.* That's just how it goes. And, anyway, if Naomi was serious about building a following, then she would have surely figured out the loopholes one way or another, without me. She might be young, but she's still an adult. She makes her own choices. I didn't make her do anything. There's a reason an influencer is called an influencer, not an enforcer. I tell myself this over and over. And yet I can't shake the memory of being in that dressing room with my mother, wearing the navy shift dress, having just been told that I'm not thin enough to wear something else. I pretty much did that to Naomi. I only have myself to blame.

I puke in the bathroom. After, I'm exhausted. I sit on the bathroom floor with my back against the tub for almost an hour.

Even though it's a beautiful day, I spend a few more hours inside, diddling around on my phone, preparing more content. I make a post for Skin Beams, a boomerang for the collagen gummies, and several posts for the next few days with easy and inventive salad recipes. I edit a video from a hike I took earlier in the week and post it to my stories so that it looks like I went for a hike today. I add some copy encouraging everyone to get outside and move their bodies.

By the time I'm done, I've missed lunch. I'm tempted to binge and purge again, but I'm too low on supplies. I need to go into Oak Bluffs later and restock.

When I emerge from my room a little while later for the garden tour, I see that Stephanie is glued to her laptop in the living room.

"Still up for the garden tour?" I ask.

"No," she says, only looking up quickly. "I wish. But shit has sort of hit the fan with my job. I've got a lot to deal with. But I'll see you guys at dinner."

"I'm sorry," I tell her. "Good luck."

Rhoda and I walk to the garden together.

"What was that about?" she asks. "With Stephanie, I mean. Is she okay?"

I pull out my phone to google her company. And it's just as I suspected: the CEO's accusers have now gone public. Not just one but four actresses are all accusing him of the same type of manipulation: film roles in exchange for . . . *blugh*. I look at pictures of him—he's a greaseball of a man. I show my screen to Rhoda, and her eyes widen.

"Oh no. Stephanie's really elbow deep in this, isn't she?"

"It would seem so. In the eye of the storm."

I feel a little bit queasy thinking about the position Stephanie is in, and I wonder if she knew about any of her boss's *behavior* before this. Her job makes her his protector, his literal defender. I know I'm no saint, and I certainly am to blame for adding to some deeply negative societal norms, but this is on another level. I decide that Stephanie must have a huge arsenal of very necessary sleeping pills, and who knows what else. There's no way she could be doing this job without it.

"I hope she quits," I add.

"Me too," says Rhoda.

A small group of guests has already gathered around the garden's entrance, including the leggings and the man always in khakis. At least today, in the heat, he's in khaki shorts. The leggings wave at us.

"Hi, Ava, Rhoda," Bronwyn says. "I'm so excited for this tour, aren't you two?" She, along with the two others, has started following me on Instagram. I won't follow back. I have to draw a line somewhere, and a lot of times it's good to not follow back. It helps to maintain my mystique. I wonder again, just for a moment, if one of them could also be mermaid1985, but I just don't get the sense that any of them could be so conniving. Plus, even though I'd never admit it to any of them, I've looked at all of their profiles, which are public, and it seems like they barely know how to use social media at all.

"Yes," I say. "Really excited."

The handsome gardener emerges from behind us, and there's a collective gasp among the women. Eliza elbows me.

"Oh my god," she whispers. "I'd like to pick *his* cucumber, am I right?" She covers her mouth to suppress her giggle. Yeah, there's no way she—or any of the leggings—is mermaid1985.

"Hey, everyone, thanks for coming," the gardener says once he finds a spot in front of us. "I'm Max. Today's tour will be about an hour, and I'll be showing you everything we grow here, and telling you how we grow it, harvest it, and other secrets of the earth, as I like to say."

We follow Max through the garden, a meticulously fenced-in rectangle with raised wooden beds throughout, lined up in orderly rows. There doesn't seem to be a leaf out of place, and yet there's a wildness to it as well. We walk past emerging zucchini and squash, and Max points out the velvety squash blossoms hidden behind the vegetable's giant fanlike leaves. He shows us developing cucumbers, egg shaped and light green, some with sharp spikes on them. One box is filled with mounds of dirt blanketed with short, leafy green stalks, which will be potatoes come end of summer, he says. Peas, beans, radishes, peppers, eggplant, five different kinds of lettuce and two different kinds of kale, and several varieties of tomato plants, not quite ready for harvesting but almost there. Nasturtium flowers burst out of the sides of many of the planters, their rounded petals cascading down the sides. He picks one and pops it in his mouth.

Most of the women on the tour are more interested in Max than the produce, and I get it: he's absolutely gorgeous, but can't be older than twenty-two. But I'm genuinely fascinated by what he has to say: the garden is so alive, so full of mystery, so full of promise. It's enough to make me want to start my own garden, to harvest my own food—as if I could ever do that living in my tiny apartment in LA. I'm reminded of what Carter said, about how nothing compares to food that you've caught or grown yourself. He's right.

"Edible flowers," Max tells us, pointing to a bed of colorful nasturtiums. "Go ahead and try one." We each delicately pick one. The flowers are silky and smooth, delicate and soft, in rich hues of purple and yellow. It feels wrong to eat such a beautiful flower, and silly, but we all timidly pop them in our mouths. The flavor is unexpected—bold and spicy. Max explains the process of planting the seeds, nurturing the seedlings in the retreat's greenhouse, and moving them into the garden once they're ready.

"And at the end of each week," Max tells us as we reach the end of the tour, approaching the entrance where we first started, "we donate all of our excess produce to the Island Food Pantry. Even on Martha's Vineyard, food insecurity is a real problem." Hearing that, I feel sick to my stomach with guilt, knowing that I'm fortunate enough to never be hungry a day in my life, and yet I choose to waste so much food.

The tour concludes in the tomato section. I check my phone again, and the news headlines about Stephanie's company have multiplied—in just an hour, a handful of other accusers have come forward. As we finish up, Rhoda chats with the leggings, and I see Sarah approach me.

"Hi, Ava," she says. "How was the tour?"

"Oh, it was really great. I loved it."

"That's wonderful to hear. And how was your hike earlier?"

I open my mouth to say that I didn't take a hike today, but stop as I remember the video I posted. *So,* I realize, *Sarah is secretly checking up on my Instagram.* "It was great," I tell her, deciding to play along.

"That's wonderful. Well, enjoy the rest of your day." She nods with a smile and turns to greet some other guests. I watch her go with suspicion and a smug sense of validation, knowing that even Sarah isn't *actually* above it all.

"That was so interesting, wasn't it?" Rhoda says as we head back to the cabin. "I could tell how much you enjoyed it, Ava. You really do have a passion for food."

We cautiously enter the cabin, afraid to disrupt Stephanie. We find her sitting on the couch, right where we'd left her, with her head in her hands. She looks up when we enter.

"Hey, guys." Until now, I've only seen Stephanie as being practically made of armor—tough, flawless, impervious to emotional setbacks. But it's clear that she's distraught. She might have even been crying.

"Stephanie, what's going on? What happened?" I ask.

"Whatever it is, you can tell us," Rhoda says.

We sit next to her on the couch, and she releases a big sigh.

"I have to go, that's what happened. I tried to take a break from work, but I can't do it. I just looked up flights, and there's one tonight to JFK."

"Hold on," I say. "Why do you have to leave?"

Stephanie tells us what happened, or at least as much as she can: she's under contract with the company—a big, fat, juicy contract—one that pays for a very nice lifestyle for her. And one that comes with a complicated employee NDA, one that was actually her idea when she started at the company seven years ago. And, of course, client/attorney privilege. But now that all the dirt has come out—things she says she truly didn't know—she feels like she morally can't sit back and do her job. But she also feels like she has to.

"Well," she says, "I'm not saying that anything you've read or heard is true. But hypothetically, if it were, I honestly didn't know the extent of it. I knew that there were some . . . questionable actions. And I helped to cover up those actions. But I'd really duped myself into believing that no one was truly getting *hurt*."

"What did you think was happening?" I ask.

"You know . . . typical Hollywood stuff. Powerful producer takes an actress to dinner to discuss a role. No one is *forced* to do anything, no one is drugged, there's no real *violence* . . . maybe there's an unspoken pressure, I guess. But my boss had always made it seem like these women were the ones coming on to him. God, that sounds so ridiculous now. But I really believed that."

"Oh, honey. You're too smart to believe that," Rhoda says. "I know you are."

"You forced yourself to believe it," I tell her.

"Well, it doesn't matter what I believe now," she says. "I'm trapped."

"No, you're not," I say. "I know it feels that way, but . . . what if you just . . . quit? What if you broke your contract? What would they actually do to you?"

"Well, for one thing, I'd be walking away with no money. A big portion of what I make comes from my annual bonus, and that would be out the window. And I'd be blackballed from pretty much every other possible job out there."

"I doubt that," I say, though I don't really know what I'm talking about. "And as for the money . . . I mean, I guess it comes down to what it's all worth."

"That's what Ralph says, too. He says I should just walk."

We sit with her in silence for a few moments.

"I think you know what you have to do, Stephanie," I finally say. "And we know you can do it."

"And in the meantime, we've got to eat dinner, right?" Rhoda says, lightening the mood. "Half an hour?" We agree and go to our rooms to get ready.

As I shower, I think about the position Stephanie is in versus my own. It's been so easy for me to make excuses for myself, to defend my actions, to find ways to justify what I'm doing. But if I had been the one sitting there on the couch, explaining my predicament to Stephanie and Rhoda, they probably would have told me exactly what I told Stephanie. I know what I need to do. I know what the right thing is. I just don't know if I can do it.

# Chapter 15

"So, did you think about what I asked you last time?" Wanda says as I sit in her office during our next session.

She had asked me to identify a moment in my life when I became aware of my own body. Over the past few days, I've been thinking a lot about that moment in the dressing room with my mother. But I still can't bring myself to talk about it.

"I did think about it, but I'm struggling to really pinpoint it," I tell her. And that's not a total lie. While the dressing-room incident might have been somewhat of a shift for me as I grew from child to adult, the real truth is that there wasn't one single moment in which I became aware of my body. Even my prepubescent years were fraught with anxiety over what to wear, how to style my hair, how to smile, what "my" smile even *was*. As I got older, middle-school sleepovers and coed dances only exacerbated this, with the absolute torture of waiting to be asked to dance, standing under the glare of the gym's fluorescent lights, my blue eye shadow only slightly more noticeable than my chin of volatile red pimples. And then, later, in high school, there was the constant, overbearing desire to look like an actress or a model or whatever pop star was queen at that time, along with the unavoidable hormonal pitfalls of being a teenager. And finally, as an adult, I have felt the constant, free-flowing criticism from men of women's bodies. To ask me to identify *one* moment in which I became aware of my body is like asking me to identify the moment I knew I was a woman. I just always *knew*. And, anyway, I can't bring myself to talk about the dressing-room incident because I'm still ashamed of how I mirrored it with Naomi.

"I understand," Wanda says. "Let's shift gears, then. I'd like to talk about your mother. When did you become aware of *her* thoughts on her own body?"

"This isn't about my mother, though," I push back. "I know what you're getting at. You tried to do this last time."

"Well," she says in a calm tone that's so flat it's starting to bug me, "you're right. It's not about her. It's about you. And yet I think there's a connection. I know it's hard to talk about it, but it might help you. Do you think there's a moment you can recall when you saw her as a *woman*, not just as your mom?"

I think about it. It's a tough question. I'd really only considered times with my mother that affected the way I saw my *own* body.

But Wanda is onto something with this question. Until now, despite being aware of my mom's habits and self-criticism, I nevertheless didn't truly see her as a woman herself, with her own insecurities. She was always my mom.

"I was watching her get dressed for a party," I blurt out, surprising myself. But the memory comes back to me as I speak. I don't even think I'd remembered it at all until this moment, but now it's suddenly at the forefront of my mind, vivid and raw, like it just happened five minutes ago. "She and my dad had some holiday party that night. I used to love sitting on their bed while my mom got dressed. She let me help her choose what jewelry to wear, stuff like that." My voice trails off as the image sharpens. "I must have been ten or eleven. Young."

Wanda nods.

"She was choosing between two dresses. One was much prettier than the other. It was dark blue with little sequins on it. My mom loved sequins, anything that sparkled. The dress had long sleeves and was knee length, but it was tight. And I think the material was stretchy, so it sort of showed everything, you know? But she looked spectacular. And the other dress was boring. Some black-velvet thing with no shape, just plain and boxy. It hid her body completely. So, I told her she should wear the blue one."

I can see my mother now, in the blue dress. When she moved, the dress shimmered, like it was made of water, like she had magic powers. She was radiant.

"She told me no," I continue. "She said that she was going to wear the black one. But I didn't understand why. I just didn't get it. She looked so beautiful in the blue one. So, I kept pushing. 'Wear the blue one,' I said. And she kept saying no. And I asked her, 'Why not?' And finally, she turned around and looked at me."

I pause. I remember feeling the punch of my mother's emotion before she actually spoke what came next. I remember feeling guilty for breaking her down, for pushing her, for saying something I wasn't supposed to say, even though I didn't understand what that was.

"And then she yelled at me. And she wasn't a yeller. My mom never yelled, not really. But she yelled at me. She said 'Because I'm too fat! I'm *fat!*' And she just kept screaming that over and over again. She took the dress off and threw it on a chair. And I just remember the dress hanging over the side of the chair, like a deflated balloon. And my mom was so mad. And she was . . . sad."

"You said she yelled at you." Wanda shifts in her seat.

"Yes?"

"Was she really yelling at you? Or was she yelling at herself?"

I try to remember how it felt to hear her voice in such a shrill tone, loud and full of anger. She had turned her back on me and looked at herself in the mirror. The look on her face was one of disappointment, failure, contempt. But Wanda was right. My mother wasn't mad at me, she never was. She was mad at herself. And in a way, that felt much worse to me. Anger from a parent was familiar to me, but seeing her vulnerability and self-inflicted pain was a foreign sensation, one that dismantled everything I thought I knew about her stoicism, about what it meant to be a grown woman.

"She was yelling at herself." I think further. "And I guess that moment wasn't so much about seeing her awareness of her body. I guess it was more about me realizing that it was possible to hate your body. That notion just wasn't something that would have even occurred to me. Until then." Wanda just nods and writes something else down. What a wild idea, I realize, that it might have been possible for me to go through life simply appreciating what my body could do, not just how it looked.

"Good," she says. "That's really good, Ava. When you got older, what do you think it was that compelled you to focus so much on your body as a means of self-worth?"

"Uh, what?" I never said that. "I don't equate my self-worth with my body."

"Well, your body is sort of the primary tool of your business, is it not?"

"I mean, I guess so. But that doesn't mean I equate it with my self-worth."

"But you're seeking approval from others, no? Would you say that's not how it works?"

"Look, I get what you're saying." I'm starting to get annoyed now. "But this is just how it *is* to be a woman now. I mean, don't tell me *you* don't think about your body." I might be crossing the line by turning the tables on Wanda, but I refuse to believe that even she hasn't experienced what it's like to feel too thin, too fat, too this, too that.

"Sure, there's certainly a level of insecurity that we all feel. Our society has done us no favors in that sense. But what I'm really asking you, Ava, is not so much whether you're seeking approval from other people in general. What I'm really asking you is whether it's possible that all this time you've been trying to seek your *mother's* approval, even though she's not here?"

I release a kind of grunt in response, the best I can muster. And I feel the same sense of frustration I felt after my confrontation with Naomi. I know that Wanda is right, but I don't want to admit it.

"Next time," Wanda says at the end of our session, as we stand in the doorway of her office, "I want you to tell me about the earliest times you made yourself throw up. I know it might be hard to remember, it might be uncomfortable, but I think you're ready to go there."

I nod, knowing that it actually *won't* be hard for me to talk about it. That's one area where I'm completely numb. I could talk about it all day without a hint of feeling crossing my face. It's become part of a routine, like swiping off my eye makeup with a cotton pad and remover before washing my face each night. It's just something I do.

I walk back toward my cabin to do some work before lunch. The memory of my mother and the sparkly blue dress is still fresh in my mind. I hadn't hit puberty yet when it happened. I had little buds for breasts, an undeveloped body whose sides ran parallel to one another, and the only makeup I'd worn at that point was my mother's lipstick once or twice when playing dress-up. I didn't yet have a body to compare to my mother's, so the incident did not leave me standing in front of a mirror, scrutinizing myself through the lens my mom had just presented to me. Rather, it showed me that to be a woman meant a certain inevitable level of dissatisfaction and self-loathing. If my mother, who was perfect as far as I was concerned, could be stung with such potent disgust at the sight of herself, then the only conclusion I could extract was that self-revulsion was simply inherent in my future as a human, as a woman. It occurs to me that I was never angry at my mother for teaching that to me. I've never been angry at her for anything, except for leaving. But maybe I should be.

Before I arrive at my cabin, I see Naomi crossing the lawn.

"Hey," I call out.

"Hi," she says. She looks the same as she does every day. I think about the photo she posted yesterday. The person in front of me is not the person in that photo. And I know all too well what it feels like to embody two contrasting selves.

"Listen," I say. She shifts her hips. She's carrying an empty tray back from the chapel. "I feel weird about our conversation yesterday, you know, about editing photos. I don't want you to think that you have to do that to be an influencer." I wait, hoping that she will say something, so I don't have to explicitly mention her new bikini photo that I've obviously seen.

"Don't feel weird," she says with an air of casualness. "It's all good, really. You know, it was actually a reminder to me that if I want to build my platform, I need to get more serious about it."

"No, but that's not true, Naomi." I want to tell her the truth, and I'm going to. "I've been wrong. You were right. My content, the way I present myself, it's not tr—"

But Naomi cuts me off.

"It's okay. I get it," she says. "Really, you don't have to explain. I know how it works now." I can see that there's been a shift within her, the same shift that I'd seen in me, and I know she won't hear me even if I do tell her the truth. "Anyway, I've got to get back to work. I'll see you later!" Even when I want to tell the truth, it's like no one wants to hear it. I wonder if I'll ever come clean.

Back in the cabin, my phone chimes. Carter asks if I can escape on Sunday for dinner and sunset watching. I want to go, but I worry that a second date—a *dinner* date—makes it a *thing*. It will create expectations for the rest of the evening—will we sleep together or not? And knowing that adds a whole layer of pressure on me that I don't think I want right now, or maybe ever. I've heroically managed to not reach out to Ben, but it's not like I haven't thought about him, or wondered why he hasn't reached out to me. It's still too fresh of a wound to think about dating someone else.

And yet . . . I enjoy spending time with Carter. And last time, when he dropped me off, I felt the *lack* of a pressure to kiss him. It just felt comfortable. Maybe there's a version of having dinner together that doesn't have to be stressful. Maybe I could just spend time with him and enjoy it, not overthink it. So, I say yes. But I tell myself that I can always cancel on him if I want to.

I load some more content, respond to a few emails, and decide that I should take the time to film a skin-care tutorial that I've been putting off doing for a while now. It just requires more effort than I've been able to give—I have to set up my tripod and ring light just right, I have to make sure my skin looks good while looking makeup-free. And on top of that, I have to go through a lengthy six-step process that I rarely actually do. In the end, I've convinced my followers that all they need to do to achieve flawless skin is spend hundreds of dollars on products and devote several hours to the process each day. *Easy!*

When I finish, I'm about to set aside my phone and watch some episodes of *Sex and the City* on my laptop before dinner. But another message from mermaid1985 comes in:

**If you don't tell the truth, I will . . . sooner or later.**

# Chapter 16

That night, Rhoda knocks on my door, asking if I'm coming to dinner. I don't want to go. I want to hide. I just want to order a pizza, and Indian food, and french fries, and binge and purge and online shop. I'm not in the mood for the communal chitchat, the forced camaraderie, the lack of privacy. And I'm scared. I finally caved and replied to mermaid1985, and of course now I'm deeply regretting it.

**I have nothing to hide**, I'd written back.

One of the major rules of being a social media star is that you don't stoop to the level of the trolls. You just don't. But I did, and now I feel petty and immature. But more than that, now I've stoked the flames. Whoever this person is—Sarah, the leggings, or someone else—now I've given them more ammunition to do whatever it is they're trying to do.

I tell Rhoda that I'll be ready in five, only because I really am hungry, and because tonight is a special dinner being prepared by a woman who owns two cafés on the island and is known to be one of the best local chefs. I'm curious.

"It's a real treat that Lucy Green herself is here to cook for us tonight," Sarah tells us as we shuffle toward the dining area. "She owns the Picnic Basket, which is an island institution here on the Vineyard, and her weddings and events are booked *two years* in advance, sometimes longer. And . . . the *New York Times* just featured her in a piece about the Black chefs changing American cuisine." I look her up on Instagram but can't find her.

I peek into the kitchen on our way to the table. The usual kitchen staff has the night off. In their place is Lucy and her team, a group of tattooed and pierced cooks, moving through the kitchen with ease. There's an energy to this group that feels different—relaxed yet productive. *Fun.* There seem to be at least fifteen different stations firing away at once—chopping and sautéing and melting and slicing.

"You guys go ahead," I tell Stephanie and Rhoda, suddenly getting an idea. "I'm going to see if I can film a little bit for my Instagram." The idea comes to me out of the blue. Normally, with the retreat's kitchen staff, I wouldn't dare ask to film anything. They're too buttoned up and seem to be under the watchful instruction of Sarah at all times. But I see Lucy, the head chef, at the back of the kitchen, and I get the sense that she might be okay with it. Lucy has a bright, easy smile, with green eyes that burst against her brown skin, and she wears her hair pulled back with a tie-dyed bandana. On her feet are pink Crocs, which, somehow, look whimsical on her rather than frumpy. Her kitchen smells of melted butter and sea salt, warm and inviting. I shimmy my way through the door.

"Hi," I say to her. She's slicing up a handful of chives with dogged ferocity. She doesn't look up. "My name is Ava. I'm an influencer, a food blogger. I was wondering if maybe I could film a few things in the kitchen for my feed?" Lucy keeps chopping. I wonder if she heard me at all, even though I'm standing right next to her. "It's great publicity. But, I mean, I don't want to impose," I add. I'm starting to think the idea was a mistake. Then she looks up.

"Listen . . ." she says. "No disrespect, but I don't do online publicity stuff." So that's why I couldn't find her profile. She doesn't have one. "I've got rules. And one of my rules is that if you're in the kitchen, you've gotta be helpful. So, Ava?" I nod. "Do you like food? Do you like cooking?" I nod again. "Well, then, put your phone away, and why don't you help me cook this dinner. How about that? Maybe you can take photos later. But if you're in the kitchen, you gotta help."

It's not what I expected, and I'm a little bit annoyed that my plan for some good content has been derailed, but I'd much rather embrace the meditative bustle of a busy kitchen than sit with the leggings through another dinner during which all I can think about is whether I'm going to binge and purge or not.

"Great," I say. "Thanks." I put my phone in my back pocket. "Tell me what to do." Lucy gives the quickest of smiles and then instructs me to roll up my sleeves, wash my hands, and put on an apron and a hairnet.

"Here," Lucy says, thrusting an armful of fresh basil at me. "Grab that knife." She points to a large chopping knife on a magnetic strip. "You're going to chop up the basil like this . . ." She takes a few leaves and starts slicing them with her own knife.

"Chiffonade," I say.

She looks up, surprised. "That's right. Chiffonade. Now go ahead and do all of these, and then I'll give you your next task." I have no idea what the basil will be used for, but it doesn't matter. I have one task right now, and one task only, and there's a freedom in that.

When I'm done, I look up to see that Lucy has already placed several cartons of wild strawberries in front of me, small and juicy and a deep pink-red color. She's cut a few of them up into discs. Without even saying anything, she nods toward the slices, and I nod back, my task understood. I wipe my knife and get to work slicing the strawberries, just as she had done. While I work, Lucy seems to be in ten places at once. One of the specially printed menus for the guests is taped up on the door of one of the refrigerators. There's a deconstructed Nicoise salad with bigeye tuna caught off the F/V *Honey Badger*, Morning Glory corn fritters with Mermaid Farm cheese, crispy GOOD Farm duck wontons in an umami broth, North Tabor Farm steak tartare with quail eggs, Cape Poge Bay scallops over a carbonara-style risotto, and wild strawberries with basil, marinated in balsamic and drizzled over buttery pound cake. My mouth hangs open.

Silently, Lucy appears as soon as I finish slicing the last strawberry, and leads me to the stovetop with her, where she tosses the strawberries into a pan. She then adds in the balsamic vinegar, coarse sugar, and other things I try to identify but can't. She hands me a wooden spoon.

"Don't overstir. Just watch, let it bubble a bit, and wait to stir when you need to," she tells me. "The pound cakes are ready and buttered. We'll throw them on the grill just before we take the dessert out later."

"Wow," I say. I'm starving now.

"And don't worry," she adds as though reading my mind, "there's always leftovers of everything for the staff. We'll eat when we're done."

"Thank god," I say with a smile. "It would be torture to cook this and not even get a taste."

"You're a natural in the kitchen," she says, watching me as I give the strawberries a slight push with the spoon. "Do you want to be a chef?"

"No," I say, "I don't think so. I mean, I just love food."

"So, you'd rather just take pictures of it? Sweetie, I can tell you love cooking and really appreciate food. That kind of love belongs in the kitchen."

Not waiting for me to respond, Lucy takes the strawberries off the heat, deciding that they're done. She runs off to assist the cook plating the steak tartare, and I find a place at the sink and load the dishwasher as best I can, trying to be helpful. It feels good to have a role, an actual job on which others rely, one that doesn't require my opinion in that moment or my stance on something, let alone my voice or my face.

Lucy isn't wrong about my love for food. But what she doesn't get is that I abuse food. Food is always with me at my highs and my lows. It's my comfort in hard times, and it's my celebration in good times. In a way, I'm a prisoner to food. Working in a kitchen would be . . . bliss. But also torture.

I look over to see Lucy testing the broth for the wontons and practically moaning in response.

"Perfect. Perfect," she tells the cook. Lucy doesn't seem like most of the chefs I know in LA. Or anywhere, really. I'm reminded of a time when Becky and I had dinner at a new restaurant downtown—a trendy, modern Italian spot with a fresh-faced female chef, a rising star, in an industrial space with exposed pipes and hand-thrown pottery plates. She came out to greet us halfway through our meal and brought with her some complimentary whipped ricotta and toast. She was rail thin, as bony as the metal chair on which I sat.

"She's one of those anorexic chefs who gets off on feeding other people," Becky whispered to me when the chef returned to the kitchen. "It makes sense, actually, like in terms of the psychology of it. She gets to live vicariously through the diners, and she gets this sick sense of satisfaction knowing she's fattening other people up but not herself." Then Becky stood on her chair to get an aerial shot of the free appetizer and our drinks.

I shamefully knew exactly what she had meant by that. Because the idea had appealed to me, too. If I had that kind of discipline and I was a chef, I'd do the same thing. How many times had I harbored the wicked, secret wish for a classmate, colleague, or even an actual *friend* to be struck by the curse of weight gain? How many times had I taken a closer-than-normal look at the backside of another woman in order to find some flaw, some lump or some extra inch, just to make myself feel better? How many times had I zoomed in on a photo of another influencer, trying to detect telltale signs of an editing mistake? How many times had I felt a smug, secret sense of victory upon eating a salad for lunch while my dining companion ate a more caloric sandwich?

The thing is, my entire platform is about lifting other women up. And the desire there is genuine. I do want other women to feel good about themselves. I know how it is to feel like shit and to take control of my life—my diet, my exercise, my habits—in a way that makes me feel better. Finding a system that works for oneself is an amazing tool, and I have always wanted the women in my life to feel the same sense of empowerment. But I don't know anymore if it's possible for that desire to coexist with the apparent jealousy I harbor for other women as well, or with my own insecurities that constantly force me into comparison with others. I don't know if I can ever be true in my pursuit of sharing wellness with others while continuing to be poisoned by my own spite.

Lucy, it seems, couldn't be further from that downtown LA chef. She's not thin, or fat. She just seems healthy. Energetic, full of enthusiasm and passion, plump but not overstuffed. But that's not the point. The point is that her cooking and her desire to feed others don't seem to come from the same place as the LA chef. They seem to come from a pure love of food, and the subsequent desire to share that love and joyful experience with others. The notion that anyone could be around food that much and still somehow maintain a healthy relationship with it almost seems impossible to me, and I envy Lucy for that. I long for it.

The rest of dinner service flies by, and although I've only just met the other cooks in the kitchen, I feel connected to them. I feel comfortable with them. As dessert is brought back in, signaling the end of the meal, I help one of Lucy's team members, a punk rock–looking girl named Vera, dry some of the dishes and tools that Lucy brought to use that night.

"I think I know who you are," she says as we work side by side.

"Oh," I say, not sure from her flat tone if she's leaning toward a compliment or not.

"Ava Maloney, right? You're different in real life, for sure." She reaches across me for a new dry rag. "I mean, you seem much more normal in person. No offense. It's just, on your Instagram, you seem very . . . *LA*." Before I can respond, Lucy comes up behind us, placing a warm hand on each of our shoulders.

"Well done, ladies. Ava, thank you for joining the team tonight. You did great. How did you like it?"

How did I like it? The evening made me feel alive, engaged, creative, fulfilled.

"I *loved* it," I practically stutter.

"Well," Lucy says, "too bad you're just visiting. I need another set of hands in the kitchen. Our season goes until the new year, believe it or not, and we're booked with gigs every week until then." She pauses, looking at me, like she can see the wheels in my own head turning. "Too bad."

Then she turns toward the rest of the kitchen and raises her arms. "Our turn to eat!" Everyone gathers around the kitchen counters, sitting where they can or standing with a plate in hand, and we all savor the fruits of our labor. The food is all just as delicious as it had smelled, as sweet and savory as it had looked. There is an air of joy in the room, and fatigue, and togetherness. A bond. It's wonderful and exciting and scary to me all at once. I had decided, a few years ago, to work alone, to basically exist alone. I didn't know that it was possible to be part of a group cleaved together by a shared, undeniable passion—in this case, for food. And I want to be a part of it.

When we're done eating, and we finish cleaning up, Lucy and her team pack up their bags and head out.

"Bye, Ava, nice to meet you! See you on the gram," says Vera. I wave.

Lucy gives me a hug, warm and strong. "I'm serious, you know. You've got a job here if you decide to stay," she says.

I laugh. "Decide to stay?" Lucy doesn't laugh, and I realize that she's entirely serious. "Thanks, Lucy, but I have to get back to LA."

"Okay," she says with a smile. "Well, consider yourself warned. This island has a way of pulling you back in. I once moved to Key West and only made it one winter before crawling right back." She gives me a final smile, and I turn to leave.

Stephanie and Rhoda are awake in the living room when I return to the cabin soon after.

"So," Stephanie says, "you disappeared on us. We heard the kitchen kidnapped you. What happened?"

"Well, I went in to film some content, but the chef asked if I wanted to help with some cooking." I collapse down onto the couch. "It was a blast." I'm suddenly overwhelmed with fatigue, but the good kind, the kind that makes me feel satisfied and accomplished. I know I'll sleep well.

"Well, that chef sure knows how to cook. Best meal we've had since we got here, wouldn't you both say?" Rhoda asks. We nod in enthusiastic agreement.

"She offered me a job, actually. Well, sort of."

"If I were your age, I'd just say yes and move here," Rhoda says.

"Me too," Stephanie agrees. "Maybe I'll go for it if you don't," she sighs.

"How are you feeling?" I ask her. "I mean, about work and everything?"

"I've got a decision to make," she tells us. "You guys have been really helpful, so thank you. I'm not going to leave the retreat early. I think I know what I'm going to do. Or, I think I know what I *want* to do."

"Sounds like you do, too, Ava," Rhoda adds. "Good for both of you."

And she's right. I know what I want to do. Now it's just a matter of doing it.

# Chapter 17

When the weekend arrives a few days later, mermaid1985 still hasn't responded to my message. But I've been in such an unusually good mood since the night I helped Lucy in the kitchen that I've barely thought about it. That is, until Becky texts me asking if I'm still being harassed by the troll.

*Whatever you do,* she says, *don't message them. They'll go away, they usually do.* I don't tell her about the message I already sent them. Why did I think it was a good idea to write that I had *nothing to hide*? The whole point is that I have *everything* to hide, and they know it. Maybe I could beat them to the punch, explain to my followers what I'm going through before mermaid1985 has a chance to expose me. But then again, what if they're bluffing, and then I out myself for no reason at all? There's too much on the line. I'd lose all my deals, lose thousands of followers, and have to deal with endless backlash. As it is, I've already lost a few hundred followers in the past few days just because I haven't been posting my usual amount of content. I simply don't have enough to fall back on. I have to keep going. I take Becky's advice, and I do nothing.

On weekends, the retreat offers brunch in the midmorning, encouraging guests to sleep in, a surprise that I've fully embraced. "Rest is just as important as work," Sarah had told us. My phone rings just as Stephanie, Rhoda, and I enter the dining room after a quiet morning of reading in the living room. It's my brother, Mike. He never calls, except on my birthday and holidays, or to give me some update on his life, which revolves around his two young boys and his wife, Darcy. It's not that we're not close, it's just that we're not the type to keep one another constantly updated. Mike isn't on social media, but Darcy and I follow one another on Instagram, and she always likes my posts and comments with encouraging emojis. We're just not the type of family that is constantly in *touch*. At least not anymore.

As I answer the call, I realize why he's calling, and what I've forgotten: it's Mom's birthday today. I'm the one who always calls Mike and my dad on this day, not the other way around. I'm the one who always remembers, the one who glues the family together when it feels like we've been apart for too long. I'm the one who remembers Mom.

The swift realization of my error throws me, and I suddenly feel ill. What have I been so busy with that I didn't even remember her birthday? Self-reflection, beach walks, and yoga? I feel a flash of anger at Wanda. In just a few sessions, she's made me feel a confusing kind of fury toward my mother that has clouded my memories, my sense of reality. I answer the phone.

"Hey, Mike. Hold on one sec." I turn toward Stephanie and Rhoda. "I'll meet you guys later. It's my brother." I point to the phone, and they nod in understanding. "Sorry," I say to Mike. "Hi. I was about to call you, actually."

"Hey, Ave," he says. "How you doing?" It sounds like he's at a kids' soccer game. I hear a whistle in the background. I won't tell Mike that I had forgotten about Mom's birthday. The thing is, even though we always speak on her birthday, we don't actually acknowledge what day it is. We share the silent understanding that it's too painful and pointless to vocalize the significance of the day; our shared grief is loud enough without saying anything at all. These yearly calls of mindless chatter, obligatory terms of endearment, and the collective, scathing burn of our bereavement have become an annual funeral.

"Good. I'm good. I'm actually at this retreat thing, and there's not a lot of alone time, or I would have called earlier. I'm gonna call Dad after this." Mike knows me, and knows when I'm bullshitting. But he's too busy with his life to care. We are worlds apart in terms of our day-to-day lives. Mike's weekends involve driving from sports game to sports game, picking up project supplies at Home Depot, watching animated movies, and giving Darcy shoulder rubs. My weekends involve no one but me and my own sick self-destruction.

"Oh yeah, Darcy mentioned you posted something about being on vacation. A retreat?"

"Yeah, I just needed to kind of hit refresh."

"Life in LA getting too stressful?" I know Mike is only joking, but part of it is true. He's always thought that my career as an influencer was silly, or "fluffy," as he once described it.

"Ha, ha. No, I just . . . wanted to get away. I'm on Martha's Vineyard."

"Oh, wow. For the week?"

"Um, a little bit longer. I've got, like, four weeks left." I hear some muffled noises on Mike's end.

"Theo, here, drink this," Mike says. I can hear Darcy in the background, too, cooing to one of their boys, who sounds hurt. "That's a long time. You sure you're okay?"

"Yeah," I tell him, though something about hearing him ask if I'm okay makes me want to crumble and cry. "I'm good. Really."

"Well, then, good for you. Sounds nice. Might as well do stuff like that while you don't have other responsibilities in your life to worry about." Mike only means it to be encouraging, but his words make me feel isolated and alone.

"Thanks," I say. "Yeah, I'm doing a lot of thinking while I'm here. You know, about my career and stuff, and Mom."

I hear more shuffling noises, and then Mike yells at Darcy.

"You told me you were packing the orange slices. No, I don't have them!" Darcy mutters something in response.

"Hey, listen," Mike says to me, "I gotta go. But, uh, take care of yourself today, okay?"

I wonder what Mike would do—what he *could* do—if I told him that I'm not sure I am able to take care of myself. Today or any day. But it's not his problem. "You too," I tell him. "Love to Darcy and the boys. Bye."

I hang up and call my dad, who answers on the first ring.

"Ava," he exclaims into the phone. "How are you?"

"I'm great, Dad. I'm great." It's the only way to respond to that question from my dad.

"That's good to hear. How's the, uh, social media business going?" I don't mind that my dad doesn't understand what I do. I don't expect him to.

"It's going well. I'm making some pretty good money."

"That's great, Ava."

I pause for a second; we both know what today is. But, as with Mike, we won't say it out loud. There's no need.

"How are you, Dad? You going golfing today?"

"Already went out early this morning. Just got back from two rounds."

"That's great." I pause again, the silence between us suddenly deafening. "Well, I've got to go. Bye, Dad."

"Wait, Ava," he says. "Penelope was helping me clean out the basement. You know, I've been meaning to do that for a while." Penelope is a woman that I know he's been dating, though I don't ask questions, and neither does Mike. We're happy for Dad that he's not alone, but we don't want to know about it. "And uh, I finally dug out the old photo albums. Penelope scanned some of the photos so I can email them to you. She thought you'd like that." I'm annoyed that *Penelope* has gone through our old family photos and that she's taking liberties with some of our most precious family items, but I have to admit that I'm excited to see them. "You know, she would have been fifty-three today. Your mom."

I'm shocked that my dad has actually mentioned my mother explicitly. I'm shocked that he even knows how old she'd be turning today. He never lets on that he thinks about her as much as I do, that he counts the days since she's been gone.

"I know," I say. "I know."

"Well, I'll let you go, kiddo. I'll email you right now. You take care of yourself."

"Bye, Dad."

After I hang up, I receive an email with a Dropbox link to the photos, clearly Penelope's tech-savvy work. But I'm grateful for it. I wait to open the link, not feeling ready yet.

I eat brunch alone, at the very end of the shift. The only other diners there now are the twins. Their plates are loaded with everything from the buffet, and they wear basketball shorts and oversize T-shirts. I give them a smile as I sit, and wonder what their mother is like, or if they have a mother at all. I wonder why they came here, and if the reason is anything like my own.

I find a spot on the lawn afterward, deciding to take some time to go through the photos. I wave as I pass by the leggings, who are gathered in a circle of Adirondack chairs, sipping coffee and scrolling through their phones, chatting. I'm still fairly certain that none of them could be mermaid1985, and yet I keep my distance just in case. As I walk by, I wonder, just as I had about the twins, what the daughters of the leggings are like, and what the leggings are like as mothers.

On a lounge chair at the end of the lawn, I load the Dropbox folder and wait for the photos to download. I'm impressed; my dad has sent me dozens, maybe a hundred photos. They start popping up on my screen in vivid color, momentarily bringing my mom back to life.

I scroll through with a level of detachment at first, but slowly I begin to let myself remember. There's the photo of her at my seventh birthday party at a bowling alley. There's a photo of all of us in Bermuda on a vacation. There's a photo of her teaching me to ski in Stowe. There's a photo of her and my dad, dressed in black tie, about to leave the house for some fancy event. There's a photo of her on Mother's Day, still in bed, wearing her Laura Ashley floral nightgown, beaming at Mike and me as we serve her homemade waffles.

She's perfect in every photo, even the ones that seem candid and unplanned. Even the ones in which she's holding me or Mike as a baby, or when she's cooking in the kitchen, or gardening outside with her hair in her face.

I click on a photo of the four of us out to dinner at Bertucci's. It's spring, just a few months after that last Christmas Eve. Mom was sick but still able to do normal things with us once in a while, like go out to dinner. I don't know what the occasion was—probably nothing—but I think it's the last photo taken of all of us as a family. We're sitting in a booth, a bread basket between us, Diet Coke for me and a regular Coke for Mike. It seems like an ordinary photo, but it's not. That was the night that Mom found out what I was doing.

Wanda had asked me to recall the earliest times I had made myself puke. Of course, the Christmas Eve buffet was the first real turning point. And immediately after that, it just got easier and easier. It became like a sport, at first, like I was always in a competition with myself and in a secret competition with everyone around me. One of my favorite spots to binge and purge was at the Cheesecake Factory at the mall. My friends and I would go there most weekends, cruising the sale racks, trying on makeup at MAC, and then tuck in to a long meal at the Cheesecake Factory, where we'd talk about boys we liked and what we were going to wear to the upcoming school dance. That restaurant really was a bulimic's dream. Before the food even came, I binged on their bread—warm and dark brown—which I'd slather in butter. Then

I'd take a quick bathroom break and return hollow, ready for more. My favorite meal was a chicken sandwich on fried bread. Literally: *fried bread.* Or sometimes I would get a creamy pasta dish. Occasionally, my friends and I would just share a bunch of appetizers. I would eat with frantic energy, stuffing and sipping and gulping. And once I hit that point of being almost too full to breathe, I would go to the bathroom again. The bathrooms themselves were what made the restaurant so exquisite. The stalls were incredibly private, like little cells, with doors that went all the way up to the ceilings. And the doors locked, of course. Even better was the fact that music played loudly in the bathroom, and outside. And finally, there must have been at least a dozen stalls, so I never felt the pressure of knowing someone was waiting for me outside the door. Those purges were the best ever. I walked out feeling light, youthful, knowing that the world was full of possibilities just for me, because I had a secret that no one else had. I had figured it out.

After those first few months, I could puke anywhere. I could do it silently, without leaving a trace of evidence behind. At school, at friends' houses, at home, at restaurants, even once or twice in the car with my family, straight into a barf bag, faking motion sickness. No one looks closely when you're puking; everyone turns away. So, it's easy to just stick your finger down your throat and cover it up with the bag in the flash of a quick moment. I was a true expert.

But the night of the photo, at Bertucci's, was the first time I got caught. And it was by my mother. I'd ordered pasta, and I can even remember what kind—pasta pomodoro—because I remember the acid of the tomatoes burning my throat later on. I scarfed it down, along with two of their bread rolls. And as we were finishing the meal, I excused myself to use the restroom. Luckily, my mom didn't come with me. The bathroom was empty, though it was more quiet than usual—no music was playing, and there was no fan. I did what I needed to do, quickly and efficiently. Somehow, during that time, I didn't hear the door open, and I didn't hear my mother come in.

I emerged from the stall thinking that I was alone. But my mom was there at the bathroom counter, applying lipstick. My reflection in and of itself seemed to me a giveaway: my eyes had watered, my chin was a little bit red, and I had the fatigued look of someone who'd just been sick. I didn't say anything, and neither did she, as I walked to the sink and washed my hands. I fished into the pocket of my jeans for some gum. I could feel my mom's eyes on me, but she didn't speak for a moment.

"Honey," she said finally, "are you feeling okay?"

I desperately wanted to burst into tears and tell her the truth, but I couldn't.

"I'm fine," I said. "My tummy just felt a little funny."

"Okay," she said. We never spoke about it again, not once, not ever. But three weeks later, she brought me to a doctor's office and told me that she'd made me an appointment with someone who specialized in *young women's issues*, as she described it. The doctor turned out to be an eating-disorder specialist. I always wondered why my mother referred to the doctor as one who specialized in women's issues. Did she think that that would make me more open to going? Or did she truly believe that eating disorders were simply *women's issues*?

We still didn't speak of it a few months later, when my dentist pulled her aside after one of my routine cleanings. I waited in the lobby, but I could hear them talking outside his office.

"Ava has severe enamel erosion, from what seems to be an excessive exposure to . . . uh, stomach acid." He cleared his throat. "And damaged gums from overbrushing."

"I understand," she said to him. "She's getting the help she needs. Thank you, Doctor, for your concern." After that, she increased my dentist appointments to three times a year instead of two, and I continued to see the therapist every few weeks. Maybe my mother thought that was enough.

But I also think she was scared. How could she not, on some level, feel that she was somewhat responsible for what I was doing? By sending me to the therapist, she was acknowledging that I needed help. She was acknowledging that I had a problem. She was acknowledging that she cared. And yet somehow, those acknowledgments only made it worse. Because, in turn, it also meant that she was turning her back on me, handing me off to someone else to take care of me, unable to truly be there for me when I needed her most. And maybe she had to do that as a kind of self-preservation. Maybe she did that because she was battling her own demons, too, and couldn't handle battling mine as well.

Still, I could have gone to her. I could have asked her for more help, more support. I could have started crying in the Bertucci's bathroom and let her hold me while I told her what was happening. But I couldn't. Not so much because I was afraid she would stop me, or get mad at me, or take it away from me. But because there was a part of me that suspected that she *wouldn't* stop me, that she *wouldn't* steer me away from my sickness. That she'd be proud of me for it.

# Chapter 18

I find myself in a state of constant rage after looking through the photos of my mom. Rage because I miss her and there's nothing that I can do about it, no one I can talk to who misses her as much as I do, or at least not in the same way, and rage because I'm angry at her. And then I'm angry at Wanda, again, for fueling my anger in the first place. Being angry at a dead mother is pointless. The anger won't go anywhere or result in anything. There's no point in resenting someone who isn't here.

That afternoon, I borrow one of the property's bikes and slog through five humid miles to a little supermarket called Cronig's, arriving hungry and drenched in sweat. My mother once told me to never go grocery shopping on an empty stomach, and it was good advice. But it's the only way I've ever done it. I have a backpack with me and the bike's front wicker basket to carry things, and I load each vessel as much as I can with whatever appeals in the moment—a jar of peanut butter, a jar of Nutella, a loaf of bread, presliced cheese, organic beef jerky, a family-size bag of Cape Cod potato chips, an Entenmann's coffee cake, containers of prepared macaroni salad and tuna salad, and some candy at the checkout, along with a jumbo bottle of water.

When I get back to the retreat, I sequester myself in my room and order a mushroom and pepperoni pizza from Porto Pizza since they're the only place that delivers and the last taxi driver I had told me it was the best pizza on the island. I meet the delivery guy at the start of the driveway and somehow slip back to my room unseen by Sarah or my cabinmates. The taxi driver was right—the pizza is delicious, some of the best I've had anywhere, ever. For hours, I binge and purge repeatedly while watching episodes of *Queer Eye* on my laptop, alternating between slices of pizza and my supermarket snacks. I don't emerge from my room until late morning the next day, too late to even make it to brunch. Stephanie and Rhoda have left a note on the kitchen counter telling me that they've gone to the gym. But that was hours ago. I return to my room, shutting the blinds, wishing that it was raining. All the *healing* that I've done at the retreat has gone to waste. I feel just as bruised and as toxic as I did when I was in LA.

Before I know it, I only have an hour until Carter is picking me up at seven. I wasted the day finishing the remnants of my food and looking through the photos again. I'm regretting having agreed to the date. The sun doesn't even set until about eight thirty, and there's an intimacy to a date in the raw sunlight that I'm not looking forward to. At least in LA, everything happened late at night, well after sunset, so I could always rely on the forgiving blanket of darkness and dim evening lighting to hide whatever I was feeling.

But it's too late to cancel, and I could use a night away from the retreat. I shower and put on a silky slip dress in a dark army green. It skims over my hips in a way that's flattering, but only when I'm looking thin, which, right now, I am. I wear a black lacy bralette underneath, and I tie my hair back in a low ponytail. I put on gold hoop earrings and keep my makeup minimal, focusing mostly on highlighting my cheekbones and accentuating the tan I've developed. I feel pretty refreshed, considering the waste of a day I've had. But I wish I could just take everything off and slip back into my bathrobe.

As I walk toward the entrance to the retreat, I see Carter standing in front of the farmhouse, talking to Sarah. I remember how she had described him as being *infamous* on the island, and it occurs to me again that they could have dated, or hooked up. I feel incredibly awkward as

I approach. I'm an outsider, a visitor paying an obscene amount to stay here, while they're locals. Sarah sees me approaching, and then Carter does as well, and they both take the tiniest step back away from one another, but it's noticeable enough to me.

"Well, hello," Carter says to me. I thought my slip dress was on the casual side, but I suddenly feel wildly overdressed. Sarah is in her usual work attire, with a makeup-free face and simple brown clogs on her feet. My confidence starts to plummet. I feel ridiculous.

"Hi," I say.

"You two have a great evening," Sarah says with a smile, like she's stifling a laugh. "Ava, I'll make a note that you'll be out this evening." I could kill her in that moment.

"Thanks."

She nods her head at me, then at Carter, and then disappears into the farmhouse. I turn to Carter.

"What are you doing here?" He was supposed to meet me at the end of the road, like last time. "I was going to walk down."

"Yeah, well, I got here a little early, and I wanted to see my painting."

"Oh, okay." Even though I know it might reveal my budding jealousy, I'm desperate to ask him about Sarah. "So, do you and Sarah know one another? Sure seems that way," I blurt out, unable to help myself. What do I care about looking jealous to Carter? I'm not even interested in him. Not really.

"Yeah, a little bit." He looks at me, and as though my face conveys exactly what I'm feeling, he adds, "No, not in that way. I don't know her well. It's just a small island." He pauses for a second. "Don't let her fool you."

"What does that mean?"

"I mean, she acts like this puritan hippie chick. But she's a bit of an island gossip." I decide not to mention my suspicion that she's been trolling me on Instagram all this time, but I feel validated. "No one on this island is entirely pure," he adds.

"Good to know," I say, though I wonder what he really means by that, and whether he's including himself in that statement. As we hop into his car, I notice he's slightly more dressed up, too, in a navy-blue button-down and jeans. I smell the faintest hint of cologne on him.

"So, where are you taking me to tonight?"

"Up island," he says.

"But I thought we already *were* up island."

"We are," he says, glancing over at me as he pulls out of the retreat. "But I'm taking you way up island. *Aquinnah.*"

The drive is about twenty minutes, and in the golden light of the early evening, it's glorious. The road dips and swells, and we pass by an old graveyard, private driveways marked with buoys, rustic stone walls, and lush wetlands. A few minutes later, the road opens up on one side to an expansive water view and, in the distance, an old lighthouse.

"Almost there," he says.

We reach what feels like the absolute end of the island. There's an old brick lighthouse perched up on a hill, and some small local shops and a restaurant at the very tip of the cliffs, overlooking the sea.

"We're taking a pit stop here to look at the view, and then we're having dinner. Not here, but close by. You'll see."

He parks the car, and we walk a short path through shops filled with artisan crafts and tourist paraphernalia until we reach a lookout point. Now it doesn't just feel like the end of the island; it feels like we're at the end of the earth. The cliffs below us are made of red clay, and they arc seamlessly down to the beach, on which boulders jut out in a style so beautiful it looks like they were planted there purposely. The water is somehow even more sparkling and clear than anywhere else, almost a pure aqua color.

"Wow," I say.

"I know," Carter responds, looking out. "I love Gay Head."

"Excuse me?"

He turns to me and starts to laugh. "Gay Head. That's what Aquinnah used to be called. Well, actually it was always called Aquinnah. That's the Wampanoag name. Then it got changed to Gay Head, and now it's back to Aquinnah, as it should be. I just forget sometimes. Habit." He pauses to take in the view. "I think the Wampanoag meaning of Aquinnah is 'village under the hill.' There's a lot of history here."

"I didn't think there could be so much difference among beaches," I say. "But I was wrong. This place is . . . magical."

We stroll up to the top of the lookout, and then Carter checks his watch and realizes it's time for dinner. We hop back in the car, and just a sixty-second car ride later, he pulls into a quaint New England–style place called the Outermost Inn.

We're greeted by a hostess who also seems to know Carter—who doesn't? I start to wonder—and she leads us through the restaurant to the back porch, where there's an outdoor bar and a vibrant green lawn that sweeps downhill, offering a sumptuous view of greenery and the ocean. On the lawn are several chaise lounges and chairs. There's even a basket of plush blankets for guests. It's the kind of place that had previously only existed for me on Pinterest boards, and a far cry from the Los Angeles version of ocean-side dining at Nobu in Malibu. Carter orders us a bottle of Sancerre, and we choose two chairs on the lawn. I have to give it to Carter: he did well in choosing this place. Really well.

"So, the deal here," Carter says as we sip our wine, "is that you make your dinner reservation for just a hair after sunset, in this case at eight thirty. And you get here an hour early and have drinks outside so you can watch it in all its glory. People say Menemsha is the best sunset spot on the island, but I disagree. Aquinnah has my vote."

"Well, I haven't seen the Menemsha sunset, but I think I'm just going to agree with you, anyway," I say.

And he's right. The sunset arrives without warning, and all at once the sky is flooded with a luminescent gold, so bold and rich that it's as if the sun itself has cracked open like an egg and spilled out onto the horizon. Every single leaf, every single blade of grass on the rolling hill, seems to be illuminated and bowing its head to the sun. A communal stillness and sense of wonder washes over the restaurant. Carter wraps a blanket around my shoulders. I can't help myself from recording a bit of the sunset on my phone, but I do it when Carter isn't looking. *Creating content is still my job,* I tell myself.

Despite the enchantment of the evening, I'm still concerned about what my plan is going to be for dinner. Just like that last dinner with Ben back in LA, I need to make a decision. I decide that I will order sensibly—something light and healthy, like a salad and fish—so that I don't feel the need to purge after. I'm dehydrated, and we've already had two glasses of wine each.

"You guys ready for dinner?" the hostess asks us as we watch the last drops of the sunset. We follow her inside, where she seats us at a cozy table by the window. But I panic when I see that the restaurant only offers a three-course dinner with a set price, and all the options, even the ones masquerading as lighter dishes, are fantastically indulgent. In just a split second, I mentally change my plan and decide to order whatever I want. Screw it. The wine has gone to my head already, and my stomach rumbles with hunger. I order chargrilled Katama Bay oysters with kimchi butter for my appetizer and the squid ink tagliatelle for my entrée, plus the chocolate cake for dessert.

"We can swap bites of everything, if you want," he says after he places his order of chicken liver toast, herb roasted hanger steak, and profiteroles with vanilla ice cream.

We order another bottle of wine, and the waitress returns with an amuse-bouche of foie gras on toast, as well as a basket of warm little rolls of bread in rich colors and textures, beckoning me to try each one, and a side of salted butter. The food is exquisite—creative and layered with complex flavors, yet simple and straightforward at the same time, letting the high-quality ingredients shine through. I quickly take pictures of each dish and post them to my stories, tagging the Outermost

Inn. Even in my wine-fueled delirium, I know that this is too good of a meal not to document.

I try to eat slowly, to savor each bite. I want to enjoy it. I want to enjoy it *normally*. But I'm restless. And with each bite filling my stomach, I become more torn between my desire to stay, to *be* here, to let myself have this evening and my instinct to run, to purge, to rebel. Before dessert comes, I know what I need to do.

"Just going to the bathroom," I say, rising from my seat. I regret wearing the slip dress now that my stomach sloshes with heavy food and wine.

I'm surprised to discover that the restaurant just has one bathroom, an impossibly small room with a rickety door. It's right off the main entrance to the restaurant, where there's a sitting area. Several people are cozied up on the couches and chairs in there, drinking wine and talking, and yet it's deathly quiet. I peer at the bathroom as I approach it. The door isn't even flush with the ground. There's someone in there right now, and I can hear every move they make as they finish up and wash their hands. Remembering what happened at Ben's, I know that this won't work, even for me. I begin to spiral, knowing that I don't have any other options. Maybe it's the wine, maybe it's the emotional turmoil surrounding Mom's birthday and the photos Dad sent, or maybe it's the fact that I just want this food out of my stomach, but I start to feel like I'm unraveling. I can't stay here. I need to escape. I turn on my heels and return to the table.

"I'm not feeling well," I tell Carter. "I kind of want to go." I hate myself as I say it, but I'm suddenly so blinded by, and consumed with, the need to purge that I don't care what he thinks or how I get myself there. I just need to *go*. My skin starts to feel pricky and hot. It's the same feeling I had when I ran out of Ben's house; it's the knowledge that I'm ruining something good, that I'm running away from it, that I'm choosing self-destruction over everything else. But just as it was before, it's now out of my control. I have no choice. I have to go. Carter looks at me with genuine concern, and I have to look away. He reaches out to touch my forehead. I pull back.

"Okay, okay, no problem," he says. "Maybe it was something you ate? I probably shouldn't have ordered another bottle of wine so soon." He motions to the waitress for the check.

At this point, I really just have a half-hour window to get the food out of my system. After that, my digestion will kick in, and the purge will be exponentially more difficult. The drive back to the retreat is almost twenty minutes in and of itself. I need to go. *Now.*

I don't bother to offer to split the meal, even though I know it's expensive. I'm angry at Carter for taking me here, for assuming that I could be the kind of girl who could appreciate this. I'm angry at him for putting me in this position. But mostly, I'm angry at myself for not knowing better.

In the car, we're mostly silent. I hold my hand to my head.

"God, you got sick really fast," Carter says, glancing over at me. I keep my eyes glued out my window.

"I'm sorry," is all I can say. I'm mortified. I can't look at him, I can't speak to him, I just need to *go.*

"Do you think you have a fever?" he asks. "Or maybe you got too much sun today? Here, have some water." He pushes a water bottle that was sitting in the cup holder toward me.

"I'm fine. Just drive, please." I hate the snap of my voice, and I want to apologize to him, but I can't.

The air between us is thick with tension, and when Carter pulls up outside the farmhouse, I slam the door. "Thank you," I yell as I run to my cabin, not looking back. I desperately want to glance back at him, but I can't. I'm too mortified, too possessed with self-pity and blame. I hear his tires turn on the gravel and drive off.

I trot through the farmhouse foyer but am intercepted by Naomi, the last person I want to see.

"Hey!" she says. She looks different. Her hair is in two tight french braids, and her cheekbones sparkle with highlighter. "I was actually wondering if I could show you a post I'm working on to see what you think."

"Not right now," I say, avoiding her eyes. "Sorry. I can't. I have to go deal with something. Tomorrow, okay?"

"Uh, okay." She follows me as I walk toward the door. "Are you mad at me?"

I just wish she—and everyone—would leave me alone. Don't they understand that *I'm* the one who needs help? That *I'm* the one who doesn't have it figured out? That the more I present myself as the person with all the answers, the less I actually know? And then I feel myself breaking, my frustration rising to a boiling point.

"No, Naomi, I'm not mad at you. But I can't help you. Because this is bullshit, okay? It's all bullshit. Instagram isn't real. What I do isn't real. It's all lies. Everything I do is phony, it's all for my brand, for my endorsements. How do you not get that? How do you not *see* that? The truth is that I don't fucking care anymore. All the girls like you, the ones who look up to me, the ones who think I'm a *role model . . .*" I release a strange noise, something close to a laugh but deeper and more guttural. "You all need to stop. You need to get a *life*. Find someone else to follow. Because I can't do it anymore. I'm sick. All the healthy stuff I post? All the photos of me? The workouts? Even the 'real' posts? They're all a lie. I'm a bulimic, okay? I'm *sick*. And maybe an alcoholic, and possibly very depressed, and definitely just fucked up in every way you can think of. Why the hell do you even think I'm *here*, anyway? Did it ever occur to you that there's something wrong with me? If you don't mind, please leave me alone."

Naomi doesn't respond. She just stands there, silent. I turn my back and run toward the cabin. Stephanie and Rhoda are in the living room reading when I barge in. I don't acknowledge them, instead just going straight into my room, and then the bathroom, where I collapse onto the cold floor and proceed to brutally purge until I am dizzy and breathless, not caring who hears or sees me, not caring about anything at all.

# Chapter 19

A knock on my door wakes me, and I slowly open my eyes. Even with my curtains closed, sunlight streams through, and I can tell it's another beautiful, clear day. Again, I wish it were raining. I can feel myself slipping back into my old routine of bingeing, purging, and wasting the day. I roll onto my side and look at my phone. It's a little past ten already. I have a string of messages, but I don't look at them long enough to see who or what they're from. I don't even care if mermaid1985 or Carter messaged me. Even though Carter might not know *why* I bolted last night, it doesn't matter. He's seen the real me, and chances are he'll respond just like Ben did . . .

*Sounds like you've got a lot to figure out . . . I just don't think I'm equipped to handle that right now. Good luck to you . . .* His words still sting me. Not because they're *his* words, but because he's right. I have a lot to figure out.

Despite having passed out and slept like a rock after my purge, I feel exhausted. My body is brittle, like my bones are made of paper, and I'm intensely thirsty.

"One sec," I groan. Who has the audacity to knock on my door? The housekeeping staff here knows better; if there's a guest in the cabin at all, they steer clear.

I walk to the bathroom, my feet tingling and my throat dry, and I spend several minutes shoveling water from the tap straight into my mouth, until I'm gasping. I brush my hair back into a bun on top of my head and splash my face with cold water. When I lift my head, my reflection in the mirror stares back at me. All I see is sadness, emptiness. I've been here before, this rock-bottom place. The morning after that last dinner with Ben. Except after that, I could run. That's how I ended up here. I ran away. What does it mean to hit rock bottom *here*? It's a new low, a new level of masochism, of loneliness. In my T-shirt and boxers, I swing open my bedroom door, sure that my puffy, bare face will frighten whoever is on the other side.

Stephanie and Rhoda stand there, dressed in their clothes from yoga. Rhoda has her arms folded. Stephanie's hands are on her hips.

"Okay," Rhoda says, peering into my room. "Get dressed. We're taking you somewhere."

Stephanie hands me a yellow Gatorade. I don't know where she got it, but I'm glad she did. I open it immediately and start chugging.

"Fine," I mutter. "Give me ten minutes."

"We'll be waiting," Rhoda says.

I take a quick rinse in the shower and then dress in jean shorts and a loose tank top. The events of last night keep playing in my mind, and I actively cringe as the images flash behind my eyes. None of it was worth it. Everything I did, everyone I hurt, everything I revealed, what was it all for? Just to empty my stomach of a few thousand calories? I got what I wanted, in the end. I purged. I ultimately went to bed with an empty stomach. But was it worth it? For most of my adult life, the answer would have been an unequivocal yes. But now, I don't know.

I brace myself and scroll through my phone, needing to at least quickly check my messages before leaving with Stephanie and Rhoda, wherever they're taking me. I check Instagram first, before my texts. Tons of positive responses have come in after my meal at the Outermost Inn. To any follower, it really looks like I had the most dreamy, magical night. It looks like I'm someone who is able to eat food with pure passion and appreciation. Someone who is able to let that food stay in her stomach and fully digest. Someone free spirited. Someone who isn't sick. Someone who isn't me. And mermaid1985 has responded:

**Tick tock.**

I start to type out a response: **fuck you** . . . But I stop myself. *Let them* out *me*, I think to myself. *I don't care anymore.*

Then, I look at my texts. Carter has called once and messaged me: I hope you're feeling better. Can I bring you anything today? Don't be embarrassed. Whatever happened, it's okay. Rest and hydrate today. Here if you need anything.

I have to read it twice, scanning it for some judgmental or angry undertone, or at least a lack of interest in me now that I've freaked out on him. But I can't find any sign of that. It's like he's totally unfazed. And I realize that I was relying on him pulling out of whatever this thing is between us. That's what I was expecting. I don't know how to process any other kind of response from him. I don't know how to process his kindness.

At least Ben's reaction made things easier for me, in a way. It drew a clear line. It allowed me to move on from him. And really, it showed me who *he* was. But with Carter, I can't just retract myself from whatever our *thing* is without some kind of conversation. I can't just accuse him of being an asshole. As much as I want to, I can't ignore him. And I can't be fake.

Thanks. I'm okay. I am so sorry, Carter. I owe you an explanation. Could we go for a walk in the next few days? Let me know. I stuff my phone into my back pocket and decide that it's time I took accountability for myself, for once. It's not really that I owe him an explanation. It's that I actually want to give him one.

"Ready?" Rhoda asks when I emerge from my room. The Gatorade has helped revive me, somewhat, but I'm starving. I grab a banana from the kitchen.

"Yup," I say, scarfing it down. "Where are we going?"

"The farmers market," she says.

I couldn't be less in the mood for a cheery farmers market, full of happy families buying fresh flowers and cherry tomatoes. But I'd rather do something distracting than sit with my own thoughts all day. As we walk out of the cabin, I pull down my sunglasses, scanning the grounds for a sign of Naomi. *She's the one to whom I actually do owe an explanation,* I think as everything I said to her comes rushing back in my mind. I *really* let her have it. And I really exposed myself to her. Where would I even begin in apologizing to her, in explaining myself?

Out front, a van taxicab is waiting for us, and there's no sign of Naomi anywhere, which makes me worried. What if she quit? What if she reported me to Sarah?

The three of us sit in the van in silence, at first, with Rhoda in the middle. I almost laugh, for a moment, thinking about how the three of us look, and how funny it is that these two other women have become my support system. I didn't ask for it, but I'm grateful for it. Stephanie looks ever regal in black metallic leggings and platform Nikes, Rhoda looks sparkly-eyed in loose track pants and a plain white T-shirt, and I look like a cranky teenager coming down from a bender. Stephanie leans over Rhoda, who is sitting in the middle.

"So, listen," she says, "we're not going to beat around the bush. We heard you come in late last night, and we've got a feeling about what's going on. We had some suspicions before." I suddenly feel hot and trapped in the van. Are they taking me on some kind of intervention? That's what the retreat already was for me—an intervention for myself. Where could they take me from *there*, a rehab facility? "This is *not* an intervention," she adds, as though reading my mind. "We've all got our stuff. Hell, why would we all be at that fucking place if we didn't have issues to work through? We just want you to be okay. And we thought that today we'd get you off campus, distract you. Enough with the meditation stuff."

"And," Rhoda says, "there's something I want to show you. *Both* of you," she says, looking over at Stephanie, too. "You'll see."

Their compassion makes me want to curl into a ball. All the stuff I preach about women supporting other women—this is it. This is real. This is what it looks like when it actually happens. I feel a lump in my throat as a wave of gratitude washes over me, knowing that I might not be deserving of this. I'm grateful for their help as much as I'm grateful for their silence during the rest of the drive.

We arrive at the farmers market, set inside and around a beautiful gray-shingled structure that's sort of a cross between a barn and a house. Outside, in the parking lot to the side, are two rows of vendors, each with their own tent and table.

"Here we are. Grange Hall," the taxi driver says. Stephanie thanks him and pays him in cash, and we slide out. The first thing I smell is coffee, and I see a Chilmark Coffee Company truck.

"First stop?" I ask, desperate for caffeine, and Stephanie and Rhoda nod. We order cold brews, and I feel somewhat better after the first sip. Coffees in hand, we stroll through the market, sampling and buying things here and there: Prufrock cheese from the Grey Barn, sourdough bread from Cinnamon Starship, a box of dark chocolates from Salt Rock Chocolate. We admire the flowers from Tea Lane Farm, the produce from Slip Away Farm, and all the seafood from the various oyster farmers and Menemsha fishermen. I notice that Rhoda and Stephanie don't treat me differently as we consume little bites of things here and there. Normally, when someone knows I have a *problem*, they treat me with kid gloves. This feels better.

As we approach the end of the market, Rhoda stops us, holding her arm out. She's staring ahead, at one of the last stands, where a woman who looks about the same age sells small oil paintings. Rhoda looks like she's seen a ghost. Stephanie glances at me with confusion, and it's clear that she doesn't know what's happening, either. Rhoda turns to face us and waves her arm for us to follow her. We step aside, away from the crowds.

"Did you girls know that my David and I were married for fifty-two years?" She smiles. "Fifty-two years. He was the best man I ever knew. And now we have nine grandchildren. That's really something, isn't it?" We nod. My confusion starts to turn to concern, and my mind reels. What is she getting at? Does this have something to do with that woman? Did David cheat on her?

"And I don't regret a day I spent with him. I loved him so much. But . . ." She pauses. And she cranes her head slightly to look toward the woman selling paintings. "But when I was in college, at Wellesley, I met someone else. Another student. Elena." My eyes widen, and now I know where this is going. In just a split second, I see Rhoda differently. She's someone with a complicated past, with a story, with struggles. She continues, "We were in love. But it was a different time. We kept our relationship secret. Even after college, when we were both living in Boston, no one ever knew. I suppose we could have run away. We could have done a lot of things. But then, I met David, and suddenly I had this opportunity for a normal life, I guess you could say. It was . . . *easier*. So, I ended it with Elena. I told her that I wasn't gay. That I never was. That it was a phase." She looks down at her feet and shuffles slightly. "The truth is, I came to this retreat because I knew that Elena is here, on the Vineyard. I tracked her down. And I decided to call her. I mean, it's a miracle that we're both still alive, in a way." She laughs a little. "She doesn't know I'm here right now. I think I used the retreat as an excuse to get myself here. And if there's one thing I want you two to know, it's that life is short. Time will slip through your fingers faster than you can imagine. You're both so young. You've got everything ahead of you. So, don't wait anymore. I don't regret my life, I don't. But I don't want you to wait, like I did."

Stephanie and I stand there in silence, mouths open, totally in shock. I'm the first one to speak.

"Rhoda, I had no idea. I just—*wow*. You're very brave. You were then and you are now."

"So, what are you going to do?" Stephanie asks.

Rhoda looks over at the woman. "Well, that's her, if you hadn't already figured that out." We all turn to look. Her gray hair is in a long braid on one side, and she wears a large straw hat. "That's my Elena."

"You're ready," I say to Rhoda. "And we'll be cheering you on." Rhoda squeezes our hands and tells us that she'll meet us out front later on, if all goes well. She makes her way toward Elena, who spots her as she approaches and freezes, as though in disbelief. We're too far away to hear what they're saying. They stand before one another for a few seconds, several feet apart. And there's a moment where I'm not sure Elena is going to be receptive. But then Elena is walking around her table and reaching her arms out, embracing Rhoda. The two women hold one another as though they've been waiting to do so for fifty years.

"Well," Stephanie says to me, "I did *not* see that coming."

"Me neither," I say. We're both still staring.

"The farmers market was her idea," she says as we stroll away to avoid gawking. "I just thought she wanted to get some local honey or whatever, and I agreed that it would be a good distraction for you. And honestly, for me, too."

"Well, I'm glad she suggested it. Fifty years . . . can you imagine?"

"Honestly, I kind of can," Stephanie says. "Which is what scares me. I mean, I think it's totally possible to live your life just sort of . . . *coasting*. Telling yourself what you need to tell yourself to get by. I think I could live like that forever. But I don't want to. And I don't intend to."

"What are you going to do?"

"I'm going to quit." And when she says it, I know she means it. "Hey, I'm hungry. Want to grab some lunch? There's supposed to be a really good spot next door."

"Sure," I say. I'm still starving.

We wander down the street to a café called 7a, tucked behind Alley's General Store. We order a few sandwiches for the three of us to share and some cold drinks. Stephanie and I go sit on the porch of Grange Hall and eat.

"Well," I say in between bites of a tuna melt on rye with banana peppers and bacon, "I'm really inspired by your decision to quit. I know it's not an easy one. How's it going to work, exactly?"

Stephanie chews and swallows. She's eating the café's signature Liz Lemon sandwich—a turkey Reuben studded with potato chips.

"It won't work, not at first. But that's not a reason to avoid doing it. I'll get another job. I know I will. I just have to go through the storm first."

I wonder if Stephanie is trying to observe how and what I'm eating. She and Rhoda didn't say in explicit terms that they know what my problem is, but it's obvious enough to me that they do. And yet I still don't feel judged or *watched* by them.

"What about you?" she asks. "Has being at the retreat helped you at all? With your eating disorder, I mean?"

And there it is: she's said it. But it's okay.

"I think so," I say. "But I've got a long way to go. What I think it's done more than anything is actually helped me to reevaluate my career choice and how that's been affecting my disease. Basically . . . my job is no longer good for me. My job is now part of the problem. So, in a way, I've got a choice kind of like yours to make. Do I walk away from what I've built, or do I stick with it, knowing that I'm hurting myself, hurting others, and that it's not really the truth?"

"Well, when you put it that way, I think the answer is pretty obvious," she says.

"I know. You're right. I know what I need to do."

And I do know.

"And listen," she adds, "I never had a real eating disorder myself, so I don't know what it's like. But I've had my fair share of insecurities, diet fads, cleanses, all of that bullshit. Honestly, Ava, I don't know one woman who *hasn't* experienced at least some of that. I'm not saying it's not a big deal. It *is* a big deal. It's life threatening, and you need to get better. But I also think you shouldn't feel guilty about struggling. It's not your fault."

I don't realize until I hear her say those words that I've been blaming myself all this time. Yes, I've been blaming my mom for her role in it, in the way I view myself and view food. But I've been blaming myself for failing, essentially, when really, I've just been struggling. I've been trying so hard to project an unflappable image of perfection and ease for so long that I've also been punishing myself anytime I wasn't close to that in reality. And in that sense, I've been perpetuating the cycle over and over again.

"Thanks, Stephanie. And you're right. Most grown women I know, in fact, especially the ones who are successful, smart, ambitious, complicated . . . they've *all* experienced some kind of eating disorder or body insecurity. It's so fucked up to say this, but it's almost as if it's just part of being a woman. But it doesn't have to be that way. It shouldn't be that way." I pause, finally feeling ready to admit what I've needed to for a long time now. "And I've played a big role in that. It's time for me to stop. Not just for my followers. But for myself."

We sit in the sun and watch Rhoda and Elena from afar. My phone buzzes. Carter has written back, suggesting tomorrow afternoon for a walk. I feel better already, knowing that I'm going to be honest with him. What do I have to lose? I think about Naomi, too, and decide that I will seek her out and tell her the truth. And give her a big apology.

As for my followers, they need to hear the truth as well. Maybe mermaid1985 has given me a gift, in a way, by making me realize this. They're right—my followers do deserve the truth. But they deserve it from me, and no one else.

# Chapter 20

As soon as we get back from the farmers market, I wait outside Wanda's office until she has a free window. Beth has told me that she's pretty booked, but that if I wait in the lobby, she might be able to squeeze me in.

"Ava," Wanda says when she emerges from a client session with one of the stocky twins, "I didn't think you had an appointment today."

"I don't. But I need some help."

"Beth? Do I have time right now?"

"You do have half an hour free, yes."

"Then come on in," Wanda tells me. It's almost like she's been waiting for me. I think they call this a "breakthrough" in therapy.

I start talking as soon as I sit. "I've been in denial," I tell Wanda. "This whole time. I haven't really been able to admit to myself the root of my problem. I've barely even admitted to myself that I have a problem. That I have a disease. And I know I haven't been able to admit it because, well . . . because of how it's all connected to my mom. That's what I need to figure out. And I've finally realized that until I do that, I'll never get better. And I want to. I really want to." It feels good to say it out loud—that I want to get better. That getting better is *possible*.

I wait for Wanda to speak, to instruct me, to give me the secret to getting better now that I've relinquished myself to her.

"So, what do I do?" I plead.

Wanda leans forward, resting her elbows on her knees.

"The first thing you need to do, Ava, is thank yourself. This takes a lot of bravery, coming here, admitting to this, being vulnerable. So, let's start there." She pauses and leans back. "The next step is going backward. We still need to talk about the root of this, like you said. You. Your mother. All of it. And it's going to feel like you're regressing. It's not going to feel like good progress. It's going to hurt. It's going to be messy. And you're going to be angry. But it's the only way forward. We've got to go through." It's just like Stephanie said: I've got to go through the storm.

"I'm ready to do the work," I tell her.

"I also want to warn you," she adds, "that this process is just like coming off any other addiction. You will have withdrawal, and it won't be a linear process."

"I know," I say. "I'm scared. Because I admit that I love the feeling—the physical feeling, anyway—that I get after a purge. And I really don't know how to enjoy food without thinking about purging. The problem is, I love food. But I hate it, too."

"We're going to work on that, Ava. But I want you to think about it as a trade-off. Sure, you might feel better after you purge. The same way you feel great when you're drunk or high. But really, afterward, you need to ask yourself: Was it worth it? Do I actually feel better in the ways that are important to me? Was it necessary? Most of the time, if you're honest with yourself, you'll find that it wasn't worth it. It comes down to how you want to live your life."

When the half hour is up, I schedule sessions with Wanda every day that week. I've just received a payment from Skin Beams, and I decide that I'm going to use that money specifically for this. No more wasting my income on things that only make me feel worse.

After that, I search the campus for Naomi, and I find her emerging from the beach with a tray of empty iced-tea glasses.

"Hey, Naomi," I call out. I can tell she's noticed me, too, and is trying to avoid me. "Can we talk? Please?" She stops and turns to me.

"Sure, what's up? I only have a few minutes. I'm working."

"Thanks, I know. I won't keep you long." I take a breath to collect myself. "I want to apologize. I am so, so sorry for what I said to you last night and how I treated you. I never should have spoken to you like that. Especially because I feel like we have been building an actual friendship. I respect you. So, there's no excuse for how I behaved. But, the truth is, I was having an episode." I realize that I haven't said this out loud to anyone before, not even Wanda, not in such unequivocal terms. "I know I said this to you last night, but I really am sick. I'm severely bulimic. That's sort of why I'm here. And when I ran into you, I was having an episode, basically. I don't know what else to call it. A panic attack, maybe. I had just had dinner and well . . ." I take a breath. "I can't believe I'm saying this, but the truth is, I just needed to purge. I won't go into details, but when that happens to me, it's like I'm just totally consumed, like nothing else matters. Like I've got blinders on. And it's no excuse, like I said, but that's why I acted the way I did."

Naomi's expression has softened, but she still looks skeptical.

"But what about the other things you said," she asks, "about everything being fake?"

"Well, that's true, somewhat. It didn't start that way. It started as being real. And then it somehow got away from me, and my sickness got worse as my success grew. But I don't want to lie anymore, Naomi. You helped me realize that. Women like you, ones who have trusted me and relied on me—you matter to me. And it's not fair to you. I'm going to make it right."

Naomi doesn't respond right away, and I'm pretty sure she's going to tell me to go fuck myself. She wouldn't be totally unjustified if she did. But then she speaks.

"I'm sorry, too," she says. "I'm sorry that you're sick. Bulimia is a terrible disease. And it sounds like you've put a lot of pressure on yourself. When really you should just be focusing on getting better."

"Thanks, Naomi. Well, that's why I'm here. Really. I want to get better. And I want to be honest with everyone."

"So, are you going to like, tell your followers or something?"

"Yes, I will, eventually. I just need to do it in my own time. I have to figure out the right way."

She nods. "Well, I think it's great that you're doing the work to get better," she says. "And what happened last night—it's okay. I get it now. And I won't tell anyone."

"Thanks for understanding, Naomi." I'm relieved that she's not as mad as she could be at me, and more relieved that she's promised not to tell anyone.

Later on, I decide to go down to the beach for a swim by myself. I need to think about what I'm going to say to my followers, to my sponsors. I need to take a break from social media altogether first, to focus on myself, like I told Naomi I would. But taking a break from social media is something I haven't yet dared to do, and it scares me.

The water is warm in the afternoon sun, and entirely flat, not a wave or ripple in sight. I've got the beach all to myself. I sit on the shore and hug my knees into my chest. I think about the advice my mom would give me now, if she were here. She might not be able to take her own advice, but I have a feeling she would tell me to do what was going to make me happiest, to take the risk, to do the work to feel my best, to get better. All the things that she never got to do.

I open up Instagram and turn on the video, facing the camera toward me.

"Hey . . ." I say, stopping myself before saying my rehearsed *friends*. "Hi." It's the first time—ever—that I start filming without worrying about what I look like, without testing out a few filters, finding the right light, the right angle. I just *go*, and that might not seem like a big deal, but considering the fact that my entire *life* has been documented through a filter, it's a pretty radical change for me. "I wanted to let you all know that I'm going to be offline for a while. A couple of weeks, probably. You know, I told you guys I was on vacation a few weeks ago. And I wasn't completely honest with you when I said that. The truth is, I'm at a wellness retreat. It's not rehab, but it's not completely a vacation, either. I'm not ready to talk about what issues I'm working on while I'm here, not specifically, but the point is that I'm here working on *myself*. Because none of us are perfect. Even those of us who seem to have it all figured out don't. And I've been wrongly giving you the impression that everything is fine—that life is easy for me—that I'm perfect. I'm far from it. And I'm here to get better. So, I'll tell you more soon, but I need to take some time just for me. I hope you're still here when I come back. In the meantime, thanks for your support. Be well."

I don't even read through the responses as they come in. I don't check my DMs. For all I know, mermaid1985 could be plotting something right now. But I don't care. It's time to move on. And before I can stop myself, I email all my sponsors and endorsement-deal reps and tell them that I'm going off the grid for a few weeks. It's a huge risk, and one that I can't really afford to take. If they all drop me, I'll only be able to get by for a few months before I'll need to scramble to get another job. But despite the risk, I know that I don't really have a choice. I *need* to do this. It's the first time in a long time that I've chosen myself over anything else. I might have just thrown away my entire career in a matter of seconds, but I also haven't felt this stable or free in years.

# Chapter 21

The next day, in the late afternoon, I walk to the beginning of the road to meet Carter. I resisted looking at my phone all night and all day—instead, actually letting myself enjoy a yoga class with Samantha, lunch with Stephanie and Rhoda, and a few hours of . . . *nothing*. It was blissful. But as I wait for Carter, I feel an overwhelming itch to just take a quick look. I check the time. He should be here any minute, so I decide to give in and glance at my phone, promising myself that I'll put it away the moment he arrives.

The first thing I see is a message from Skin Beams: Ava, we're very sorry to do this, but we're going to have to terminate our partnership with you. Our company prides itself on being authentic, and choosing partners who reflect that core value. Please be well.

I'm shocked. I know that I said I was going off the grid, but what does that have to do with being inauthentic? They can't just drop me for no reason. I pound a response:

> I'm sorry, but what have I done that isn't aligned
> with your core values? I'm taking a few days off to
> restore, but I'll be back with content soon, and I
> thought our agreement allowed for that. Can you
> please elaborate on why this isn't working out?

I hit "Send" just as I see Carter driving up. I put my phone away, but I can feel my addiction to it pulling me like a magnet. Bailey pants in the passenger seat, and Carter shoos her toward the back as I climb in. I take a deep breath, trying to put the news from Skin Beams behind me, trying not to obsess about why they dropped me, trying not to fixate on my suspicion that mermaid1985 was somehow behind this.

"Before you say anything," I tell him, "I want to apologize again."

"It's okay." He starts to drive. He's taking us to a nearby trail that he'd said is one of his favorites. "You don't have to explain. Things happen."

"No, but I want to explain. If we're going to be friends . . ." I pause, letting that word linger, considering it. "Then I want to be honest with you."

"Okay," he says. "Whatever it is, I'll understand."

"I have an eating disorder." It's not easy to say it, but I feel triumphant as the words come out. "That's why I'm here, at Island Wellness. I'm . . . bulimic. That's a disease where you . . ."

"I know," he says before I can finish. "My little sister was, too, for a long time. She's better now. At least, I think so."

"Oh." Carter had only mentioned his sister a few times. "So, you knew? I mean, you could . . . *tell?*"

"No," he says, giving me a glance as he drives. "I didn't assume anything. It wasn't obvious that that's what was going on. But you know, spending six weeks at Island Wellness probably means that you're working on something. I guess what I'm really trying to say, though, is that I'm not *freaked out* by you, Ava. Don't get me wrong, it's a big deal. And getting better should be your priority, not dating some local guy." He pauses, stops himself. "Not that we're dating. But, uh . . . I just mean that I don't think this defines you. And I know you're going to get better."

Carter understands, and that's that. The conversation is so easy, so supportive, that I don't even know how to respond.

"Well, thanks." It's all I need to say.

He pulls off North Road onto a dirt path marked MENEMSHA HILLS.

"Listen," he says, handing me a full water bottle, "this is a three-mile hike. It's not crazy hard, but are you up for it? The final destination is worth it, I promise."

"I'm up for it," I say.

I decide to leave my phone in the car on purpose, even though my mind is still reeling from the endorsement drop. That one is going to hurt financially, too. I was relying on that income. If my instincts are right, and if mermaid1985 was behind this, then what's next? I should be focused on damage control right now, not off hiking in the woods. But I'm here. There's nothing I can do about it in this moment. And after the stunt I pulled on Carter last night, I owe it to him to at least be present today, just for the hike. I can do that. I think.

Without my phone, we begin the walk. And after a few minutes, I actually forget about it altogether. Maybe it's all in my head, but I swear that the air smells fresher than usual, the sky appears bluer, the leaves on the trees are a deeper green. Through the thick woods, the path suddenly opens up to a clearing atop a hill, overlooking the ocean. Its wide-open face glistens under the sun, and the waves beat gently against the smooth beach-stone shore. At the bottom of the hill is a lofty tower built of bright-red bricks, ancient looking and somewhat decaying, like a long-lost, secret ruin. Bailey runs ahead of us.

"This is the Brickyard," he says. "There was an entire harbor right here at one point, a huge shipping port." He points out toward the sea. "Massive docks where cargo ships would come in, and up there was a grist mill. It was all powered by the Roaring Brook, it's called, which still runs fresh water to this day. Most of the oldest buildings on the island, and a lot off island, too, were built with the bricks that were made right here."

"So, what happened?" I look around at the brick-and-stone ruins.

"Times changed. The island changed. But it's still here. That's what I love about it. Everything around the Brickyard has evolved, but the Brickyard itself has weathered every single storm. And it's still standing."

We stay on the path as it curves around the Brickyard, past the brook, and down a staircase to the beach, where we can watch the water from the brook flow out, over the rocks, and into the sea. It's that perfect time of day, right before sunset, when the air is somehow full of both possibility and nostalgia.

"You know," I say to him, "I can understand why people never leave this island. I'm starting to get it."

"I had a feeling you would."

Later that night, I succumb once more to checking my phone. Just a peek. Skin Beams hasn't responded to my message, and I have a feeling they never will. Their mind is made up, the deal is over. I flip through some of the DMs I received in response to my story about taking a break. They're mostly positive and supportive. But buried among them is one from mermaid1985:

> **Too bad about Skin Beams. But they needed to know the truth, too. Let the countdown begin.**

# Chapter 22

The next morning, I wake up in a panic, certain that it's all over, that this time I'm really going to lose it all. But that morning, and every morning after that for the next few days, everything is fine. Nothing happens. I never responded to mermaid1985's last message, and they haven't written to me again, either. My social media is quiet. *Too* quiet. No new messages, no deal drops, nothing alarming. At first, this fills me with more panic. But soon, I grow used to the silence. I let myself relax a little bit. And I tell myself over and over again: Everything is going to be fine. I'm not going to lose anything.

I still want to puke after most meals, but I resist it as much as possible during the next few days, succumbing only a few times. I still want to binge and purge in the darkness of my own room; I still want to have four portions of pasta salad at lunch instead of one sensible serving. And, more than ever, I want to get drunk. I am desperate for the powerful numbing effects of both food and alcohol.

But I don't give in to it. The work is hard, but now there's an equally powerful part of me that *doesn't* want to throw up. Every meal, every snack, every bathroom trip is a challenge. I have to rewire my entire brain, my entire way of functioning. I start to realize how much time I spent focusing on the logistics my disease required—the when, the where, the how, the what of every binge and purge. I've spent so much mental and emotional energy on it, not to mention sheer *time*. Without all that, I'm freed up to focus on other things, and that, in and of itself, is terrifying.

But with each passing day that I don't puke, it becomes just a tiny, tiny bit easier. The process is the hardest thing I think I've ever done in my entire life.

Wanda and I have mostly talked about my mom for the past few sessions, and I've almost come to peace with the realization that my mom was part of the problem but that it's up to me to do the work. I can be angry at her, but I can't blame her. And that anger, Wanda tells me, can coexist with the love I have for her.

"I think I've been using bulimia as a way to be closer to my mom," I realize in one of our sessions. I'd told myself, somewhere along the way, that if I had a bad relationship with food, just like my mom did, then we were more connected, somehow. "Like I was using it to hold on to her."

"Your relationship with your mother will never not be complicated," Wanda tells me. "But that's okay."

We've moved on to talking more about *me* now. What I want to do, where I want to go from here. Wanda keeps telling me to think of food as fuel. *Fuel for what?* I ask her. She tells me that it's my fuel for living my life, for doing all the things I want to do. And this is where I get stumped.

"Maybe that's part of the problem," she says one morning. "You need to find your passion. Except I think you've already found it. You just need to let yourself go for it."

"I don't know, Wanda. That's easier said than done."

"Well," she says, "you've told me that you're not happy with your career. That you're no longer passionate about the work you're doing. So, it would make sense, then, that fueling yourself to live each day to achieve all the things you want to achieve is no longer a priority. But what would happen to you if you were doing something you really wanted to be doing, something you believed in, something you thought made a difference? Something that made you *happy*, Ava. Do you think that maybe then you'd want to do whatever you could to be more present and more alive in your life?"

"Okay, sure, but don't you think that's a little bit of an indulgent perspective?" I shift in my seat. "I mean, I already have a pretty great life. It's not like I'm miserable."

"But you're not happy," Wanda continues. "If you could do anything, what would you do? Go back to the beginning. What used to bring you joy?"

"Well, that's the problem. *Food.* Food is the thing that's always brought me joy. I love cooking, I love eating, I love it all." I think about this for a second. My greatest passion has been my greatest detriment. "But how can that be good for me?"

"Food isn't the problem, or the enemy. Your disease is the problem. You need to get out of your own way," she says. "Think about that for a second, Ava: food is not the enemy. If you love food and want to do something food related for work, you *can.*"

"I'm scared," I tell her. "What if I can't do the work in the real world? I have less than a week here."

"We're going to do everything we can to prepare you over these last few days, Ava. It's not going to be easy. But you can do it." She pauses. "You know, after this, there's no reason why your life has to look like it did before. You can change things." We end our session there. I wonder how my mom felt about her own life at my age, and if she wanted to change things, too.

Later that night, I eat dinner with Stephanie and Rhoda.

"Girls, I've got some big news," Rhoda tells us. We've seen less of her recently because she's gone to meet Elena for dinner or a trip to the beach almost every day. They're making up for lost time, she has told us. "I'm not leaving," she says.

"What do you mean, not leaving?" I ask.

"Elena has asked me to come stay with her," she says with a grin. "Or . . . live with her, really. Ever since we reunited, it's like we've never been apart. So, why go back to Florida? There's nothing there for me anymore. I don't want to be where she's not. So, when the retreat is over, she's coming with me to pack up my things, and then we're moving back here . . . for good."

"Rhoda, I gotta give it to you," Stephanie says. "You have surprised the hell out of me."

"I take that as a big compliment," she says.

I think about Rhoda's words—how there's nothing left in Florida for her. And I wonder where I would go, what I would do, if I decided to abandon my old life in LA.

"I've actually got some news, too," Stephanie says shortly after. "I told you guys that I was quitting. Well, I went ahead and put some feelers out, you know, for other jobs. And I've got an interview next week back in the city with another production company. It's an all-female-led company. I've known the CEO for years, and they just so happen to be needing new counsel."

"Wow," I say, "that's great!"

"Yup. If all goes well, I'm going to break my contract and leave those bastards high and dry. They've got too many other things to deal with right now to worry about me leaving. I'm not going to let it stop me. It's time to get my life back. I might even consider having kids."

I can feel the attention shift to me next, like it's my turn to announce my own big plan for my future.

"That's so great," I say. "Both of you. Just, wow . . ." I look down. "I really don't know what I'm going to do next. I've still got to figure it out."

"You will," Rhoda says, patting my arm. "You will."

The three of us take our time finishing dinner and dessert, and walk back to our cabin just as the stars begin to emerge in the sky.

"Ava!" I hear from behind us. "Ava! Wait!" It's Hadley. We turn and see her trotting toward us, Bronwyn and Eliza behind her. They catch up to us.

"Ava," Hadley says again, almost out of breath, "we just saw . . . and we, well, we just wanted to say we're so sorry. And obviously we had nothing to do with it. I mean, I did tell my cousin in New York that you were here, and she's definitely a talker, but she's not responsible for *this*."

"What are you talking about?" Not only have I resisted puking every day, but I've also stuck to my plan of going off the social media grid. I've barely looked at my Instagram at all since I made that last video on the beach, and I've only checked my email a handful of times. I even put up an automated "Away" message. But I know something terrible has happened.

Hadley, Eliza, and Bronwyn look at one another, their faces clenched.

"Oh, just show her," Bronwyn says, nudging Hadley.

"What are you guys talking about?" I look at Stephanie and Rhoda. "Do you guys know?" They shake their heads.

"It's on the internet," Eliza says, like that explains anything. "We thought you knew. Here, look," she says, and hands me her phone. "Someone . . . *outed* you," she whispers. "I'm really sorry . . ." She keeps talking, but I don't hear it. I knew I shouldn't have relaxed, I shouldn't have let down my guard. The tranquility of the past two weeks was just to trick me. I should have seen this coming.

I look at her phone. Her browser is open to The Cut, and my stomach drops to my feet as the image on the screen comes into focus. It's me, just a few weeks ago, screaming at Naomi in the farmhouse lobby that night after dinner with Carter. It looks like it's from a hidden security camera that I somehow missed. My voice comes out shrill and vicious: "You need to get a *life*. Find someone else to follow . . . All the photos of me? The workouts? Even the 'real' posts? They're all a lie." Stephanie and Rhoda watch the video over my shoulder, while the leggings cringe and bite their nails in distress as they watch behind us. The video shows our entire altercation, ending in me storming out. The headline is Wellness Influencer Ava Maloney Meltdown in Rehab Caught on Camera. The article continues by describing where I am and even what my initial application said. It describes Island Wellness as "bougie rehab for rich women with eating disorders and addictions." Somehow, there's a screenshot of part of the application, the part where I specifically say that my entire platform on social media is a lie.

I put the phone down. My head spins.

"When did this break?" I ask.

"Like, literally two minutes ago. I got one of those news notifications from The Cut," Hadley says. "We had to come tell you. You don't think . . . I mean, it must have been someone here. Right?"

"Obviously, Hadley," snaps Eliza. "But *who?*"

"Well, it must have been a staff member," Bronwyn chimes in. "Who else would have access to her application?"

"A lot of regular people are hackers now, you know," Hadley says. "Could have been anyone."

"Well, we've got your back, Ava," Eliza adds. "We know that this isn't really who you are."

"Thank you," I say, though my mind starts to leave my body. I can't believe it actually happened. Mermaid1985 actually went through with it.

"So . . . what are you going to do?" Bronwyn asks.

I can't even open my mouth to speak. I feel dizzy. I look at the leggings, at Stephanie and Rhoda. Could it have been any of them?

"It's late," Rhoda interjects, a look of concern on her face. "The only thing you should do right now is go to sleep. We can figure all of this out tomorrow morning." She glances over at Stephanie, who shares her worried expression. "Come on, let's go." She takes my arm, Stephanie takes the other, and they lead me back to the cabin. My phone begins to ding with messages as we walk, one after another, a relentless barrage, reminding me that this is *actually happening*.

I undress for bed like a zombie. Stephanie and Rhoda come to check on me a few minutes later. I still haven't looked at my phone. I can't bring myself to. They sit on the edge of my bed.

"You know," Rhoda says, "maybe this is a blessing. That this came out."

"I wouldn't say that it's *good*," Stephanie interjects. "Just being honest . . ."

"No," I say, "I agree. Maybe now I can let go of all the pressure I'd been putting on myself. Stop being fake. Start just . . ."

"Living your life?" Rhoda asks.

"Yeah," I say. "Something like that."

I agree to go to a sunrise meditation with them tomorrow morning, based on Rhoda's advice that it will be a good way for me to clear my head and to strategize next steps. I put my phone on silent before I fall asleep.

There's only one person I'd want to talk to right now, only one person who could help me. Only one person who could comfort me. And she's gone.

# Chapter 23

The sunrise meditation does, in fact, clear my head. I open my eyes at the end of it and know exactly who did this to me.

But I also know that it doesn't really matter. What it's made me realize—unexpectedly, and more than anything—is that I miss my mom, and that I no longer want to hold on to anger toward her. I want to let it go. I *need* to let it go. And I'm ready to.

"So, feel any better?" Rhoda asks as we walk back to the van.

"I do, actually."

When we pull up to the farmhouse, I tell Rhoda and Stephanie that I'll catch up with them later.

"I need to talk to Sarah," I say. I hang back until all the guests have unloaded from the van and it's just the two of us.

"We need to talk," I tell her as she shuts the van door. "I know it was you."

I should have known from the start. It's so obvious now, thinking back on it. The profile fits her to a T. She's one of the only people with access to my files, and, most important, she's had it out for me from the beginning. When she saw me on the date with Carter, the night I went off on Naomi, that must have sent her over the edge with jealousy.

But she just gives me a blank stare.

"Ava, it wasn't me. If you mean whoever leaked the video. I had nothing to do with it. I'm so sorry this has happened to you. That said, you can't speak to one of our staff members like that. That doesn't give anyone the right to break into our security system and leak things to the press, but still. You owe Naomi an apology." She pauses. "But I've been worried about you all morning, since I saw it."

"Sarah, you can stop pretending. I'm not proud of the way I spoke to Naomi, and I've apologized to her, but I know you did this. You've *never* liked me. You've had a problem with me since before I even got here."

"That's not true," she says. "That's not true at all, Ava. I've never had a problem with you."

"I know you're mermaid1985. Just admit it!"

"What? I don't know what you're talking about."

"Come on, Sarah. I know you lied about having Instagram."

"Okay, fine," she says with a sigh, and I'm sure I've got her nailed now. "You're right. I did lie about that. I do have Instagram. I just . . . I guess I just wanted to convey an image of professionalism to you, to everyone. And . . . well, I don't know, an image that I was better than all that. I'm not, obviously."

"So you're admitting it, then? It was you?"

"No, I lied about having Instagram. But I'm not this *mermaid* person. I truly don't know what you're talking about." I still don't believe her. It doesn't explain everything. She's the *only* person who could do this, who's capable of it, who would *want* to.

"So you haven't been trolling me, threatening me this whole time?"

"No, Ava. I'm telling you, I wouldn't do that."

"Well, then, how do you explain how my application was leaked? Or the security-camera footage?"

She looks around and then steps closer. "Ava, I wasn't going to say anything to you. I was going to wait and talk to the owners of Island Wellness first. It's not really my place to do so. But . . . there's only one person who could be responsible for this. You see, this morning I checked the security-camera footage from that night. And the file was removed. It was removed *that night*."

"Okay . . . *and*?" I still don't believe her. I *can't* believe her.

"There was only one person working the night shift when the file was removed. Think about it, Ava."

And then it hits me: *Naomi*.

No, there's no way. As hard as I was on her that night, I don't think she'd do this to me. We had formed a friendship. I had . . . trusted her. But then again, *she* had trusted *me*. And I ruined that.

"No," I say. "That doesn't make sense. You—mermaid1985—started threatening me long before that night."

"Ava, I'm sorry. I don't know why she would have done this. But it wasn't me. I'm telling you. There's only one person who could have deleted that file that night. And it was Naomi."

I feel sick to my stomach. How could I have been so blind? This whole time, I've been focusing on Sarah, thinking that she was fixated on me. But really, *I'm* the one who's been fixated on her. I built her up in mind to be a representation of all my insecurities and jealousies. And it turns out, the person I've made her out to be isn't even entirely real. She's just as concerned with projecting a certain type of image as I've been. In a way, we're exactly the same, and we have been, all along.

"But y-you," I stammer. "I just thought . . ."

"Look, I know I can come across as sort of . . . *judgy*," she says. "But I really do believe in the work we do here. I've only wanted to help you. Ever since I saw your application, I *wanted* you to be here, to get better. And you have, Ava. You really have. I'm sorry I lied to you about being off social media. I guess that's sort of pathetic of me. Lying to make myself look a certain way."

"No, it's not. I mean . . . I get it. I understand. I've been doing the same thing, obviously. None of us are entirely . . . *pure*."

Suddenly, we hear footsteps from the front door of the farmhouse and turn to see Naomi. Her eyes are filled with tears. Sarah and I look at one another, and I know in that moment that she's right. She shuffles away, leaving me alone with Naomi.

"Ava," Naomi says, "let me explain."

"You're mermaid1985," I say, and now I understand. Naomi wanted me to think it was Sarah this whole time. Long before the night I went off on her. Everything about the Instagram profile made it seem like it was Sarah and not her. "How could you do it? I thought . . . I thought we were friends."

"I didn't mean for it to get so out of hand. I changed my mind after we talked and you apologized. I . . . I sent the video to a writer I know that night, in the heat of the moment. I was so mad, my feelings were so hurt. But then, after we talked, I called her and begged her not to run it. But it was too late."

"But . . . Naomi, you've been threatening me long before that—since the day I got here. And the Skin Beams deal, that was you, right? You blew it up? You realize the domino effect that's going to have, right?"

She looks down, and I almost feel sorry for her. Almost.

"Yeah, that was me, okay? I didn't mean for it to go so . . . public, like it did. I just wanted you to be held accountable by someone."

"Accountable? Accountable for *what?*"

"For selling a lie, Ava! You get paid to *lie*. And it's not fair."

"But I . . . I thought you were a fan." I still can't reconcile this angry person in front of me with the young woman I thought I'd gotten to know over the last few weeks. "How could you do this? *Why?*"

"You don't understand what it's like for my generation," she says, her voice shaky, silent tears now streaming down her face. "Everything is about social media for people my age. Before I do anything, I think about how I'd caption it, how I'd photograph it, whether or not it would be cool on my feed. Social media is our *reality*. That's why I liked you at first. You seemed real. I believed you. But then, something changed . . . and you became like everyone else. *Fake.* And I guess . . ."

Her tears subside a little and begin to give way to what I can tell is authentic anger. "I guess I just felt like you needed to know that you were hurting people. You *are* hurting people, Ava. You make people feel like they need to be perfect all the time." Her accusations sting, but she's not wrong.

"But you told me that I had helped you, Naomi. That you wanted to be like me."

"The old you. I wanted to be like the *old* you. Before you got caught up in whatever it is that made you change. I could tell, I could see through it. And at first I just wrote you off as another generic influencer. I forgot about you. But then when I saw that you were coming here as a guest, I looked at your application. All my suspicions about you were right. And once you were here, I still hoped you'd prove me wrong. But then everything you showed me over the last few weeks only confirmed that again. You're just another phony, profiting off the vulnerabilities and insecurities of people like me. The people who *believed* you. The people who wanted to be like you."

Her words cut me, making me feel open and exposed, raw and ashamed. I can see her pain, how real it is. I recognize it because I've felt the same way. I know that I should hate Naomi in this moment, that I should be filled with rage toward her for doing what she did, but I actually just feel . . . *relief.* Everything she's saying is true, whether or not I meant to hurt anyone. And now, there's nothing left to hide.

"Naomi," I say, "I'm sorry. You're right. I did change. I lied. And I need to do better. I need to *get* better. That's why I'm here."

"Well . . . you owe everyone an explanation."

"You're right. I do. And I will." I start to turn away from her before she can respond. There's nothing she can tell me that would change things. I don't want an apology from her; it wouldn't make a difference. I just feel remorse for pushing her to this point. "Hey, Naomi," I say, "for what it's worth, I understand why you did what you did."

I go to my cabin and head straight to my room. I shut the door, needing to be alone. I open my snack drawer and examine the contents: a bottle of wine, two bags of chips, some old cookies, and a scone from yesterday's breakfast. Instead of stuffing it all down my throat, I take everything out of the drawer, bundling it in my arms, and storm out into the kitchen, where I dump it in the trash. It doesn't feel right, not really, and yet I know I have to do it. Stephanie and Rhoda watch me from the living room couch but don't say anything. And I sigh with relief as I slam the trash can shut.

I know that I should feel overwhelmed with stress, but I'm suddenly overcome with gratitude. Hitting rock bottom might be the best thing to have happened to me in a while, I realize. There's nothing to do from here but change, start over, redirect myself. And what a gift, in a way, I think, to get to start over.

My mother never got a chance like this. She never got to have a clean slate, she never got the chance to face her insecurities, to get help, to learn how to love herself and feel beautiful and confident, and to know that she was enough. She never got a chance to ask herself who she really wanted to be.

I know that if she were here now, she'd squeeze my hand and tell me to never give up. She'd tell me to keep going, to grab hold of that second chance and to never let go. She'd tell me to be *me*, and to never lose sight of who I am again.

It might have been too late for her. But it's not too late for me.

# Chapter 24

The next twenty-four hours are a frenzy of DMs, emails, calls, and texts, as well as a constant barrage of alerts informing me that yet another article, tweet, or post about me is up for the world to see. I decide to wait a few days to read them all and respond to anything. I have two choices: I can try to brush the whole thing under the rug, blame it on being drunk and overwhelmed, having chronic anxiety, and succumbing to the pressures of social media that we all feel. Or I can admit to having a real problem. I can admit to the actual truth. And I can make a change.

The easier choice is to brush it under the rug, of course. So many public figures out there, especially ones on social media, have gotten busted for airbrushing themselves in photos or claiming to be somewhere in a photo when they were actually somewhere else. It ends up being old news in a heartbeat. No one cares after a few days. As soon as another story hits, the world forgets the mistakes of their idols. And in the end, followers still want the same content they got before, so they'll keep coming back for more, even when they know they've been fooled. Maybe it's because they never actually *believed* it to be real. Maybe, deep down, no one ever thought it was real; maybe they just got swept up in the aspiration of it. I never had a platform of 100 percent truth, and while I take responsibility for that, I'm not sure that can even exist on social media at all while being totally real. Some people can, and do, but not me. There's always going to be something in my content that's scripted, edited, curated, schemed; maybe that doesn't make it a lie, but it doesn't make it entirely truthful, either.

The next afternoon, after a quiet morning of yoga, lunch, and a session with Wanda, I bring my phone with me down to the beach and decide to speak into the camera. It's time.

"Hey, friends," I begin. I'm so used to this flowery opening that I almost automatically slip into my choreographed recitation of what I've consumed that day, what I'm wearing, what's on my face. "By now, most of you have probably read the article about me and seen the video. First of all, I want to say to each and every one of you that I'm sorry. I am so, so sorry. Let me back up and explain."

I take a deep breath. I haven't planned this speech, not exactly, but I can't help the words from pouring out of me. It's like they simply need to be said if I want to survive.

"When I was fifteen, my mom died. I'm not telling you this for sympathy. Just hear me out. I really idolized my mom. To me, she was perfect. But she wasn't perfect, not even close. None of us are. She struggled with her self-esteem. She was always on a diet. And right before she died, my own body changed. I didn't feel good about myself. So I started making myself throw up. I became bulimic. I still have a lot to figure out," I say, pausing, accepting those words that once hurt me so much. "And I might not ever really figure it out, but I think a big part of why I did it was for my mom's approval . . . and then, to feel closer to her somehow, after she was gone. I just never wanted to let her down.

"Anyway, later on, after college, I got better, for a while. And I really did get healthy. I always loved food, and cooking, and wellness. That's why I started TheGratefulAvocado. It really came from a good place, and from a passion for food. From a sincere desire to feel strong and healthy and to want others to feel that way, too. Everything started out real. But somewhere along the way, I don't know . . . I slipped. I fell back into it. I started bingeing and purging again. But by then, I had so many followers, and this whole platform. I didn't know what to do. I just pretended like I was okay.

"And then finally I felt like I hit rock bottom, so I checked myself into this wellness retreat. That's where I am now, where I've been for the past six weeks. And I've been in therapy almost every day. I've learned a lot, about the roots of my issues and where I want to go from here." I pause, looking out at the water. "All I know, for now, is that I shouldn't have lied to you all. I gave you this idea that it's easy to be perfect, that it's effortless to be healthy all the time . . . but that's not real. That's not human. That's not life. You might not like the real me, but at least now you know who that is. I'm working on liking myself, too. I hope you understand. I hope you forgive me. And most of all, if you are struggling with an eating disorder, I hope you reach out to someone for help. I hope you know that you can find a way to get through it. But it's a hell of a lot easier if you don't fight it alone."

Before I close out Instagram, I post a few links to resources for eating-disorder help. And then I lie back on the warm sand and shut my eyes. All the followers I've amassed over the years have made me feel important. They've made me feel like I matter. But I don't matter to them, not really. It's all transactional. I think about the accounts I follow, and how quickly I forget about them once I stop following them. It takes only a few days of someone being off my feed for me to not think about them at all. They evaporate into the virtual galaxy, like they were never a real presence in my life to begin with. When I take away the control and power that I've bestowed on my followers, their influence on my self-worth, I'm left with myself. The most challenging relationship of all. I prop myself up on my elbows and look down at my body. I think about how much stronger I am today than my mother was when she got sick, and how grateful I am to have a body that will allow me to run, swim, taste delicious things, have sex, laugh, cry.

And suddenly I know the answer to the question Wanda has been asking me for the last few weeks. I know why I need to fuel my body. I know what I want to do with my life.

The next day is the final full day of the retreat; the following morning, early, we're all packing up and going our separate ways. Before yoga, there's a knock on our cabin door. I'm up early, already drinking coffee and packing. I open the door to see Leon, Wanda, and Sarah, and I panic. By now, Leon and Wanda must have seen the video and discussed it with the owner of the retreat. They're kicking me out, I know it. Even though I was wronged, I know I never should have gone off on Naomi like I did.

"Ava," Leon says, "good morning. Sorry to disturb you so early, but could we come in?"

"Of course," I say, opening the door. Stephanie and Rhoda are in their rooms, but I'm pretty sure they're awake. Yoga is in half an hour. Leon, Wanda, and Sarah go straight to the couch and sit. Wanda beckons me to join them in the opposite chair. I'm disoriented by seeing them here, in my cabin, outside of their offices.

"So," Wanda begins, "Sarah took the liberty of letting us know what happened. With Naomi."

"I'm sorry," I blurt out. "What I said to her that night . . . I never should have spoken to her that way, and I'm sorry—"

"No," Leon interrupts. "It's not about that. It's about what she did to you. She broke into confidential files, stole private information about you, and then leaked it to the press. That violates every single employee rule we have."

"It goes without saying that she's no longer an employee here," Wanda says.

"You see," Leon says, "Wanda and I are actually the owners of this place. We just don't like to advertise that to our clients because our focus is really on the therapy. We are doctors first and foremost. That's why we opened this place twenty-five years ago. So, when Sarah told us what happened, we not only handled things immediately with Naomi, but we wanted to come talk to you directly, too. Make it right."

"Yes," Wanda adds, "our priority is the safety and wellness of our clients. We're so sorry that this happened to you. We hope it hasn't completely tarnished your experience here. We want to make it up to you, somehow."

I consider demanding a refund, just as I tried to do with Sarah six weeks ago. I think about threatening to sue. There's a lot I could do in this position, and I know it. But that's not what I need from them, not anymore. That's not what I want.

"Well," I say, "I'm grateful to you. This place has done a lot for me. Wanda, our sessions have really helped me. And when I first got here, I didn't think anything or anyone could help me. I've still got a long way to go, but you got me started." I pause, an idea forming in my mind. "There *is* something you can do, though, to make it up to me."

I tell them exactly what I want and how they can help. They're surprised, I can tell, but they say that they're happy to oblige. Before they leave, Wanda gives me a hug. "I'm proud of you," she says. And I know she is. For the right reasons.

Even though it's the last day, I agree to meet Carter for a quick afternoon swim before the retreat's final dinner that night. He picks me up and swings a left when we drive out of the retreat, then proceeds to zigzag down several winding roads before turning onto a shaded road deep in the woods.

"Ice House," he says as we park. "You can't leave without a swim here first. It's a freshwater pond."

We walk from the car up a wood-chipped trail through the trees, until it opens to a broad, glassy pond bordered by lush greenery. It feels like we're in Vermont, not on Martha's Vineyard.

"Technically, we're not supposed to be here right now," he says, pointing to a sign that indicates that lifeguard hours are over and swimming isn't allowed. "But even I break the rules once in a while."

A dock with a ladder at the end extends out into the pond. I shimmy out of my shorts and lift my T-shirt over my head, dropping them on the ground, and I start running toward the water. "Come on," I say. "We came to swim!" He follows, and we leap off the dock. The water is crisp, not cold. It smells like rain and feels like silk. We swim out toward the middle of the pond.

"So, you ready to go back to LA?" he asks me as we tread water.

"Yeah," I say. "I'm ready to go back. Just not sure how long I'll stay." I give a quick smile and duck under the surface for a moment.

"What does that mean?" he asks when I emerge.

"You'll just have to wait and see."

Without any warning, clouds begin to roll overhead, and we hear a crashing of thunder, and then suddenly the sky erupts into a steady and swift rainfall, out of nowhere. The water around us becomes a field of jumping raindrops, each of them reflected in the surface of the water. I touch my feet to the mucky floor and stand. With my eyes closed, I lift my arms and face up to meet the sky and embrace the rain. It's silly, and I might have felt embarrassed doing this six weeks ago, but now, standing here in the water, with Carter, I feel totally free of inhibitions.

Carter inches closer to me. I know he wants to lean in and kiss me, and I consider it. I really want to as well. His hair is slicked back, and I think about how his long, tan arms would feel wrapped around me right now. But I let myself fall back onto the surface of the water instead, and I just laugh. He starts laughing, too. And it feels good, maybe better than any kiss ever could.

When he drops me off at the retreat, he gets out of the car. We're in front of the farmhouse; the moment for a kiss is gone. I embrace him in a firm hug, pressing my face against his chest.

"Thank you," I say. "For being such a great friend to me."

"Friend, huh?" he asks.

"Yeah, friend," I say, sheepishly. "Just don't go anywhere."

"What do you mean?" he asks as I walk away, looking back over my shoulder. "Where would I go?"

I shrug my shoulders with a smile. "I'll see you soon."

# Chapter 25

That night after I leave Carter, I go to dinner with Stephanie and Rhoda. We toast our iced teas to our collective courage and the changes we've all decided to make. Stephanie is ready for her interview at the women-led production company, and Rhoda is gearing up for her new life with Elena. When I tell them what I'm going to do next, they react with a mix of shock and admiration.

"Okay, well, that finalizes it for me," Stephanie says. "This is really inspiring, Ava."

"Agreed," says Rhoda. "And you won't regret it. I know you won't."

"Thanks," I say. "I owe a lot to the two of you. I didn't think I even wanted roommates when I first got here, I have to admit. I was pretty pissed about it. But you two have become some of the most amazing friends I've ever had." The three of us, perhaps the most unlikely of trios, share our final cup of tea together before returning to our cabin. Stephanie has the earliest flight out of all of us, the 7:00 a.m. to JFK, and Rhoda is leaving a few hours later for Elena's. My flight's not until nine.

I wake naturally the next morning at dawn, feeling excited and nervous. Since I stopped consistently throwing up, I wake up more often during the night and early in the morning to pee. My body is adjusting to being hydrated again. Each time I'm reminded of what it feels like to be healthy, I feel a kick of temptation to slip back to my old ways, but so far, I have resisted. I cleaned out my snack drawer and the fridge weeks ago. One day, I hope to be able to be around junk food without wanting to binge on it. But for now, I can't, and I find comfort knowing that I can recognize my limitations.

I put on a bathrobe and sit outside on the cabin's front step with a cup of hot coffee. And I decide to check my phone, finally. When I filmed my confessional video on the beach, I didn't read any of my messages or emails that came in afterward. I just posted the video and then closed the app. I have no idea what kind of reception I've gotten, what the aftermath has been, what fires I need to put out. But I'm ready to face it now. I brace myself for the angry notes of blame, disgust, outrage. And there are those messages, for sure.

But, to my surprise, there's something else, too. There's an outpouring of support—far greater than anything I've received before. Not just from existing followers, but from new ones as well. There's also a slew of offers from my current endorsement deals and prospective ones asking me to collaborate, to partner up on projects. There's even interest from The Cut on a chance to write my *own* side of the story in an article for them. Somehow, this disaster has blown up my platform exponentially. I feel a sense of triumph—that old feeling of *winning* the social media game. But I know what I have to do. Part of me—the old me—is tempted to take advantage of this new angle, and I immediately envision the rebranded content I could post, the new endorsement deals, the expanded base of followers I could gain. This version of me, though, today, isn't tempted at all. The only thing I can do is the one thing I would have never dared do before.

I go into my settings on Instagram and, with just a hint of hesitation, I select *Delete TheGratefulAvocado*. Just like that, with one press of my finger, TheGratefulAvocado is gone.

I decide to take one final walk down to the beach before I pack up to leave. I don't even bother changing out of my bathrobe. I remember the first time I walked this trail. It was only a few weeks ago, and yet everything feels different now. *I* feel different now.

There's a stillness in the air when I reach the shore. The water is calm, and the sky is peppered with slowly drifting white clouds. I take it all in one last time. A slight breeze hugs me, and I dig my hands into the pockets of the robe. And then I feel something in there, something small and slippery between my fingers: a penny. I don't know how or why it got there, but there it is, glittering in the sun. I laugh a little, and with one quick glance up toward the sky, I shut my eyes, make a wish, and toss it into the vast ocean.

# Chapter 26

*One year later*

I forgot to mince the shallots. I did the onions, I did the garlic, but I forgot the shallots. And Lucy will notice. I start dicing them maniacally, hoping that if I finish them in time, I won't have to delay her cooking process: onions, shallots, then the garlic. They're going to be the base of the paella she's making for the beach rehearsal dinner on Chappy that we're catering tonight.

It's a hot July day, and our twenty-first wedding dinner of the summer season already, including wedding cocktail parties and rehearsal dinners, too. I've never worked harder, but I've never felt more exhilarated by work, either.

Just before I left the retreat last year, I asked Leon and Wanda to help me with one thing, in return for what Naomi did to me.

"I want to come back here," I told them. "Not *here* here, but to the island. I think I want to try living here, at least for a little while. Start fresh. And I was hoping that you could help me figure that out. Lucy, the caterer who was here that one night, well, she offered me a job, sort of. Maybe you can put me in touch with her, help me find housing?" Leon and Wanda almost laughed with relief.

"Of course," Leon said.

"I think I know how to help," Wanda added. And she did. She put me in touch with her niece, a nurse at the hospital. She needed a roommate in the house off Main Street in Vineyard Haven that she already shared with three other women, a teacher at the Chilmark School, a pastry chef at State Road Restaurant, and a real estate agent, all fellow washashores in their midtwenties. I flew back to LA to pack up my apartment. It took me a few months to get sorted, but that was for the best. During that time, I got used to living my life offline. At first, I continued to check Instagram and Twitter daily on my fake accounts, and I googled myself obsessively. Becky advised me to *pivot* from this, telling me that I could *rebrand* and create a new lifestyle blog. I told her I'd think about it, but that wasn't really the truth. Even if I'd been interested in staying on social media, once I moved to the island in the early spring, I didn't have *time* for it. Days went by where I completely forgot to check anything online at all. And yet I was still there, I was still living my life. I realized that social media wasn't vital to my existence. It wasn't even part of it anymore.

I started work as soon as I arrived on the island. Lucy was thrilled to have me on board, she said, but she insisted that I work at the Picnic Basket, her café in Edgartown, until the catering season was in full swing. There, I learned the ropes of the kitchen: the pecking order of chefs; how to keep my station organized; the stark difference between smoked paprika and regular paprika; how to use my core, not just my arms, when lifting a heavy delivery box or stack of dishes; how to sharpen my knives; and how to run an onion under cold water to stop myself from crying. It was line-chef 101. All I did for those first few months was think about the kitchen. I became addicted to the energy of it, the passion, the flavors, and the smells. And I realized that this was what it felt like to have a calling.

My roommates have made me realize it, too. I'd forgotten what it was like to be around people who care about what they do for a living. In the evenings, when we have time to cook dinner together, we share stories about the people and things we encountered at work that day: an eighth-grade student organizing a Black Lives Matter rally during morning assembly; a West Chop estate passed down for three generations, now being sold by five quarreling siblings; a young mother in labor who had to be helicoptered to Mass General but who now has a beautiful baby boy.

Rhoda, too, reminds me of what's important. She and Elena came into the Picnic Basket almost every day for coffee and a scone when I worked there. If I had time, I sat with them for a few minutes and heard about their adventures. Rhoda left Florida entirely, and she and I share a special bond in being new year-round islanders. When she and Elena told me that they plan to get married in the fall, with just a small ceremony and only two dozen guests, including Stephanie and Ralph, they asked me if I'd do the cooking. *Of course!* I shrieked. Stephanie told us they were going to come for two entire weeks. That's something I do now, she texted us. Take *vacation*.

That night, when all the lemon tarts and individual crème brûlée have been eaten, and the bride and groom have gone off to sleep, Lucy and I and the rest of the staff load up the vans outside.

"Thank you," I tell her. "For giving me this shot."

"Thank *you*," she says. "You've been a great addition. You're a natural, like I told you. I know a passion for food when I see it. And you've got it."

She's right. I've continued my sessions with Wanda, once every two weeks, outside of the retreat. We meet at Owen Park in Vineyard Haven early in the morning. I bring her a blueberry muffin and a black coffee from Mocha Mott's, and we talk for an hour. She's helped me to realize that my bulimia was never really about food. It was about my mom, about connecting with her, holding on to her through it. It was about my sense of self. It was realizing that in order to feel like I was in control of my own life, I had to relinquish control of many other things. Food was just how all those things manifested themselves. Once I was able to realize that, I could appreciate food in a new way.

I ask her, one day, about Naomi, and if she knows what happened to her.

"I do," Wanda says. "In fact, I worked with her for a few months after she left Island Wellness. As a therapist, I mean. She clearly was in a lot of pain. Not that it excuses what she did."

"I'm glad," I say, and I mean it. I had recognized myself in Naomi when the truth came out. I had recognized her anger at me, at the world, at the hypocrisy of social media. She was in just as much pain as I had been in. "I hope she's okay."

"She is," Wanda says. "She moved off the island, which I think was the right thing for her to do. But she's doing okay." I think that maybe one day I'll reach out to Naomi, to let her know that I forgive her.

After all, I've even formed a friendship with Sarah, of all people. Once we both stopped looking at one another as competition—for what, I don't know—and started respecting each other, we were able to have a relationship. She even helped me get settled when I moved to the island, taking me to the Chicken Alley thrift shop to look for a bedroom dresser.

Every time I see Wanda, I feel a little bit better, but I'm also reminded that I'm still in the midst of the struggle. That it's still difficult. But I'm committed to getting through the struggle, and that's what matters. I know that some people say that they've completely overcome their eating disorder and have truly found a way to free themselves from it, from the relief of the old habits, the muscle memory of it. But that's not me. At least, it's not me yet. Maybe eventually it will be. Until then, I take it day by day. I haven't been perfect, but that's no longer the goal. The goal is to be happy.

When we're off the Chappy Ferry, we drive to the Picnic Basket and unload our gear there. At almost midnight, we're finally done. And when we step outside the café, just off Main Street, where the

Edgartown bars are still alive and bustling with people searching for something, Carter pulls up in his Land Cruiser, with Bailey salivating in the front seat.

"Right on time," I say.

He parks the car and gets out. And this time, I run into his arms and we kiss.

"Let's go," I tell him. I spend the night at his place a few times a week, but I still sneak out early in the mornings, hopping on my bike and pedaling home as the sun rises. I'm working on intimacy. But I think I'll get there.

A few months later, I suggest to Mike and my dad that they come to the Vineyard for Christmas. "We could start a new tradition," I tell them.

They agree to it, and I book them all rooms at the Harbor View Hotel in Edgartown. When they arrive the day before Christmas Eve, I wait at the ferry terminal and wave to them as I watch them disembark down the ramp. My nephews run toward me, with Mike, Darcy, and my dad, along with Penelope, following behind.

"Thank you all for coming," I say between hugs. I even hug Penelope. And it's actually nice.

"It's good to see you, kiddo," my dad says, giving me a squeeze. Carter lets me borrow his car for the night, and we all pile in for the drive to Edgartown. The island is lit up for the holidays, and snow has just started to fall. When we reach Edgartown, I drive down Main Street on purpose so the boys can see all the Christmas lights, and the lobster-trap "Christmas tree" down by Memorial Wharf. They're all tired from the trip, so I drop them off and tell them that tomorrow we'll go for a walk and then have Christmas Eve dinner at four.

Lucy has generously agreed to let me use the Picnic Basket to host them the next night. I'm doing the cooking all by myself, though. Along with some of the classics, I'm making several dishes with local ingredients: clam chowder made from quahogs that Carter and I raked the day before in Sengekontacket Pond, oysters on the half shell that I picked up fresh off the farm from Signature Oysters, codfish from a Menemsha fisherman, and bay scallops that I painstakingly caught and shucked myself in November and then froze.

When my family arrives for dinner, I've just finished lighting the candles on the table. The café smells of freshly baked bread. I pour some wine as everyone takes their coats off and settles in.

The meal is spectacular: flavorful yet simple, authentic to the island but inventive. I'm proud of what I've done.

"Ava," my dad says, raising his glass, "thank you for having us and for cooking this incredible meal."

"*Incredible* meal," Mike echoes. "I mean, I knew you were a good cook, but wow, Ave. You're a *chef*."

"Not yet," I say, "but I'm working on it." I raise my glass, but before we clink glasses, I think of Mom and how much she would love this.

And as though he's read my mind, my dad lifts his glass and says to me, "You know, your mom . . ." He pauses and looks down for a moment. When he lifts his head back up, his eyes glisten, just slightly. "She would have been so proud of you, Ava. *I'm* so proud of you."

It's only one sentence—the most he's really said to me about Mom since she died, and the most he might ever say. But it's enough.

"To Mom," I say with a smile.

"To Mom," my dad says. "And . . . to *you*, Ava. To *you*."

I think about our Christmases with Mom. I think about the ordinary days with her, too. I think about how she always knew the right way to bandage up our scraped knees when we got hurt. I think about the bedtime stories she read us every night when we were little. I think about the way her eyes watered whenever she laughed really hard. I think about how committed she was to us, how she gave herself completely to us.

There was far more good than bad, far more love than hurt. And I know that just because she didn't entirely love herself, it doesn't mean that she didn't love me. And just because she wasn't able to overcome her pain doesn't mean that I can't overcome mine. I don't say it out loud, but I decide in that moment to let my mom off the hook. *It's okay,* I tell her. *I'm going to be okay.*

I exhale. I forgive her. And it's only once I've done this that I suddenly know what I've needed to do all along. Forgive myself.

As I do, I get this funny feeling, a strange sense of contentment. And then I realize what it is: I feel full.

# Acknowledgments

I wrote most of *Full* while I was pregnant, and finished it during the first few months of my son's life. I struggled with postpartum depression and almost gave up on this book many, many times. Thank you to Casey Elliston for not letting me, and for understanding that during the rare moments when we finally had free time together, I needed to use that time to write, alone. Thank you to Rebecca Spiro for reminding me that "it's all temporary." (You were right.) Thank you to Laura Spiro for always asking me how I was doing, not just how the baby was. Thank you to Vivian Spiro for your time, your endless support, your belief in me, and your singular ability to somehow make everything better, always. You are the best mother in the world (and I will tell you for the thousandth time: you are not the fictional mothers in my books). Thank you to Lionel Spiro for buying me groceries and fixing things around the house so that I could focus on my book. Where does someone find a guy like you? Thank you, Elise and Robert Elliston, for being the greatest "in-laws" and for always helping out when we've been in a bind, which has been a pretty frequent occurrence, though you'd never say so. Thank you to Miriam Ritchie and Molly Valle for your validating reads, which allowed me to exhale after months of insecurity. Thank you to Cassie Bradley and Maggie Morrison for literally guiding me through early motherhood—I could not have survived without you two. Thank you to Caroline Davey Hannah for taking such good care of Winston. Thank you to Kim Januszewski for getting me back in the saddle. Thank you to all my generous, loving friends—and a few in particular—for your support: Isabelle Esposito, Fahad Missmar, Sam Morel, Phoenix Rogers, Betsy and Heather Cabot, the Rukeyser family, Sofia Warner, Melissa Lewis, Colleen Macsuga, Clare Bast, Maddy Boudreau, Caroline Vik, Annie Sylvia, Melissa Thomas, Tommy Ward, Griffin Hughes, Bree Taylor, Charlie Melvoin, Jayne Wolfson, Chris Baker, Sarah Maguire, Liz Backup, Emily Graff, and Kiran Pendri.

Alicia Clancy, my superb editor: Thank you for somehow always knowing where my story and characters are going, even when I'm not so sure. Thank you for your honesty, your commitment, and your vision. During the times when I lost sight of this book, you steered me right back on track. Your patience is endless, and your advocacy is steadfast. I am incredibly fortunate to have your faith in me, as well as access to your brilliant mind.

None of this would be possible without two people who told me *yes*, they would read my first book back in 2017; and *yes*, they would help me: Cait Hoyt and Michelle Weiner. Cait, thank you for never doubting me and for being my strongest advocate. I like to think that I haven't needed hand-holding thus far, but it might only be because I always know that your hand is there for me, just in case. Your support has made what is sometimes a lonely and isolating process feel like one of collaboration and celebration. Michelle, thank you for never letting me settle and for always making me feel like my words matter. And thank you to my friend Ali Trustman, as well, for your support behind the scenes.

Thank you to the entire Lake Union team for bringing this book to life and making it infinitely better than I ever could have on my own: Nicole Burns-Ascue, Sossity Chiricuzio, Gabriella Dumpit, Sarah Engel, and Jill Kramer. I'm so grateful to you for your keen attention to detail, your candor, and your creativity.

Thank you to Brooke Lea Foster for your dazzling and very kind blurb.

Thank you to my son, Winston, for reminding me to hold on tight to what's important and to let go of (most of) the rest.

# BOOK CLUB QUESTIONS

1. What role do you think Ava's followers have in the way she views herself?
2. What do you think *wellness* has come to mean in the age of social media?
3. If it's Ava's job to promote and sell products on social media, is it dishonest for her to edit her content to be as appealing as possible? How is that different from a billboard or an advertisement in a magazine?
4. Do you think Ava would have ever changed if she hadn't been outed?
5. Was Naomi somewhat justified in outing Ava?
6. It's clear that Ava's mother struggled with body dysmorphia and possibly an eating disorder. How did those issues affect Ava's own perception of self?
7. How would you describe Ava's relationship with her mother, and her thoughts on her mother now?
8. Ava seems to have a love-hate relationship with food. Do you think it's possible for her to ever find a healthy relationship with food?
9. Ava, Stephanie, and Rhoda form a (perhaps) unlikely friendship. How do the different perspectives and backgrounds of these characters unite them?

10. Why do you think Ava is initially jealous of Sarah? What does Sarah represent to her?

11. What do you think about the ending? Is it possible for Ava to ever get "better" and overcome her demons, or will this be a lifelong battle for her?